I0771559

REDEMPTION
POST MORTEM

EMIL BUCHMAN

To Julie, Michael & Daniel

PART I

THE PILOT PROGRAM

CHAPTER 1

Craigburn Forest, Moffat, CO

People don't usually hate weather. True, everyone uses superlatives talking about a season but no one really experiences intense feelings toward a few raindrops. Yet, the howling wind and freezing rain chilled me to the bones and I was royally pissed at Uriel and his Heavenly Department of Energy for this ungodly chill. San Luis Valley, Colorado, in early November was not at its best and my body craved warmth, the finest hiking gear notwithstanding. Unfortunately, driving in a well-heated car was not an option because my targets likely used drones to patrol Route 708, and hiking from Moffat was the only sensible way to avoid detection. A heavy bag with an arsenal suited for a small army didn't make the hike any more pleasant.

Finally, I saw my destination—a small meadow lit by campfires. The guards were no doubt armed to the teeth and I had to move stealthily, which at times involved crawling on the freezing ground, adding to my foul mood. Still, the mission is the mission, and a few inconveniences were not going to stop me. I made it to the meadow around 11:30 p.m. and surveyed my surroundings.

The meadow was packed with people standing in three concentric circles. Armed guards wearing an emblem of the Order of Nine Angels on their Kevlar vests occupied the outer perimeter. I cursed under my breath. Kevlar vests meant I had to aim for headshots—not an easy task in the darkness of night.

The next circle consisted of figures in dark hooded capes. Finally, in the center stood a makeshift altar with something moving under a rug thrown on top of it. The altar was flanked by a tall figure in a purple cape—must be the grand master of the U.S. chapter performing the ritual—and a few of his hooded assistants.

The guards stood at ease, quietly waiting, the hooded figures milling about, whispering quietly at times, all eyes focused on Purple Cape who quietly directed his assistants. There was no wild-eyed chanting or agitated dancing, no drug-fueled frenzy, although I could smell a light whiff of a joint or two. Everything was orderly, almost businesslike. After all, the ONA was a paramilitary occult organization with superb discipline and military training.

Thirty minutes until midnight should be plenty to get organized. First, I strategically placed a few of my favorite gadgets—devices that imitated the sound of gunshots and barrel flashes—around the perimeter. These were my secret weapons, capable of disorienting even the most highly-trained adversary. Satisfied with their placement, I turned my attention to finding a suitable vantage point. A sturdy oak tree caught my eye, its thick branches providing ample cover and support. I climbed up into the crown of the tree, feeling the rough bark against my palms as I ascended. After assessing each branch for stability, I settled on the perfect one to stand on and carefully positioned my weapons on the upper branches. My watch showed five minutes to midnight. So far, everything had gone as planned.

A trumpet announced the beginning of the ceremony. Purple Cape took out what appeared to be a carving knife. One of his assistants handed him a folder. It looked somewhat out of place, as one would normally expect an ancient dusty manuscript with burned edges and other indicia of Satanist ritual books. Then again, in this day and age, it could have been a digital tablet. Purple Cape first raised his hands heavenward reciting some sort of incantation, then opened the folder and started reading in a strange language. The crowd around him chanted and rocked in unison. The assistants removed the rug from the altar, revealing the shape of a young woman tied up there, apparently designated as a sacrifice. The woman was partially hidden from my view by the rows of worshipers but she must have been drugged as her movements were sluggish and feeble. She whimpered quietly and wriggled, feebly trying to free herself.

As he finished reading, Purple Cape raised the knife, preparing to sacrifice the woman. At the sight of it, the crowd hollered and gyrated, ecstatic with the bloodlust and anticipation. Now it was my turn. I didn't enjoy killing. With my recent reeducation in the Movie Room, my soul had a very keen sense of right and wrong. Alas, I had no choice. It was either them or me facing Oblivion, and when it comes to this kind of choice, the instinct for self-preservation always gets the upper hand.

With my back pressed firmly against the rough bark of the oak tree, I reached into my pocket and activated the remote control. The air was instantly filled with the deafening sound of the gunshot imitators I'd placed throughout the meadow. With precise aim, I took out Purple Cape in a single shot before unleashing a barrage of bullets from my XM-7s with extended magazines. Chaos erupted as the hooded figures dove for cover and the guards scrambled to identify the source of the rapid gunfire and the number of shooters. I was aiming primarily for the guards, as they presented the biggest danger to the mission.

I dropped expended magazines and reloaded. A few seconds of respite almost allowed guards to organize, but the next wave of bullets brought new chaos to the ranks of the worshippers. It was now time for the grand finale, the grenade launchers on my XM-7s. The grenades blew up with a deafening *boom*, killing more of my targets. But just as I was about to reload again, the grenade launch produced too much stress on the branch and it gave way. Losing my balance, I slipped and fell to the ground.

Crap! Pain pierced my leg. I may have broken something.

Overcoming the pain, I took my two Glocks out of their holsters and continued with the killing spree. I was now exposed to the guards, and they ran toward me firing their rifles. My Kevlar vest protected me, but the bullets threw me off balance. Getting on one knee behind the closest tree stump, I shot a few approaching guards. The pain subsided—either the fall had been lucky or the adrenalin had put my body into overdrive. I had to do a bit of a ballet, moving around guards, ducking their bullets, diving between them, hitting them with elbows and knees, all the while shooting them at point blank. I steadily reduced their ranks. They may have been well-trained but the body I was using had the best training and muscle memory that the Heavenly Department of Health and Human Services could assemble.

After a few minutes that felt like an eternity, everything went quiet. I surveyed my surroundings. Most of my targets were either dead or dying, sputtering blood and desperately clinging to life. I went to the altar, grabbed the folder from Purple Cape, confirmed the kill, and put the folder into my backpack. It was time to finish the job, but something drew me to the sacrifice on the altar.

Now I was able to get a better look at her. She appeared young, probably in her early twenties, but with an aura of innocence that made her seem even younger, like a teenage girl. Her hair was long and wavy, a rich dirty blond that cascaded down her back in loose curls. Her face was attractive, but the most striking part of her appearance were her huge blue eyes. Wide with fear, pupils dilated, they exuded supernatural magnetism. Her body was slender, not the perfect curves of a supermodel, but more reminiscent of a teenager's lithe frame. The nipples on her small breasts stood up from the cold, and her body was covered in goosebumps. Some strange letters had been carved on her belly with a knife. Damn savages!

She was hyperventilating and thrashing helplessly, trying to remove the bonds. While the shooting and chaos had given her a glimmer of hope, and thus added to her strength, she was still too weak to free herself. Her helplessness made me want to protect her, to shield her from the terror surrounding her.

My instructions had been clear—no survivors. Yet, somehow I couldn't bring myself to end the life of this girl. I took out my knife. At the sight of it, she shuddered and closed her eyes. I cut her restraints and helped her off the altar, throwing the rug over her shoulders. I looked around. The carnage was so complete that I had a few minutes to reach the nearest car, put the girl into it, and let her drive away before I finished my job.

"Can you walk?"

She nodded but stumbled almost immediately. I grabbed her waist to keep her steady and started looking for cars. These guys must have come here somehow. Turning around, I spotted a bunch of cars and trucks parked nearby. The cars were unlocked, but too many of them were modern keyless models. Finally, I found an older truck with keys tucked under the visor.

As I helped her to the truck, a bullet whizzed by. Damn.

Someone was still alive and capable of shooting. I couldn't see the direction the bullet came from, so I pulled the girl down behind the truck. A few slugs hit the fender. Judging by the sound and shot frequency, this was a shotgun, not an assault rifle. The bullets betrayed the location of the shooter. I turned to the girl.

"Stay here. Wait for my signal, then get in the truck and drive like hell. The highway is that way." I pointed in the direction of Route 708. "The town is just a few miles away. Can you drive?"

She couldn't understand anything. Shock must have set in.

I shook her and repeated louder, "Can you drive?"

She finally snapped out of her shock and nodded.

I patted her on the shoulder.

"Good girl. Remember, the highway is that way and the town is in that direction."

I crawled quietly toward the shooter. In a few yards, I could see him. It was one of the guards, badly wounded but still capable of fighting, standing behind one of the trees. I came from behind, lunged at him, and sliced his throat in one move. I stepped out from behind the tree, waved to the girl and yelled, "Go! Go now!"

I watched her open the truck door and stagger into the driver's seat. I caught a glimpse of her eyes filled with fear and a burning desire to get away from this place as fast as possible. She hit the gas and took off like a maniac, hitting the shrubbery and driving over the bodies lying around. The tires screeched as she made a sharp turn toward the highway and sped away.

I was about to start the gruesome task of finishing off any survivors when the sound of the speeding car, the image of the terror-filled blue eyes of the girl, and the carnage around me triggered a strange sensation of déjà vu. It must have been one of the less pleasant episodes from the Movie Room. The scene looked painfully familiar, causing my stomach churn, but no matter how much I struggled to put my finger on it, the memory was enveloped in a thick, impenetrable haze.

The attempt to jog my memory distracted me from the mission, making me hesitate for a few seconds and lower my guard. Payback followed almost immediately. One of the wounded guards must have come to his senses, saw me standing in plain view, and squeezed the trigger. The bullet hit me in the neck, severing my brain stem. My head exploded and everything went dark.

CHAPTER 2

Department of Justice – HA Department

As I slowly regained consciousness, I found myself sitting on a couch in a waiting room, near the receptionist of the Head of Human Affairs, Heavenly Department of Justice. My head hurt like crazy even though there was no head…or body, for that matter. I was a pure soul, and what surrounded me was not corporeal either, but somehow my mind's eye assigned images to my surroundings.

Finally, the receptionist motioned me inside. "The boss is ready for you."

The office of the head of the Human Affairs Department was large with a heavy mahogany desk standing opposite the door. Azazel was sitting in his executive chair looking away from the desk, watching the footage of the mission. Maintenance routinely recorded our missions and Azazel had the option of watching them live or via the recording. He looked dashing, his muscular body dressed in a fitted cashmere navy-blue suit with a starched white shirt and a powerful red tie. Sometimes I wondered whether I had been a mid-level bureaucrat in my past life because all Angels looked to me like impeccably dressed white-collar executives.

Azazel, however, stood out even among the Angels. His shaved head, gaunt cheeks, dark eyes with a piercing gaze, and strong chin betrayed his rebellious nature. No wonder in human lore he was identified as Prince of Hell. The Creator's favorite, the only Angel mentioned in the Sacred Texts, Azazel looked like an Archangel but he was not. Because of his rebelliousness, he had lost Satan's chair to a more boring and predictable Samael and now had to be satisfied with the number two undersecretary position in charge of human affairs. Still, he was an important member of the Heavenly Offices, such that even Samael was careful not to mess with him.

Azazel continued watching the footage, immersed in the action on the screen, oblivious to his surroundings. I politely coughed. He finally noticed my presence and turned to me. He was visibly annoyed. Without any introduction, he barked, "Why did you run after the girl instead of finishing the mission? Or, do you think mission objectives are now optional?

I feebly protested. "I did complete the mission, didn't I? The grand master of the U.S. chapter is dead, and so are most of his underlings. The others were either dead or dying."

Azazel banged his fist on the table. "Did you check every single body? Who do you think shot you, a dead man?"

The was nothing to say, he was right.

Further incensed by my silence, he continued his rant. "And most of all, why did you think the no-survivors policy didn't apply to the sacrifice? Just because she was cute was not a justification for letting her go. You monkeys are unbelievable. Even dead you are still distracted by a cute pussy, unable to do what you were tasked to do."

It was better not to argue with a pissed-off Angel, so I kept my mouth shut but, for some reason, he was getting angrier by the minute.

"You were given a special honor to participate in the Pilot Program instead of suffering in the Movie Room burning yourself into Oblivion. Sometimes I think the Creator is way too lenient with you talking monkeys. Some Pinnacle of Creation—" he sneered contemptuously "—unable to rise above their animal desires."

His mention of the Movie Room made me cringe and sent shivers down my spine. If only the living knew about the Movie Room! Contrary to popular belief, there is no Hell as humans imagine it, where a bunch of furry Demons roasts poor souls on a simmering fire. Instead, a newly-departed soul is shown its life in all its most embarrassing details. Once the animal shell is shed, the right and wrong become crystal clear and the soul judges itself. It is impossible to describe what one's soul feels in the Movie Room. Imagine a fifteen-year-old girl madly in love with an upperclassman football jock. She finally gets a date, he takes her to a motel, undresses her, and, to her horror, she realizes the whole affair was a hoax being streamed on TikTok for the amusement of the entire school. Whatever she feels the next morning when she goes up on the roof and walks off the ledge is a thousand times more pleasant than one minute in the Movie Room. Of course, if you are Mother Theresa, your movie is fifteen minutes long and you happily leave for Heaven, a little sad about a few minor infractions. On the other hand, if you are a hardened criminal, you are made to watch the maximum length of the movie—the entire twelve months—and when it ends, just like the shy fifteen-year-old girl embarrassed by the football jock, your soul walks off the ledge into Oblivion… whatever that means.

I knew that feeling all too well. My soul had burned with shame and embarrassment, and was about to walk off that ledge when I was snatched by an Angel and placed into the Pilot Program, my ticket out of the whole conundrum.

No, it was not an experience I wanted to live through again, so I decided to pacify Azazel.

"Okay, okay, I am sorry, I screwed up. Next time I will be more careful."

"Should there be the next time? Maybe I should report you to Samael, kick you out of the Pilot Program and back into the Movie Room. Or better yet, straight to Oblivion."

Now he was bluffing. Reporting me to Samael, the Heavenly Attorney General and Azazel's direct boss, wouldn't bode well for him. After all, Azazel was in charge of the training and the missions in the Pilot Program, and any SNAFU would be on his books. Still, the very notion of Oblivion, an absolute nothingness with no chance for salvation, terrified us human souls more than the fires of Hell, and even the slightest chance of such an outcome was an unacceptable risk. Besides, calling Azazel's bluff wouldn't be a smart move under any circumstances.

Instead, I said conciliatory, "You have to admit, Azazel, that notwithstanding my screw-up, the mission was a success. Or was it not? Didn't we eliminate the U.S. chapter of the ONA and stop the ritual? Was there any stink afterward?"

Azazel grudgingly agreed, "It was not the worst one, all things considered. Your dumb luck held. Most of the ONA's U.S. leadership was dead, and those who survived didn't feel like talking. The FBI is crawling all over the place, but they will write it off as gang warfare. The girl, however..." He raised his voice on that last bit.

"What about the girl?"

"She survived thanks to you. For now she is in complete shock and hazy about your valiant entrance, but who knows what can happen with her suppressed memories in the future. She may still be a danger to us."

I prudently decided to let the last remark go—the last thing I needed was to be assigned to her termination. Even though once the mission was complete, she was considered an innocent bystander and her murder should be prohibited, it was up to Samael and Azazel to interpret the rules and they were good at making persuasive legal arguments.

I decided to switch topics. "So, who was this girl, anyway?" I asked innocently. "She looked older than a typical sacrifice."

"Some broad from Denver, a medical student from a well-to-do family. Her parents reported her missing a week ago."

"A medical student? Why wouldn't they have picked up some virgin trailer trash?"

"You've got to ask them. Maybe there was something about this ritual that required a middle-class medical student." He snickered.

I politely laughed with him and played along. "Or, maybe, the local trailer trash gets their cherry popped before they even reach puberty."

Azazel laughed. Like any asexual Angel, he loved salacious jokes. "Actually—" He abruptly stopped laughing. "She wasn't a virgin, believe it or not."

That was a shocker! Even though not entirely obvious to normal human beings, every self-respecting Satanist knows that evil is attracted only to the blood of virgins. Could it be that the occult scientists had found out that virgins have lower cholesterol in their blood, which would appeal to health-conscious evil spirits? I raised my brows.

But Azazel simply shrugged his shoulders in response to my silent question. "Who cares?"

Indeed, who cared? Maybe, this girl had the cholesterol level of a virgin, or maybe the dumbasses from ONA simply goofed. Still, my natural curiosity got the better of me, and now that Azazel's mood had improved somewhat, I decided to find out more,

"Okay, even assuming that a virgin is no longer mandated by an Occult Sacrifice Manual, what was it in the folder, and why wasn't it one of those Satanic manuscripts?"

Azazel winced. "Please don't use the word Satanic. You know how much Samael and I hate when those occult dumbasses associate themselves with us."

I raised my hand in apology and nodded.

"I haven't had a chance to review the folder. I will, in due course. It may very well lead to another assignment. In the meantime, go to your Demon friends and enjoy your poker game."

Poker game? How the heck did he know about our Texas Hold'em meets?

Seeing, my confusion, he scoffed. "Can you possibly think I don't know what you monkeys and those Demon apes do when you are not working? By the way, what are you playing for? Neither, of you have, or have any need for, money."

"Uh, you know, we just play for points."

"Points?"

"Yeah, like a tournament. Whoever gets the most points wins the tournament."

"And what's the prize?"

"Nothing. Just the pleasure of winning."

Azazel raised his brows incredulously. After all, the pleasure of winning was utterly foreign to a rational Angel. "You monkeys and Demons are even dumber than I thought." He waved to the door in a gesture of utter annoyance. "Just go. I have stuff to do."

As I was walking out of the door, I asked one last question, "So, what was carved on the sacrifice's belly?"

He waved in irritation. "I told you, I have not had a chance to study the materials. I will tell you what you need to know when it's necessary. Get out of here!"

Something in his response sounded suspicious. He had clearly been watching the footage. How could he not see what was carved on the girl's belly? I didn't dwell on these thoughts for too long. After all, Texas Hold'em was waiting.

CHAPTER 3

Maintenance Department

As I walked out of the boss's office, I kept coming back to the feeling of déjà vu I had experienced at the end of the mission. The sensation was hazy, but powerful enough to point to something significant and traumatic that had happened to me before I died. Could it be the actual moment of my death and the reason for my induction into the Pilot Program? This was not something that I could ask Azazel, even though he could easily enlighten me on my past life's story. That would be against the rules, though, and Angels don't break the rules. Or so I was led to believe.

Trying to recall the scenes from the Movie Room was not helpful either. The Movie Room does not operate in a Hollywood style—it is not like *Gone with the Wind*, where the close-up of Vivien Leigh and Clark Gable makes everything abundantly clear. It does not give you clear images—just blurred shapes evoking piercing emotional responses, focusing mostly on feelings and moral lessons from one's life experiences. The more I tried to nail it, the more it slipped away from me, so I finally gave up. Whatever had happened, happened, and the reality is that I am dead now and facing the very scary prospect of ending up in Oblivion, especially if I had failed with the mission.

On top of that, because of my hesitation, I wasted a whole Reincarnation Right, leaving me with only two more. Was it really worth it? I was not at all certain.

I was so immersed in my thoughts I didn't even notice when I reached the basement of the Heavenly Offices building where Beelzebub, Baphomet, and Abaddon were waiting for me. I am sure that in reality Demons looked different, but in my mind's eye they looked like hairy goats with hoofed hind legs, horns sticking out from their furry heads, front paws with huge claws, and the obligatory glowing red eyes, just like in Medieval paintings. Unlike the Medieval paintings, however, they wore greasy overalls and heavy cigar smoke hung over the card table. And unlike fully spiritual Angels, Demons bore a material shell and were part of the material World, which limited their powers.

Demons were a product of another human misconception, either imagined or carefully crafted by the Heavenly Offices. Unlike those scary creatures who must be exorcised or who can be called upon to commit an atrocity, Demons were simply maintenance workers servicing the machinery of the Creation, assigned to the Maintenance Department under the auspices of the Heavenly Department of Justice. I could never understand why they wouldn't be reporting to Archangel Uriel, the head of the Heavenly Department of Energy, but then again, when does government structure make any sense to anyone?

As with any well-run system, the Creation had a network of service passages, allowing Demons to quickly reach any destination and fix whatever needed to be fixed. They spent most of their existence in those service passages, oblivious of what was happening on the surface, except when they received maintenance tickets and went to fix a malfunctioning part of the Creation. Most of what they knew came from eavesdropping on Angels' conversations when they worked on the upper floors of the Heavenly Offices.

Seeing me, Beelzebub said, "Finally, where have you been? How did the mission go?" He was shuffling cards with his huge furry paws.

After slapping their paws in an obligatory high-five greeting, I shrugged. "I did all right, though I got chewed by Azazel for not checking on all the bodies."

They nodded. Demons didn't like the Angels considering them conceited, stuffed-up assholes whose privileges they didn't deserve. The dislike was mutual, with Angels calling Demons grease apes, since they reserved the term monkeys for us humans.

"What else could you expect from that prick Azazel?" said Baphomet sympathetically. "But I wouldn't worry too much about him if I were you. He is an ass but he is afraid of his own shadow. Doesn't want to fall out of favor again. Had he not screwed around, he could have been promoted to Archangel, sitting in Samael's chair. Now, he has to be satisfied with being second in command so for the most part, he keeps his mouth shut and lays low."

"Yeah," chimed in Beelzebub, "although you should have checked on the bodies. What if someone survived and used the ritual for an FMC?"

An FMC, or False Maintenance Call, is the only way for humans to contact Demons and for Demons to get in touch with humans. Normally, Demons only respond to maintenance tickets issued by Angels with a proper Demon call sign, and even then only after the ticket is authenticated by Ashmodai, head of the Maintenance Department. However, over the past six thousand years, humans have been able to learn call signs of some Demons and to figure out how to fake those maintenance tickets. When an unsuspecting Demon, certain he is being called to a bona fide maintenance job, responds to an FMC, he gets trapped. That's why they always look so pissed and angry when called by humans. The worst part, however, is that once the Demon's call sign is identified, the Maintenance Department has no choice but to terminate him, literally excising the poor fellow out of the Creation. That is why exorcists, ignorant as they are, always insist on learning the Demon's name, as it bears the immediate fruit of excision, though for reasons no exorcist could possibly fathom.

"Oh, please." I waved dismissively. "You guys are yourselves at fault, with your inferiority complex. You are so eager to respond to those FMCs to satisfy your bruised ego with Satanic worshippers. And for what? For a few minutes of pleasure, just to be wiped out for eternity? Then you bitch that Angels don't treat you right and the whole process is unfair. I bet both you and your boss could see the difference between the fake and real maintenance tickets if you really wanted to."

"Go fuck yourself!" Beelzebub violently threw the cards on the table.

Trying to defuse the tension, Baphomet changed the subject. "So, in your mission, who were those assholes trying to call on?"

"Don't know. There was a folder containing some ancient pages, and the sacrifice had some characters, I would guess Aramaic, carved on her belly. Azazel is looking into it."

Beelzebub snorted. "Can't even read Aramaic. What kind of dumb monkeys do they use in the Pilot Program?"

I didn't need this crap. After having been chewed out by Azazel, the last thing I needed was a lecture from this Demon goat. "Look who's talking. The incantation with your call sign is probably a nursery rhyme by now among humans. I am surprised you are still around—should have been excised a long time ago."

Beelzebub roared and jumped up raising a clenched fist.

I looked at him defiantly. Demons cannot hurt a disembodied soul.

"Come on, guys, let's stop bickering and play," Baphomet said conciliatorily.

"Yeah," said Abaddon with a sigh. "Things got really bad out there. Satanists, paganists, you name it, all swarming to get a shortcut."

"That's why the Creator set up this Pilot Program and filled it with the best monkeys," Beelzebub said sarcastically, looking at his gathered cards and puffing his cigar. He turned to me. "Which is a really lucky thing for you because you should have been in the Movie Room getting ready for Oblivion. Oh, well. This is no doubt just an extension. You'll be back there in no time, the dumbass you are."

I got up and violently pushed my chair. "I've had enough of you mongrels. I am leaving."

Finally coming to his senses and realizing he was about to miss today's entertainment, Beelzebub laughed and grabbed my hand. "Stop behaving like a hard-to-get pussy. Sit down and play. I am going to win today, I can feel it."

"Oh, yeah? Then shut up and deal."

Demons were not good poker players. I couldn't say I was an expert, and it was highly unlikely I was ever in the World Championship Poker Tournament during my lifetime, but playing with Demons was easy, even for an amateur. You could always read their faces, and they could not count cards if their lives depended on it. Yet, they loved to gamble, and I loved to win. I guess I also had an inferiority complex and a bruised ego in need of validation.

This time was no different. I was ahead, as always. Just as I was about to call, holding two pairs, the bell rang and a maintenance ticket materialized out of the thin air. Abaddon grabbed it, looked at it, and cursed. "Every time I want to have a quiet game, something happens," he said bitterly. "Department of Energy, again. Uriel has issues with earthquakes in the Pacific." He turned to Beelzebub. "Come on, you hairy bitch. Your call sign is also on the ticket."

Beelzebub folded the cards. "Don't go anywhere. We will come back soon and I will still whip your ass."

"Yeah, yeah, I'll be right where you left me."

As Beelzebub and Abaddon took off through a maintenance channel, the bell rang again and another ticket materialized.

"What the heck is going on?" said Baphomet. Since he was the only Demon left in the room, the ticket was clearly for him. "What, the whole Creation is falling apart?" However, as he read the ticket, his face brightened. "This is a good one. They need to clean up the Courtroom. A soul made a mess there when they read its judgment." He paused, then coyly winked at me. "You wanna see the Courtroom?"

Of course, I wanted to see it.

The Courtroom was the heart of the Heavenly Offices, where the Creator judged all creatures, human and Angel alike. Including recently departed souls being sentenced to a number of months in the Movie Room. It was, in fact, the only place in the Heavenly Offices the Creator would regularly bless with his presence.

"Can I?"

"Sure, why not? They are too busy arguing cases to notice some lowly monkey there. Just put on some work overalls and follow my lead."

CHAPTER 4

The Courtroom

As we entered the Courtroom, my mind saw a stately Hall lined with ministering Angels on both sides of the room. Samael sat in the prosecutorial chair on the right. He had a pinstriped tweed suit, a white shirt, and a blood-red tie, apparently emphasizing his image of Satan. As an attorney general heading the Justice Department, a large part of his job was to prosecute souls. When we walked in, he just finished his summation.

Archangel Samael was too big of a boss to deal with us monkeys. I'd seen him only once before, when I was inducted into the Pilot Program. He had spoken in a low, quiet voice, the trick used by all big bosses to make you strain your ears to hear what they had to say.

"You have been given the great honor of participating in the Pilot Program established by the Creator, Blessed be He," he'd said. "Your job is to find and eliminate Devil worshipers,—" he cringed in disgust when he said the word Devil "—sorcerers, and other pagan worshippers who meddle with the works of the Creation and do not deserve to live the full term of their lives. While you won't have any supernatural powers, you will be given bodies with superior combat skills and an arsenal of weapons that would make action movies boring and unimaginative. Your bodies will be able to speak all languages necessary for a specific mission. And, as a major perk, you will receive three Reincarnation Rights. Should you die during a mission, the first three times you will be able to come back to the Heavenly Offices and get your body fixed and ready for the next mission. Should you die more than three times—" Samael grinned menacingly "—you will go back to the Movie Room, to the exact moment we extracted you, right before you burn yourself into Oblivion, with no credit for the time served."

As if anticipating our questions—not that we were allowed to ask questions anyway—he continued, "You have only one mission, one shot at redemption, and if you fail, Oblivion will be your only option. On the off chance you succeed—" his face displayed complete disbelief mixed with utter disdain for human ineptitude "—upon the completion of your mission, you will be honorably discharged. While you will still have to go back to the Movie Room, you will no longer face imminent Oblivion, and your time there will be shortened for the time served in the Program, with some of the most reprehensible episodes of your prior life deleted. If the Creator deems you worthy, you will then be allowed to go to Heaven."

At that, I'd felt a sudden trickle of hope but Samael quickly dashed it.

He paused for greater effect. "I do not like this Program and I think scum like you, who were on the verge of Oblivion when we brought you in, should go back to suffer and perish in the Movie Room while we Angels deal with idolaters and paganists. But I cannot question the judgment of the Creator. Do not think, however, that you have gotten a get-out-of-jail-free card. You are not allowed to use your skills for anything other than the mission, and any attempt to do so will result in immediate expulsion and return to the Movie Room. Most important: Under no circumstance are you allowed to murder innocent bystanders. Your kill rights are limited to the targets of your mission along with anyone who stands in your way and actively and maliciously interferes with it. What constitutes actively and maliciously? That would be decided by my Department in each individual case. I won't give you a benefit of the doubt, so try to avoid murder at all costs. In addition, the Creator has allowed me to remove you from the Program for any, and I mean *any*, infraction, and I won't hesitate to use that power." His nostrils flared and his eyes glowed red.

During that induction ceremony, Samael had the look and aura of an all-powerful Satan, the very embodiment of the destructive forces of the Creation, instilling fear and awe in everyone present.

However, now, standing here in the Courtroom watching

him, I saw a completely different personality. Samael looked like just another servant of the Creator striving to please. His face was full of genuine adoration and dedication.

After Samael finished his summation, Archangel Michael stood up. He ran the Heavenly Accountability Office, serving as Solicitor General and Comptroller General. His job in the Courtroom was to defend a soul being judged and reduce the sentence. He wore a suit and tie, the standard Angel uniform. For some reason, he reminded me of the renowned civil rights lawyer, Ron Kuby, a bespectacled, fiery advocate with unruly gray hair gathered in a ponytail. It's funny how stereotypes affect our mind's eye, assigning human images to non-corporeal Angels.

Michael started delivering a passionate speech but I couldn't understand a word. I turned quizzically to Baphomet.

He snickered. "Can't understand the lingo, ah? They speak in the Angels' tongue, very similar to the language of the First Man. Even I have trouble understanding it."

I could see he was struggling to catch a few words. Dumb ass! Demons always try to eavesdrop on Angels, so when humans call on them they can pretend they are in the know. Of course, most of the time they get it wrong, which is why Satanic rituals rarely produce real results. What wouldn't a creature do to stroke his ego? Even though they know it can get them excised, deep down they still strive for the moment of glory when people worship them.

Lost in my musings, I suddenly realized that something,

or someone, was missing from the Courtroom. I turned to Baphomet and whispered, "Where is the Creator?"

He silently tipped his head toward the podium at the center of the Courtroom. Flanked by rows of honorary ceremonial Angel gurads stood the diamond-encrusted Throne of Glory. A luminescent ball of light shrouded in a cloud hovered above the Throne.

"You cannot see him, no one can. You can only see the products of Creation, both spiritual and material, but He is outside of time and space and cannot be seen, even by the Angels. The Throne of Glory is all you can see, and even that is only because you are no longer alive and have shed your mortal shell. You can feel his presence though. Come closer, just don't stick your head out."

I crawled closer to the Throne, keeping my distance. Suddenly, a feeling of warmth and indescribable happiness, the likes of which I had never experienced, overwhelmed me. At the same time, a sharp pain of embarrassment over my past transgressions pierced my soul. Yet, the pain was not the same as what I'd felt in the Movie Room—it was more of a sadness for not following His rules, along with a clear sense that, ultimately, He would fix all the wrongs.

I was frozen. No doubt, the all-knowing Creator was aware of my presence but he didn't call on his ceremonial guard nor did he interrupt Michael's passionate argument.

I looked at Baphomet, frazzled and unable to understand my own feelings.

"Yeah, it is impossible to break the bond with the Creator," Baphomet answered my silent question. "Every creature vies for his closeness, as the greatest joy in existence, even though we are all embarrassed by our lowliness in his presence."

Hearing a poetic speech from a Demon was something new but, I guess the Creator had this effect on all his creatures.

As I experienced an intense high, something pulled me out of the Courtroom. The feeling of losing the temporary bond with the Creator was immensely painful, sort of a psychic withdrawal on steroids, more powerful than a junkie would ever experience. I didn't want to lose the bond. Yet, I couldn't resist the pull.

CHAPTER 5

HA Department

As the bond broke, I found myself back in Azazel's office.

"Enjoying the bond with the Creator?" He grinned. "The closeness to Him must be earned, monkey, and there are no shortcuts to it. Also, don't get too chummy with your Demon buddies," he said matter-of-factly. "They can invite you along but the consequences will be suffered by you alone. Didn't you learn in Sunday school that Demons are great tempters, as dumb as they are?"

I sat silent, still experiencing the aftereffects of the bond with the Creator.

Seeing my unresponsiveness, Azazel added, "I will let this one slide but next time, I will report you, and your stint in the Program will be over."

I kept my mouth shut. Let him vent. He clearly hadn't called me just to chastise me for a trip to the Courtroom.

He had plenty of underlings to carry out such lowly chores, including that deranged sadist, Uzza.

Azazel switched topics. "I reviewed the contents of the folder and what was carved on the body of the sacrifice. The first few pages were mostly gibberish in Medieval Latin but it also contained an Aramaic translation of a few passages from the Book of Remedies, which we thought had been destroyed a long time ago."

"What's the Book of Remedies?" I asked without thinking.

Azazel winced. "None of your damned business. Your mission is to find out from what source they copied those passages and destroy the original, together with any other copies. For this mission you will receive a Right to issue maintenance tickets, and Ashmodai will assign a Demon to help you with the investigation."

A right to issue maintenance tickets and assistance from the Head of the Maintenance Department himself? Holy shit! This must be something very serious.

"Your body is being fixed and upgraded. You can pick it up at the Heavenly Department of Health and Human Services. In the meantime, Uzza will have your weaponry ready at Requisitions. I will send the requisition order now."

Azazel had no intention of spending another minute with me and motioned me out of his office. Seeing that I hesitated to leave, he asked, "Anything else?"

"What was carved on the body of the sacrifice?"

He shrugged. "Some dumb stuff. They carved the name of Naama. Makes no sense but then again, with you monkeys nothing makes sense."

Uh-oh. I could definitely feel that Azazel was faking his indifference.

Naama was a human from Cain's seed who had hung out with Fallen Angels and Demons in pre-Diluvian times. No one knew for sure, but the rumor had it that she had been Azazel's girlfriend and had born a child, Ashmodai, from him. Azazel was well aware of the rumor, even if it was just a rumor. The story may have been concocted by Demons envious of their own, but the fact remained that three millennia ago Ashmodai had answered an FMC from King Solomon and, instead of being excised, had been appointed Head of the Maintenance Department and the boss of all Demons. Someone important in the Heavenly Offices must have pulled some strings for him.

But still, why would those ONA guys call on Naama in their ritual? She was not part of the Heavenly Offices, and I was not even sure whether or not she'd been sent to Oblivion, notwithstanding her boyfriend's connections. Strange, indeed.

But not something I needed to worry about right now.

I nodded and went to the Heavenly Health and Human Services Department to get back my body.

The HHS looked like a whitewashed building with an immaculate white interior. As Surgeon General in charge of the Heavenly Health and Human Services, Archangel Rafael ran the Department in his own image as a clean-freak and germaphobe—whatever that could mean in the case of an Archangel. His subordinates, striving to please their boss, kept the place sterile. A crew of Demons on the janitorial ticket worked the cleaning equipment, attacking every speck of dust in the building.

At the sight of a soul walking in, the receptionist in a white robe, face mask, and nurse's cap cringed as if she had just seen a cockroach. I handed her the body order, which she took with her fingernails, afraid to touch anything soiled by a soul. She examined the order and squeamishly raised her hand for me to wait. There were no chairs in the reception area so I had to stand. In a few moments, another Angelic being in a white robe, face mask, and nurse's cap showed up and took me to the ICU.

The wait had been long, but the procedure itself was short. I was stuck into a humming capsule, heard a few clicks, and emerged in the body of a stately-looking elderly gentleman. I had specifically asked Azazel to order the body of an elderly gentleman instead of the body of a jock I'd used for my Colorado ONA mission—which I wanted to save for something more action-oriented—and even though the HHS was very stingy with new bodies, they begrudgingly accommodated the order. Wearing the body of an older man whom no one would suspect of fighting skills was a great disguise. Inside, however, the body was superbly made. I flexed the muscles and did a few shadowboxing moves. Yeah, the accouterments were all there. I could feel the power of this body, its perfectly honed combat skills, and its enormous intellect. That was exactly what the doctor ordered, literally.

Body testing, however, was not part of the procedure. Angels felt offended that some monkey could doubt their ability to sculpt a body in perfect compliance with the order specs.

"Do you also want to try an IQ test?" asked one of them sarcastically, after which I was quickly kicked out of the Department.

CHAPTER 6

Maintenance Department

Unlike the HHS, the Maintenance Department was loud, filthy, and packed with Demons going in and out of various maintenance jobs. However, even amidst this chaos, the corner office of the Head of Maintenance was as spacious and posh as any other office of a department head. A well-groomed she-Demon served as the receptionist. As any Demon with an inferiority complex, she couldn't let me in right away. She didn't even bother to buzz her boss but instead showed me to one of the chairs in the reception area.

The door to the office was slightly open and I could hear Ashmodai talking to someone in the Angelic language. By the tone of it, it sounded more like a social call and I was here on business. Demons were a lower class and had no right to treat me as if they were Angels.

"Are you going to tell your boss I am here?" I demanded

impatiently. "I have an order from Azazel and don't have time to wait."

"You'll wait your turn, monkey. Can't you hear he is on the phone?" she retorted contemptuously.

"I may be a monkey but Azazel is not going to appreciate that the social calls of your boss take precedence over his business. Do you want me to call him and find out?"

Not knowing the substance of my business, she decided to play it safe. Azazel could easily send any Demon to Oblivion if he so chose. She buzzed the boss.

I heard Ashmodai's irritated voice, "What's so urgent? Can't you hear I am on the phone?"

"Pardon me, sir, but there is a monkey claiming he is here on urgent business from Azazel."

After a moment of silence, probably weighing his fear of Azazel against his disdain for human monkeys, Ashmodai finally barked, "Tell him to wait a couple of minutes. I will be right with him."

I was now fuming. Ashmodai or no Ashmodai, I got enough crap from Angels to be given the run-around by a Demon. A few minutes turned into a good hour before I was finally called in.

Ashmodai was sitting behind a large desk in an office that was almost a carbon copy of Azazel's, down to the smallest details—a testament to Ashmodai's desire to be like an Angel.

I had never seen him before. He didn't look like the rest of the Demons. He wore the same dark navy-blue suit as the Angels, and his hair was meticulously combed. Only his glowing red eyes and the fancifully polished horns sticking out of his hair betrayed his true nature. His behavior was very much like that of an Angel, arrogant and dismissive of all other creatures. No wonder other Demons didn't like him, considering him a backstabber and a snake.

"So, what's the rush, monkey?" he asked with a smirk. He didn't even offer me to sit, making me stand in front of his desk.

"Didn't you read the maintenance ticket? It had everything you need to know," I retorted.

"Oh, the maintenance ticket. I see," he said sarcastically. "I have so many of them that I cannot remember each one, especially one involving a monkey."

"You should have remembered this one, as it came directly from Azazel. I need a Demon assigned to me to find the Book of Remedies."

He shuffled through the papers on his desk pretending to look for my maintenance ticket even though I was sure he was well aware of it. He clearly didn't like my tone any more than I liked his.

"So, the monkey is tasked with finding a valuable book of ancient wisdom, and on top of that, he wants a Demon to be his errand boy. Well, that's a first." His voice had become louder and more menacing.

"You know, I don't have time for this shit," I said. "You got the maintenance ticket, just do what Azazel ordered or I am going back and telling him you defied his direct orders."

This was the last straw. Ashmodai growled and clenched his hairy fists. "Don't be too cocky, monkey. Azazel *asked* me to help you and if you behave like this, I will send you straight to the Movie Room. You are a fucking nobody and should behave accordingly." He pounded his fist on the table.

"Whatever." Fighting Ashmodai was probably not prudent either, especially if the rumor of Azazel's paternity was true. "Just get on with the program, will you?"

I could see in his eyes that he was tempted to pound me into dust, but damaging a body just outfitted by Rafael's Angels and still bearing HHS's tags could cost him dearly. He might try to look like an Angel, but he was still just a Demon.

So, I sat down in a chair and crossed my legs.

Still fuming, he hit the intercom button and asked the receptionist to call Abaddon.

Abaddon appeared right away, looking at his boss with the devotion of a well-trained dog.

"Take this monkey to the Records and find him whatever we have on the Book of Remedies. Get him out of here. I cannot stand his human stench anymore."

Abaddon obsequiously bowed and took me to the Records Room.

CHAPTER 7

The Records Room.

The Records Room was situated in Archangel Uriel's shop, the Department of Energy. I surmised that Uriel was in charge of the Records Room because he was in charge of light and energy and, therefore, all natural occurrences in the Creation but this chain of command made as little sense to me as putting the Maintenance Department under the Department of Justice.

Oh well…

The Records Room looked like an ancient dusty library with manuscripts and scrolls placed on the many shelves and file cabinets, all arranged in neat rows. I briefly wondered why my mind's eye didn't imagine it as a supercomputer with multiple screens. Maybe, I was born before computers came into use?

A bespectacled Angel librarian looked at us suspiciously. A monkey and a Demon coming to the room filled with the sacred records of the Creation wasn't an everyday occurrence. She carefully studied the maintenance ticket, confirming its authenticity, and then, still uneasy, pointed us in the direction of the relevant shelving units.

Abaddon peered intently at the shelves, and they started shifting until the shelf we needed finally opened up. Some of the folios flew into the air and landed on a reading console.

"So, what did you find?" I asked impatiently.

Abaddon looked puzzled. "This is a hard one—there are no records."

"What do you mean, no records?"

"Well, there is a general description of the Book of Remedies in the catalog. The Book is credited to Noah's son, Shem, who received it from Azazel—one of the screw-ups that cost him the Attorney General position."

"Azazel?" No wonder he had been so cagy about the contents of the Book. "Why would he do that? Give it to a human?"

Abaddon gloated anticipating the pleasure of sharing a gossip and showing his familiarity with the system. "Guess who was Shem's mom? Naama, no less. Our stiff-necked Azazel had a soft spot for his girlfriend and she thought her kid might need it after the Deluge with no one around."

Struggling to remember my Sunday school education, I asked "Wasn't that a different Naama, from Seth, rather than from Cain?"

Still enjoying his mastery of the secrets of the Creation, Abaddon waved his hand. "That's what your Sacred Texts say but have you ever thought why the names were the same? Naama's relationship with Azazel was a huge embarrassment for the Heavenly Offices so the story was slightly altered. Not to mention that no one wanted to admit the seed of murderous Cain was alive and well in you monkeys. In the grand scheme of things, it didn't matter anyway, as the entire pre-Diluvian civilization was wiped out, so the Creator chose to overlook the previous shenanigans of his Archangels."

Things were getting curiouser and curiouser by the moment. Now, I was genuinely interested. "So what happened to the Book afterward?"

"According to the catalog, it made its way through Mesopotamia, ended up in Judea, and was then destroyed as heretical by King Hezekiah, the ruler of the Kingdom of Judah in the 7th century BCE. After that, nothing."

"Nothing? How?"

Exactly what I said. There are no surviving records of either its contents or its whereabouts. Someone carefully expunged all records about the Book."

"You have got to be kidding. How do you expunge the records from the Creation?" I asked incredulously.

"Beats me, buddy. The Archangels are the only ones with unrestricted access to the Records Room, so they are the only ones who could possibly have tampered with them."

"And the Creator would allow that?"

"Your guess is as good as mine. No one knows what the Creator would or wouldn't allow. For you monkeys, there are the Sacred Texts that contain all the rules of the Creation applicable to humans, even if the storyline may be…well, allegoric in certain places, to emphasize the point. For us, Demons, there is the Maintenance Manual. Beyond those, only Archangels interpret and apply the law."

"So, it must have been one of Samael, Michael, Rafael, Gabriel or Uriel who did it?"

"Look at you, genius," Abaddon laughed sarcastically. "Did you figure it out on your own or that is what they taught you in the Pilot Program? Of course, it was one of them."

"The question is which one," I said mostly to myself.

"Brilliant. You monkeys never disappoint when it comes to stupid ideas. Are you now going to investigate the Archangels? Good luck, buddy. Just don't scream too loudly when they stick you back in the Movie Room before sending you to Oblivion."

He had a point. It was not like I could barge into the offices of one of them and ask. I started thinking of the alternatives, when suddenly a lightbulb clicked in in my head.

"Wait. The ritual where I got the folder was performed by the ONA, right? Or, to be precise, by their U.S. chapter. They had to have gotten the excerpt from somewhere. If that's the case, maybe we can figure out the source by checking with their headquarters in the U.K."

"Hmm." Abaddon nodded and quickly checked the ONA records. "Good idea. Looks like you are going to Whitchurch."

"Going where?"

"Whitchurch, England, Headquarters of the ONA."

What a great location for an occult organization! With all the mystery surrounding the Book, I was anxious to get to the bottom of it.

Before we left, however, I had one more question. "What language was the Book written in?"

"It is not listed in the catalog but judging by the time it was written, it must be the language of the First Man, which was a variation of the Angelic language. Why do you ask?"

"Azazel said the excerpt was written in Aramaic. Was Aramaic the language of the First Man?"

"Not at all. It sounded a bit like a mixture of Sumerian, Aramaic, and ancient Hebrew but you wouldn't be able to understand it if someone spoke it in your presence, just as you couldn't understand Michael and Samael in the Courtroom."

I looked at him quizzically. How did he know about the Courtroom? Did that big-mouth Baphomet blabber to everyone about our adventure?

"Word spreads fast in the Heavenly Offices, you know." Abaddon winked. "Anyway, being born before the Deluge, Noah and his sons spoke the language of the First Man, but it was lost when the Creator confused the languages at the Tower of Babel. After that, no one understood it, save for a few Chaldean and Jewish mystics, who safeguarded the knowledge, but even they eventually lost it. Do you want a religious education class?"

"Not really. But, that would mean whoever translated it

must have been one of those mystics who had the knowledge, right? Which would limit the time and locale of our search, don't you think? Maybe Azazel can give us some leads."

Abaddon shook his goat head. "Nah, I don't think so. I wouldn't trust him too much on this topic. The whole Book affair is a very sensitive subject for him. It's probably why he decided to get a Pilot Program monkey involved, so word won't get to his higher-ups. I'll bet he didn't even report the finding to Samael."

His reasoning sounded logical. "So, let's go to the UK," I said as we left the Records Room after being carefully searched by the Angel librarian who was still suspicious of us.

The prospect of finding the Book of Remedies that had mysteriously disappeared from the Records Room along with all traces of it piqued my natural curiosity, but that was not the only reason I was anxious to start the search. Somehow, deep down, I felt this mission might provide me with the answers that cost me a Reincarnation Right at the Moffat forest ONA ritual in Colorado. I knew mysteries tended to come in pairs, so why would this one be any different?

There was one more stop I had to make before I embarked on the journey.

The Requisition Room was located next to the Movie Room, with both being supervised by Uzza, a Fallen Angel and sadist par excellence who had been caught screwing earthly women in pre-Diluvian times. For all his escapades, he had been demoted to Movie Room supervisor—not that he was capable of any real job anyway—deriving minor pleasures from the screams of souls suffering through watching their wretched lives. The Movie Room was not soundproof, and as I passed it, the sounds of tortured souls brought back unpleasant memories of my experience in this accursed place. I felt nauseous and my body retched.

""What, cannot hold your guts?" Uzza was grinning at me. "Don't worry, you will be back here in no time for the full experience. For you Pilot Program monkeys, I will make it 3D with special effects—an Uzza special!"

I chose to ignore him. No reason to argue with assholes. Instead I asked,

"Have you received a requisition order from Azazel? I need my weapons."

Oh, yeah." Uzza smiled. If there was anything he enjoyed more than the sounds of wretched souls coming from the Movie Room, it was looking at maiming and killing devices, imagining the carnage they could inflict. "Here you go." He unlocked the Weapons Room and let me in. "Choose whatever you want."

I picked a few Kevlar-lined items of clothing, then looked for something suitable for my mission body. In the corner of the room stood an exquisitely carved cane with a fancy silver handle.

I pointed. "What's that?"

Uzza smiled. "Oh, a monkey with taste," he quipped. He took the cane, and in a fast move, unsheathed a sharp narrow blade hidden inside. "Just don't forget to limp when you carry it."

Excellent. The cane would do nicely. I picked it up. As every extra minute in the proximity of the Movie Room made me sick, I hastily ran out, hoping my mission would succeed and I would never again need to suffer in the Movie Room as I had suffered the first time around.

CHAPTER 8

Whitchurch, UK

Use of the maintenance tunnels that would have provided instantaneous access to any location in the World was not allowed for non-Demons. No matter. Travel in the Pilot Program was one of the more enjoyable parts of the job. A nice perk of the Pilot Program was an unlimited expense account. So, the next day, I awoke refreshed in the morning after a restful flight to Manchester in a first-class seat. After a short hour-and-a-half train ride, I got off at the Whitchurch train station.

It looked like the quintessential English countryside in late autumn. The air was crisp and cool, and the vibrant colors of gold and red painted the trees surrounding the station. With each step, my feet crunched against the fallen leaves that carpeted the ground. This was one of those rare dry days on the English Isles with no sign of rain in the immediate forecast. For a moment, I felt like an ordinary tourist soaking in the picturesque surroundings and relishing in the pleasant weather.

I had called the ONA before my trip asking for an appointment with their CEO, Mr. Anton Long, to discuss certain financial matters, as I put it. The guy on the phone had sounded polite but asked too many questions, to which I'd answered that the matters were best discussed in person. I kept hinting at a large bequest I was considering leaving to the organization. Finally, he'd given up and made the appointment to come in and talk.

Finding ONA headquarters was not easy. The nondescript building stood inconspicuously nestled among the lush greenery, resembling more of a quaint English manor than a center for occult rituals. No menacing gargoyles adorned its roof, nor were there any pentagrams or other signs of demonic worship in evidence. The entrance was free of cobwebs, instead welcoming visitors with a well-manicured lawn and a set of sturdy oak doors. Yet, looks could be deceiving, and this innocuous image clearly was.

I surreptitiously cased the house and its surroundings.

The door was not guarded from the outside, but two cameras masterfully hidden on nearby trees were trained straight at the entry. In fact, the whole building was covered by cameras. The NFL games on TV didn't show as many angles as this extensive surveillance system. In addition, it looked like laser motion detectors covered all accesses to the house, set up high enough not to be triggered by rabbits but low enough to pick up any approaching human. I didn't need to play limbo, though, to avoid laser beams and cameras. I had a legitimate appointment and a great disguise of an old man. I went straight to the door and rang the bell.

Whoever was watching the cameras saw an elderly grey-haired, slightly hunched gentleman with a limp, leaning on a cane and wearing a brown fedora—with Kevlar lining—and a long, badly fitting, worn-out trench coat—also hiding a Kevlar lining. I had purposefully avoided carrying weapons, as a body search at the entrance was a virtual certainty. The combination of a fanciful cane and a worn-out outfit created the impression of someone who came from money but had successfully squandered his fortune. Who would be worried about this relic of a bygone era?

The door was opened by a muscular, brutish-looking guy with a buzzcut and a bulging jacket barely covering his nine-millimeter holstered on his left side.

Putting on my best smile, I touched the brim of my hat. "Good day to you, sir. I was wondering if I might perchance see Mr. Long." My body spoke the king's English with a noticeable Oxford accent. Nice touch.

The brute was not impressed. "You got an appointment, mate?"

"Oh, yes. I called and spoke with a chap whose name I cannot recall. I think he was someone in your public relations department."

"Wait here," the guard barked and picked up his walkie-talkie.

I couldn't make out the conversation, but in a few minutes, a man came out to greet me. His impeccably tailored suit hugged his frame, accentuating his broad shoulders and trim waist. His clean-shaven face was graced by an obligatory smile, and his hair had been carefully combed into a sleek style. He exuded an air of refinement and civility, most likely tasked with maintaining a polished public image for this organization.

"Hello, sir. I am a director of public affairs for the ONA. May I ask who you are, and to what we owe the honor of your visit?" His voice sounded the same as that of the fellow on the phone a few days ago.

Ignoring his request for my name, I reminded him of our conversation. "I believe I spoke with you on the phone. I wanted to talk with someone in your organization regarding a monetary matter, a bequest of sorts. I don't know whether you are a person in charge of financial affairs, but perhaps we could go to your office and speak in private?"

My experience that greed combined with complacency opened even the most tightly closed doors didn't fail me. The guy smiled and motioned me to come in. The brute at the door took another look at me as an old piece of harmless junk and lazily patted me down without even looking at the cane. Good. He'd saved me a few moments of unnecessary work killing the entire crew manning the entrance.

We went upstairs and Mr. Sleek Suit showed me to his office. As he opened the door welcoming me in, I made sure to let him go first.

"After you sir, I insist," I said smiling, and closed the door behind me.

The office had a sofa and two cushioned chairs around a glass coffee table. He picked up a bottle and glasses from the credenza. "Whiskey?" He poured a generous serving to himself and me.

I nodded and raised the glass. I toasted making his acquaintance, all the while lightly navigating him to the sofa, away from phones and the panic button doubtlessly built into his desk. Once we dispensed with pleasantries, he sat on the sofa and I on a chair, sitting slightly above him as I'd wanted.

"So, what is the monetary matter that brings you here, Mr…?"

Ignoring his question about my name for the second time, I went straight to business. Everything was in place and there was no reason to play games anymore.

My Oxford accent disappeared and I squinted my eyes. "I have a confession to make. I lied to you. What I really need is to see your boss, Mr. Long, so I can beat the daylights out of him to get some information I need. And you will give me his whereabouts right now, or my beating the daylights will start with you." I winked and unsheathed the blade from the cane.

The guy was not impressed. I am sure he'd had too many dealings with both thugs and law enforcement to be scared by my tirade or the look of the blade. Notwithstanding his cultured appearance, he probably had some martial arts training and was surrounded by a formidable security force in the building.

Thus, an old man armed with a sword didn't seem to bother him too much. Putting an expression of contemptuous boredom on his face, he got up.

"Oh, Please. Don't bother with your ridiculous toys. Who are you anyway? Police, MI-5, a disgruntled customer? You know what? Don't answer. Security will figure it out." He went casually to his desk.

It was time to disabuse him of his preconceived notions about my capabilities. Without getting off the chair, I hit his chin with the handle of the cane. His head shook violently. I jumped up, blocking his way to the desk, and put his head in a lock before he could even move. The guy was shocked either from the suffocating headlock or the speed at which I jumped at him, or both, it didn't matter.

"Please don't do anything stupid, my friend. Just tell me where Mr. Long is, and I will be on my merry way."

"He is not here," Mr. Sleek Suit said in a hoarse voice, struggling to breathe.

"Wrong answer." I squeezed his throat a bit more.

His face turned purple.

"Have you ever seen a python killing its victim?" I said calmly while continuing to apply pressure. "They squeeze and squeeze and squeeze, slowly crushing the life out of the body of their prey. It is a very painful death."

He gasped for air. He tried to scream but couldn't.

Covering his mouth to prevent any noise, I whispered, "Did you get the point, or should I squeeze tighter?"

He started gurgling, his eyes consumed with fear. Yet, the fear of his boss was apparently still stronger than his fear of me. The fool.

I squeezed tighter. "Nod if you know where Mr. Long is and, if you play games with me, I will crush the life out of your worthless body, so you better give me the right answer."

He finally nodded. I eased my grip still keeping my palm over his mouth to prevent screaming.

"Should be in his office," he said wheezing.

"Which is where?"

He moved his eyes to the right. "In his office. The corner office at the end of the hallway."

Naturally, the big boss had to have a corner office.

"Are you absolutely sure? Because I am going to tie and gag you while I check, and if your memory is faulty I will come back and finish what I started. Am I understood?"

He nodded emphatically. I could see in his eyes that the fear of me had finally overshadowed the fear of his boss. "He is there. I am telling you the truth, mate, trust me."

Famous last words.

Rather than gagging him, I dealt him a measured blow to the head. That should keep him down for at least fifteen minutes, enough time to get to the boss's office and start my interrogation.

I walked out of the PR office and went straight in the direction he gave me. The hallway was full of people walking back and forth, but no one paid me any attention after I smiled and touched the brim of my hat, welcoming each passerby. I quietly opened the door to Long's office and went in. This room was in stark contrast to Mr. Sleek Suit's elegant office. It was filled with Nazi paraphernalia and occult implements. Demonic symbols were painted on every wall, along with strange-looking hieroglyphics.

Anton Long sat in the middle of the room on a rug in the Lotus pose, legs crossed and arms hanging freely, surrounded by candles. He wore a free-flowing robe, and a large skull cap perched atop his head struggled to contain his wild and unkempt locks of hair. A pungent odor emanated from him and, judging by the smell, he may not have washed recently. His blank stare, fixed on some distant point, gave off a feeling that he was trapped in a trance-like state, oblivious to everything around him.

I slightly touched his shoulder. "Mr. Long?"

He didn't react. I shook him stronger, after which he raised his head, his gaze remaining unfocused. "Who are you?" His speech was slightly slurred. He may have been under the influence of drugs. If he was indeed high, it would present a complication. Beating the information out of an intoxicated person was much more arduous than out of a sober one.

"Well, let's say I am a concerned citizen here to inquire into the Moffat, Colorado incident a few days ago."

"Ah." his voice was devoid of any emotion. "What are you, FBI?"

I was growing impatient. "No, I am not but I do know that

people at the Moffat ritual were affiliated with your shop. I don't care about your issues with the law. All I need to know is how the grand master of your U.S. chapter led the ceremony using a passage from the Book of Remedies."

"Book of what?"

This circus started to bore me and I decided to nudge him a bit. I hit him over the head with the cane. He whimpered and started sobering up. "Hey, what the fuck, man?"

I hit him again. "Stop playing games with me. I don't have the time or the patience to deal with you. So, tell me where you got the passage from the Book of Remedies while I am still asking nicely, or I will beat you up so badly your own mother won't recognize you in the morgue."

He started laughing, a mixture of demonic laughter and the squeaking of a junky. I lost my patience. As I was about to hit him again, I heard heavy stomping outside the office. Either I miscalculated my blow to the PR man or his skull was thicker than I expected. He must have come to his senses and alerted security. I grabbed Long, unsheathed the blade from the cane, and put it to his throat just as the door opened. A handful of security guards rushed in with guns trained at me.

I pressed the blade against Long's throat. "Tell your men to drop their guns or I will slice your artery like a pig."

He snickered again. "And, what then? If you kill me, they will riddle you with bullets."

"That wouldn't be your concern, would it?" He kept

snickering. Seeing I was not dealing with a rational man, I decided to speak directly to the guards.

"Drop your damn weapons, mates. Your boss seems to be indisposed, but you should have enough sense to understand that I will kill him before you get the chance to kill me."

The guards hesitated. I was beyond impatient and wanted to bring this stupid standoff to an end. I looked around. Two guards were inside the office, the others crowded around the entrance. This was as amateurish as it could get. Who in Zeus's name had given them the tactical awareness training?

Oh, screw it!

I moved closer to the only chair in the room, threw it up in the air using my talus, and kicked it straight into the guard closest to the door. The man stumbled, lost his footing, and conveniently blocked the men at the entrance. Throwing Long toward the stumbling man so they had no choice but to hug each other, I jumped at the remaining guard and slashed his throat before he could pull the trigger. I whipped to the second guard blocking the door and pierced him through. I grabbed Long again, and using him as a shield, lunged the sword at one of the guards blocking the entrance. The blade pierced his throat right above his Kevlar vest. As he was slowly falling to the floor, I hit the door shut and dragged Long backward, away from it.

A swarm of bullets whizzed through the door, and one of them hit Long's shoulder.

He squealed. "Stop it, you bloody idiots! You are going to

kill me for Chrissake," he yelled finally coming to his senses.

The shooting stopped.

"Well, looks like you finally sobered up, Mr. Long, so we can talk like civilized people. Let me repeat my question. Where is the Book of Remedies?"

Instead of answering my question, Long rolled his eyes, his head shaking violently, and started chanting something. Was he having a seizure?

Suddenly, the room was engulfed in thick, acrid smoke that stung my eyes and filled my nostrils with the smell of sulphur. The rug where Long had been sitting floated up in the air, revealing a blazing pentagram. Through the haze, I could see Long's body convulsing, his lips twisted into the eerie smile of a madman. What the hell…

As the smoke cleared, a familiar wooly head with glowing red eyes appeared through the pentagram. My jaw dropped. Seriously?

Beelzebub's face glowed in anticipation of the upcoming worship complete with Long prostrating before him and calling him the Prince of Hell or something like that. Then he saw me. His jaw dropped just as mine had done. "Oh, no," was written all over his face.

I recovered first. "Pause?" I mouthed silently.

Invoking a Pause meant that we slipped out of the flow of time, thereby pausing it. Humans can only go forward in time…at least for now. While no one other than the Creator can exist outside of space and time, Angels can travel back and forth in time. The lower creatures such as Demons, as well as we bodiless souls, cannot time travel, but we can get out of the flow of time for a short duration.

As we went into the Pause, the room froze and we could talk freely.

Beelzebub broke the silence first. "I guess you are on assignment." He sounded apprehensive, trying to assess how much trouble he was in.

I nodded, trying to figure out how to turn this encounter to my advantage.

"So, what's next?" His gaze betrayed his anxiety.

"You know the answer to that, my friend. You have two choices. One: You kill me, or I kill myself if you don't want to do it, and I go straight to Azazel's office on the reincarnation ticket to report you for an FMC, which, by the way, you seem to enjoy. You know the consequences. Or two: you help me find out from this Anton Long what I need to know, and I forget all about this whole incident."

"You are bluffing," said Beelzebub in a tone that sounded more like a question than a definitive statement. "You are not going to waste your Reincarnation Right just to rat me out to Azazel."

"Oh, really? Why don't you try me, you dumb goat?"

He growled. "A monkey blackmailing a full-fledged Demon? This is new."

"Your choice, buddy. If you want to stroke your ego by disobeying the Maintenance Manual, then get used to suffering the consequences, and pray that next time you won't encounter someone who is a stickler for the rules."

"Fuck you." The way he said it made it clear that he knew I'd pinned him to the wall. "What do you want to know from him?"

"I need to know where they keep the Book of Remedies."

"The Book of Remedies? The one that was lost a long time ago?"

"Yep, that one."

"How do you know they have it?"

I was not in a very talkative mood, but Beelzebub had a right to know, if he was going to help me. "Remember my Colorado assignment?"

Beelzebub nodded. "What about it?"

"They were all members of Long's ONA organization. They used a passage from the Book of Remedies in the ritual. My guess is that Long was well aware of the ritual and the incantations they used."

Beelzebub thought about that.

I decided to prod him a bit. "Hey, just do your dog and pony show with sulphur stink and Demonic roars and whatnot, and get me what I need." Seeing he was getting pissed at me, I added, "Please, with a cherry on top."

"I guess you got me." He rolled his eyes and sighed. "Give me a moment."

As we came out of the Pause, he didn't disappoint. Instead of attacking me, he turned to Long and made one of the scariest faces I'd ever seen, grabbed him, and raised him in the air. He then threw me out of the pentagram where we were all standing, so I landed at the farthest end of the room. His way of getting his petty revenge on me, no doubt.

But it worked. Long now looked really scared.

I turned and looked out of the window, whistling some lively tune. I couldn't hear what was going on inside all the smoke and roaring, but in a few moments, Beelzebub dropped an unconscious Long on the floor and turned to me. Judging by his face he'd gotten some information.

Before he opened his mouth, I raised my hand. "Let's get out of here and talk somewhere quiet."

He looked at me suspiciously.

"Don't worry, I am not reporting you, I just want to get out of this wretched place. Let's use a maintenance tunnel. There's a bunch of armed guards standing outside the door, and we don't need any extra noise, do we?"

"But humans are not supposed to use the maintenance tunnels," he objected, "especially in the presence of other humans. We cannot just vanish into thin air, exposing these people to the supernatural."

I scoffed. "Oh, so responding to an FMC from an occult junkie is fine, but using a maintenance tunnel after you showed your horned head and beat him into unconsciousness is not? It is too late for following by-the-book protocol, don't you think?"

"All right." Beelzebub reluctantly agreed. He opened up a maintenance tunnel but before we went in, he pointed to the desk. "Grab his smartphone, will you? Might be useful."

CHAPTER 9

Detroit, Michigan

As Beelzebub and I walked into the basement of the Maintenance Department, I grabbed his paw. "So, what did you find out?"

"Not much," he said. Seeing my disappointed face, he added, "But some of the things he said should be useful." Knowing his precarious situation, he was desperately trying to please me.

"Spill."

"Long came across a piece of parchment with Aramaic writing at some antique dealer's place in Syria in the late nineties, and he'd been trying to decipher it ever since. While in Syria, he tried getting it translated by people speaking Syriac, but since modern Syriac is different from the Aramaic in which the parchment was written, he was only able to figure out the gist."

"Which was?"

"Some incantations to call on Naama. As always, the ritual required a full moon at midnight, and a sacrifice—a young woman who's sexually mature. Long said if you do everything right, Naama will take possession of the woman's body and become bound to you, divulging to you ancient knowledge. Whatever that means." He waved a paw.

"How did it end up in Colorado?"

"The incantations were complex, and the approximate translation may have ended in some kind of occult disaster. Not wanting to experiment himself, Long gave it to the grand master of the U.S. chapter and let them do the ritual. You know the rest."

I frowned. "So, all they had was a translation?"

"Yeah. Long tried to get to the Book itself, did some major research, but came up with nothing. By the way, that last part might not have been true because he became very fidgety and his eyes blinked."

"Why didn't you get the truth?" I demanded.

"He passed out. You can't expect me to gauge precisely a man's strength. Some of you monkeys can withstand pressure better than others."

"Yeah, that is not very helpful," I said, disappointed.

Beelzebub looked scared. "But it's something, right? Besides, maybe this translation is all there was. Anyway, we had a deal, and I did my part."

"Don't worry about your furry hide. I am a man of my word, unlike you freakin' Demons. If I said I wouldn't tell on you, then I won't. But I definitely need a better lead."

I had to succeed at this mission. Hitting a dead end was not a good thing. Azazel would be delighted to pin a failure on me, and I could kiss goodbye to my chances of avoiding Oblivion. My only defense—claiming that someone expunged the record—I knew wouldn't sit well with the Archangels.

Thus, a dead end meant a quick trip to the Movie Room, with the sure ticket to Oblivion.

Seeing my frustration, to his credit Beelzebub tried to be helpful. "What about Long's cellphone? He said he was trying to find the Book, so he must have contacted someone. Maybe we can find something useful in his texts or emails."

Not that they had smartphones in the nineties. Still, Long might have continued to pursue the Book ever since finding the page.

"You know, you are not as dumb as you look, my friend," I said.

Beelzebub was so proud of his suggestion that he let my insult go.

"The only question is how can I open it? Can you do it for me?"

He smiled coyly and grabbed the phone. For a quick moment his face turned into Long's face, and the phone's facial rec ID instantly unlocked it.

After changing the password to something I'd easily remember, I started poring through the phone's archives. Most of his texts and emails contained ordinary occult crap, but one email caught my attention. It had been sent from the University of Detroit Mercy Aramaic Studies Department, thanking Long for his recent donation and suggesting that he come in and discuss the research he was interested in. The email bore the signature of an assistant professor, Dr. Shamoun Khoshaba.

This was promising. A thug like Long wouldn't have any scientific aspirations unless they were needed in his occult rituals and contacting the Aramaic department of a University was too much of a coincidence, definitely worth exploring.

A quick search in the University of Detroit directory showed Dr. Khoshaba was a post-doctoral graduate of Harvard's Divinity School with a specialty in the gnostic sects of early Christianity. He was a project director focusing on Apocrypha.

I replied to his email from Long's phone, expressing my interest in meeting with him. The response came quickly, thanking me again for a generous donation and offering a few dates for a visit to discuss my particular interest. I scheduled a meeting and was soon on my way to Detroit.

As I walked through the University of Detroit Mercy campus, spread over a few acres of wooded area and teeming with noisy young people, I experienced a strange sensation of sadness and a stinging feeling in my heart. A sense of fresh air and bursts of vitality filling to the brim this institution of young and vigorous human beings reminded me of how much I missed being alive. Yes, my body's senses were in working order and I could smell the same fresh air and experience the same vitality, but it was not real. Deep down, I knew this world was not mine, and the body was just a well-made suit disguising me as one of them but not capable of making me one of them..

And it made me ponder. Since I will never be alive again, why was I so scared of Oblivion? After all, isn't nothingness better than an endless and futile sense of want? Why should we always assume that a carefree life in Paradise is better than a struggle on earth? That being a soul devoid of physical desires is better than experiencing the intense feelings of having sex with a partner you are attracted to, or enjoying the adrenaline rush when you skydive from a plane? What is it in us humans that drives us to abstinence and deprivation in order to earn a few moments of languishing through a boring and pointless existence in a place not one of us has ever seen or experienced? Even though I have never been to Heaven, and chances are I never will, I bet every soul that has actually made it there would give their entire Heavenly abode for a whiff of fresh air caressing their cheeks or the smell of perfume on their lover. If the Creation is rigged in such a way that there is no going back to physical existence, maybe Oblivion is not such a bad place after all.

On the other hand, the fear of Oblivion and craving for Heaven has been ingrained in our genetic makeup to such an extent that no rational thinking could overcome those primal feelings. No matter how much I tell myself the only alternative to life worth pursuing is nothingness, I will never convince myself of that.

Or, is there an alternative—a true reincarnation and a

return to the physical plane? Nothing I've seen or heard in the Heavenly Offices has suggested such a possibility, but instead of a ticket to Heaven, is there a way I could negotiate a second chance at life…even if it cost me another trip to the Movie Room? After all, the One who created life could surely give it back.

Clearly, this Book of Remedies is a big deal for the Heavenly Offices, and when I find it, maybe I will have enough leverage to swap it for a second shot at life. Who knows? *There are more things in Heavens and Earth, Horatio, than are dreamt of in your philosophy…*

My head got heavy from all these thoughts and I brushed them off for the time being and focused on the task at hand.

Dr. Khoshaba's office was hidden deep in the bowels of one of the campus buildings. The room was covered in reams of paper and books lying everywhere, a sure sign of an academic dedicated to his work. He was in his late forties, of medium height and slight of frame, with unkempt jet-black hair and piercing dark eyes. A photo on his desk showed him with a good-looking woman and two cherubic little girls, proudly standing on the deck of a sailboat under the sign for Gross-Pointe Yacht Club and holding some sort of trophy. They had probably just finished a race, as they were all wet. Their shiny smiles were so contagious I couldn't help but smile myself.

I walked in and introduced myself as Anton Long. As I had guessed, he must never have seen Anton Long in person. He greeted me and shook my hand, thanking me for my donation.

We started out talking about the books of the Bible that hadn't made the Canon. The more he talked, the more I realized I was dealing with a scientist who had nothing to do with the shady world of the occult. All my ideas about enlisting him into my mission disappeared. First, exposing a decent human being to a cesspool of filth that no detergent can wash off your skin would be terribly unfair. Second, the Book of Remedies had to be destroyed, and no academic would ever stand idle while an ancient artifact was being destroyed. That meant I would have no choice but to orphan his beautiful family. Not a good choice, either..

I asked him if he'd made any interesting discoveries while researching the gnostic sects. Nothing was easier than leading an academic to talk about his favorite subject. His eyes lit up. He described his latest examination of the Nag Hammadi library of gnostic gospels and how he'd deciphered some of the texts.

Seeing a puzzled look on my face and happy about the opportunity to speak of his favorite subject, he clattered as a machine gun. "Oh, you've never heard of the Nag Hammadi library? It was the find of a century, in my opinion, rivaling the Qumran discovery. It was a library of gnostic gospels hidden in Nag Hammadi, Egypt. I wrote a book about the discovery." He glanced around. "Where did I put it? Oh, here it is. Let me gift it to you. No, please, I insist. I don't pretend to be a great writer, but the very topic lends itself to an exciting narrative."

This went on and on and on, and I didn't have the heart to stop him. But as fascinating as the subject may be to academics and history buffs, it was not what I had come for. I needed to pivot him in the right direction.

As he paused to take a breath, I delicately interjected, "The way you talk about it, doctor, can excite even someone as thick-skulled as I am."

He smiled and opened his mouth but I didn't want to get another history lecture.

I quickly went on, "Yet, I was wondering what you thought about the piece I sent you."

This was purely an educated guess since I had no way of knowing whether Long had, in fact, sent him a copy of the parchment, but thankfully I got it right..

"Oh, yes!" he said. "The excerpt that you sent me. I did look at it."

Now he'd gotten my undivided attention. "And?"

"The text appears to be a translation of a chapter from the Book of Remedies."

No kidding. But I wanted to test his expertise. "So, it is not the original?"

"No, no. The Book of Remedies was destroyed in the seventh century B.C. by the Judean King Hezekiah, who believed the Book was too heretical to be read. However, the translation was written in the Mandaean variant of Aramaic language used in Babylonia and Persia in the second century A.D."

I couldn't help asking despite risking another lecture. "Which variant?"

Dr. Khoshaba regarded me with the expression of a grown-up looking at a child still learning their ABCs. "Mandaeans were an early Christian sect that flourished in Mesopotamia and Babylonia. Their language was a variant of Aramaic and that was the language in which your piece was written, Mr. Long. They believed that Shem, the Son of Noah and the presumed author of the Book of Remedies, was a prophet. Not many of them are left but they are still around and are protected by Islam as People of the Book, along with the Jews and the Christians. Nowadays, those who haven't emigrated from the Middle East live mostly around southern Iran and southwestern Iraq."

"So, they must have found the Book?"

"No, I didn't say that. But this piece piqued my interest and I did a quick research. As I looked at some lore regarding Mandaean holy writings, I came across an interesting mention of Jezebel, the evil queen of the Northern Kingdom of Israel, who used the Book of Remedies to access *Senyavis*, the place of evil creatures in Mandaean theology, thus desecrating the sacred wirings of the Prophet Shem."

"And?"

I got another look of a patient adult helping a child take his first steps in the art of reading. "Well, that would mean that even though Hezekiah destroyed the Book, the Northern Kingdom must have had its own copy. I am sure that a powerful witch like Jezebel found plenty of uses for it. Apparently, Jezebel's copy still existed at a much later time. Otherwise, there would have been no way to translate it into Aramaic. That being said, the Book is said to be written in the language of the First

Man, the knowledge of which was lost a long time ago. So, the translation you saw must have been done by the last speakers of that language, deep in antiquity."

I frowned. "So, how could the Mandaeans come into possession of Jezebel's copy of the Book?"

Excitement lit Dr. Khoshaba's face. "Now you are hitting on one of the most fascinating subjects that has concerned historians for many centuries. Legend has it that the lost tribes of the Northern Kingdom of Israel exiled by the Assyrian King Sennacherib most likely went to Persia and Afghanistan by way of Mesopotamia. While proof of that remains elusive, if the legend is true, some of them may have settled in Iran and Iraq and morphed into Mandaeans. So, the Book may have been kept by those settlers, or it may have been taken elsewhere by the lost tribes, but some bits and pieces remained in the memory of the settlers who assimilated into the Mandaeans. This is, of course, speculation since no one has ever done serious genetic research, but the parchment you sent me may be circumstantial proof of the story."

"Do you think there's a way to track down the Book through the remnants of Mandaeans?"

"I tried, but the Australian Mandaean diaspora had no records of the Book, and researching in Iran or Iraq was very challenging. Mandaeans are tolerated, but their rights are not particularly upheld, like any minority in that neck of the woods. So, they keep mum about their religion, trying to avoid undue attention from the government."

Okay, so I needed to check on Mandaeans in Iraq and Iran and track down people who were not particularly keen on being discovered. Sounded like too much sleuthing, but with Abaddon's help I might be able to narrow the search.

As if hearing my thoughts, Dr. Khoshaba added, "There is a great Mandaean library in Iran at the Mandaean Council of Ahwaz but I don't think Westerners are welcome in Iran."

Bingo. I had my first stop. I energetically shook his hand. "Thank you, doctor. You've been extremely helpful. Let me see if I have better luck with the research."

He looked puzzled. I guess I didn't strike him as a bookworm type. Yet, due to the sizeable donation and a promise for more, he was polite. "Good luck with everything, Mr. Long, and please do let me know if you find anything."

PART II

THE MISSION

CHAPTER 1

Ahwaz, Iran

Now that my mission had received a boost from Dr. Khoshaba, I came back to the HHS.

The receptionist recognized me with a scowl. "What do you want?"

"Need an upgrade."

"What?" My audacity offended her to the core. "First you ask to get a new body even though your original body could have been restored and refurbished, which is already highly irregular. We gave you everything you asked for, and do you know how hard it was to sculpt an older body with the muscles and intellect of youth?" She couldn't stop ranting. "We spend so much time and effort outfitting you monkeys with the best bodies the HHS can produce—for Heaven knows what purpose—and now you *still* need an upgrade?" She mocked me with a contemptuous grimace.

"The body is fine but I need additional language skills. Farsi, Arabic, and, oh, the Mandaean dialect of Aramaic."

The receptionist looked incredulous. "That's it? How about we throw in a few sub-Saharan dialects, for good measure?"

""Funny. Look, lady, I am on an official mission and I need what I need.""

"Do you have an upgrade order?"

Damn bureaucrats. "No, I don't, but just check with the HA at the Department of Justice. Call Azazel's office and they will confirm the request."

She winced. "I don't have time to deal with this nonsense. You go and get the order and then we will talk."

I wanted to smack her so badly but she was an Angel who could handle me with her hands tied behind her back…not to mention that any ruckus at the HHS would not bode well for me. Cursing under my breath, I went back to Azazel, listened to another of his lectures on how dumb we monkeys were, got an order, and came back.

I stuck the order under her nose and she instinctively leaned back, afraid of being contaminated by an impure soul. She barely touched the order, holding it with her long, polished nails. After carefully examining it and finding no other excuse to give me another run-around, she squeamishly pointed to the triage reception. "Wait there."

After an eternity of waiting in triage—the emergency rooms with the worst wait time in the U.S. worked faster than this one—I finally got the download. My head hurt slightly, but I now spoke every conceivable language I might need on my journey.

A few days later, an Emirates flight from Johannesburg brought a stately-looking older gentleman to the Imam Khomeini International Airport in Teheran, a Sasol employee on a business trip to the Assalyeh Petrochemical complex run by Arya Sasol Polymer Company, a South African-Iranian joint venture. I carried a South African passport in the name of Jan Van Boeren. The burly-looking customs officer quickly looked at me and my passport and asked the purpose of my trip.

The gentleman replied that he was on his way to meetings with local ASPC management to discuss a new polymer production line at the facility and that he was in a rush to make the connecting flight to Assalyeh. The gentleman sounded like a proper South African, not that the customs officer would recognize the accent. I was a stickler for details.

Getting to Iran wasn't easy, with all the sanctions in place. The idea of being a tourist from a Western country didn't appeal to me because any Western tourist would be under constant MOIS surveillance. Changing my identity to a Middle Easterner would require a new body, and I loathed the idea of going back to the HHS and dealing with their conceited attitude. The South African joint venture, touted as one of the successes of industrial development in Iran, provided a much safer cover. Sasol Polymer employees were flocking to Iran like migratory birds in winter.

Just to be on the safe side, I checked the latest projects and scheduled a meeting with the local managers. Mr. Van Boeren was in fact an employee of Sasol, except that he had never been to Iran and, at the time of my trip, should have been on a two-week vacation in Maldives. However, MOIS could easily confirm my employment with Sasol and the meeting. Hopefully, that would stop all further inquiries. I purposefully flew in on a Wednesday so I could make it to Assalyeh on Thursday, and the earliest meeting would be on Monday. The Pars Special Economic Energy Zone, of which Assalyeh was part, respected Fridays, but also Sunday as a weekend for Westerners.

Once in Assalyeh, I checked into the posh Cherif Hotel, where I had reservations for a nice waterfront room, though not a suite, which would be beyond the expense account of a mid-level executive. Now I had three days to wrap up my business in Ahwaz and return to Assalyeh for my supposed meeting.

That same evening, Mr. Van Boeren rented a car at a local car rental company recommended to him by his colleague, whose name I was too happy to mention. As I said, I was proud of my attention to detail, and had combed through a secure Sasol intranet site for any messages regarding a stay in Iran. The rental company owner, flattered by the fact that a Western visitor had recommended his business, didn't ask any questions and, I was certain, would forget reporting my car rental to MOIS, especially since I paid in cash.

As I got into a car, I quickly changed into something less Western and less conspicuous—jeans, sandals on bare feet, and a worn-out T-shirt—a typical Iranian man of modest means going about his business. The drive to Ahwaz was over 680 kilometers, and I drove very carefully, just slightly over the speed limit, so as not to attract attention. Save for a few trucks, Iranian Route 96 was mostly empty throughout the night, and my not-so-new, non-descript sedan didn't catch the eye of the highway patrol.

Driving all night made me tired but I couldn't lose any time. Once there, I parked as close as I could to Nazirpor Street, leaving the car a few blocks from the Mandaean Council of Ahwaz.

The Council was open notwithstanding the early hour. An elderly gentleman in a white shirt, grey slacks, and a large white skull cap, possibly one of the priests, opened the door.

Introducing myself as Dr. Shamoun Khoshaba of the University of Detroit, I apologized for my unannounced visit and told him that, as an American, I'd had to come incognito. The story was flimsy, but thanks to HHS's thorough job, my Mandaean language was very good and the gentleman was impressed. Still, he was suspicious. Not too many Americans barged into an Iranian town unannounced unless they were part of some clandestine service.

"Why didn't you connect with our offices in Australia?" he asked.

"Ah." I waved non-committedly. "The trip came together too quickly, and I didn't have a chance. You are welcome to check with them. They should know me and my research on Mandaean scriptures."

Another flimsy excuse. I cursed myself for not being more prepared. When I'd concocted my story it had sounded convincing, but in Iran where everyone, especially minorities, is suspicious of everyone else, and with MOIS being omnipresent, it sounded awfully amateurish. Yet, notwithstanding this load of foul-smelling bullshit, no doubt mostly owing to my Mandaean language skills and grey hair, the gentleman decided to trust me. At least for now.

"So, how can I help you?" he asked politely.

"I would love to spend a few days in your library. I am particularly interested in your early records. Would you be kind enough to point me to the library?"

The library of the Mandaean Council of Ahwaz was indeed famous throughout the research community although very few Westerners did actual research there. Mostly, they would send inquiries and the Council was obliged to share information, which was a good source of income, the only source for the needy community other than the assistance from the diaspora.

I produced a sizeable traveler's cheque issued by Standard Chartered, a British bank licensed in Iran.

"I know how much you need money, so please accept this modest contribution for the privilege of being allowed in this hallowed place."

There was nothing modest about the cheque and the gentleman immediately warmed up to me.

"Please, this way, sir."

He took me to a large room on the second floor of the building stuffed with bookshelves and permeated with the musty smell of an ancient library. He quickly gave me a tour and excused himself to attend to his daily responsibilities.

I couldn't have wished for anything better. Being alone in the library gave me the freedom to search for what I needed. Yet, once I started, I realized the search would be anything but easy. The library was huge and poorly cataloged. It would take weeks if not months of research to come up with what I was looking for. I needed a shortcut. So after my host's steps died down, I sent a maintenance call to Abaddon.

He appeared in a cloud of sulfur, and as usual, with a very loud *bang*.

"Hey, careful, you idiot! Save your schticks for the satanists." I spent a few seconds listening intently but there was nothing. It appeared my host had left me to my own devices and didn't hear the noise.

Abaddon was about to curse me but having been instructed by Ashmodai to provide full assistance, he snapped his mouth closed and let my outburst pass. "What do you need?"

"Help me with the library, will you? You know what I need and you are a faster reader."

Abaddon grinned and started peering intensely at the books, humming something demonic. In a few moments, he pointed to an old manuscript. "There. It has references to Jezebel, Shem, and the Book of Remedies. You read it. I have other business to attend to."

"What? Wait a minute, didn't Ashmodai order you to assist me?"

"Yes, and I did. But it is very busy in the Maintenance Department. A few Demons called in sick—"

Whatever that meant.

"—and I have six tickets to attend to today. So, good luck, my friend."

Abaddon disappeared, again with a loud *bang*, leaving the distinct smell of sulfur. I could only hope the ventilation system didn't carry the odor throughout the building and cause the fire brigade to appear on the scene. What a moron!

Time was at a premium, however, and I couldn't dwell on Abaddon's lack of discretion. I opened the manuscript and started flipping through it, mustering all my Aramaic skills to decipher the bad handwriting on the decaying paper. The manuscript was a second-century compilation of letters between the Mandaeans in Mesopotamia and the tribal elders of the Yousufzai tribe in Kabul. To my surprise, the letters were written in flowery Aramaic, and the Yousufzai elders referred to themselves as "Bani Israel," claiming their ancestry from the lost tribes of Israel.

One of the letters in particular caught my attention.

> *Our beloved Brothers! We were distressed*
> *upon learning of the plague that afflicted your*
> *community. Regarding your inquiry of the*
> *writings of our forefather Shem whom you*
> *worship as a Prophet and we revere as a righteous*

forefather of our peoples, blessed be his Soul in Heaven, which may be of assistance to you in this calamity, we confirm that we do, indeed, possess the Book of Remedies written by this blessed man. We inherited it from the witch Queen Jezebel and her wretched husband, King Ahab, may they both rot in Hell, who obtained this Book by means of black magic not known to present generations. Unfortunately, we cannot send you the Book as it contains many remedies that our people use in treating the sick. We can, however, share with you a translation, if you allow us some time for our Sages to complete it. Beware that it contains many Demonic rituals not proper for God-fearing people, lest some of your righteous congregation succumb to the temptation of allying themselves with the forces of Evil.

Bingo!

The subsequent letters contained translations of passages from the Book into Aramaic, which had been further translated into Mandaean by the community leaders of that time. The translations were included in the manuscript, and I immediately noticed the passage that had been used by ONA's U.S. chapter in the Moffat, Colorado, ritual.

I called on Abaddon again. He came back with the same huge *bang*, even angrier than before. "What? Again?"

"I want you to take this book back to Azazel. I need to

consult on it with the experts at the Department, and carrying it safely out of Iran would be challenging."

Abaddon stopped being angry and gave the manuscript a strange look.

Something in his demeanor made me suspicious. Not sure of what, but suspicious.

"Remember, give it to Azazel and no one else. I will be back soon, and if it is not delivered—'"

"All right, all right, stop being so whiny. I will deliver it to your friend, Azazel." He sighed. "What terrible times we live in. A monkey sending a Demon on an errand."

His genuine bitching lulled my suspicion. Maybe it was nothing. Maybe I was just being paranoid in this paranoid country.

Abaddon had barely left when I heard the distant wail of sirens. It was too much of a coincidence. I guess the priest didn't completely trust my fairytale, or maybe was simply scared of an American snooping around in Iran.

I quietly left the library and peeked through the hallway window. Three police cars with blinking flashers were blocking the street at the entrance to the Council building.

I called on Abaddon again. If he opened a maintenance tunnel I could escape and leave these people wondering what happened to the nosy American.

Naturally, now, Abaddon was truly pissed. "Can't you figure out everything you need in one shot? Stop calling on me every five seconds!"

"Shut up and open the maintenance tunnel. I need to get back to the Department."

"Oh." Abaddon grinned and plopped down on a nearby chair, legs crossed and hands behind his wooly head. "Sorry, buddy, no can do."

"Are you fucking kidding me? And what's with this R&R pose? Get your ass up and get me the fuck out of here."

Abaddon didn't move. "As I said, no can do. As the Maintenance Manual states, maintenance tunnels are exclusively for the use of Demons engaged in bona fide maintenance operations. The Manual further states," he continued in a deliberate monotone, "that our actions should not attract undue attention from humans or lead them to believe in supernatural forces. Your disappearance will clearly make these people even more superstitious than they already are."

I heard car doors slam outside.

"Oooh! It must have been Jibril himself who came to test our faith," mimicked Abaddon in the spooky voice of an imaginary local shocked by my disappearance. "No, my friend, you are on your own. Besides, what do you have to worry about? Just get yourself killed and come back."

"Yeah, except that I have only two reincarnations left. Not to mention, it hurts like Hell."

At the reference to Hell, Abaddon gloated happily.

I ground my teeth. "You know what? Go screw yourself, and don't call me for the next Texas Hold'em, as I am sure there is nothing in the Manual that permits you furry goats to play poker."

"Hey, easy buddy! Why are you blaming me? You know I am not allowed to break the rules. And, unlike your friend Beelzebub, I am not the one sneaking around answering FMCs. I am a kinda by-the-book guy."

"Yeah. Sure." I was pissed, but Abaddon was right. Going back through the tunnel and starting all kinds of rumors here was not an option. "All right fine. Just get out of here."

I was unarmed, as bringing weaponry on a flight was not possible. I could have had Requisition drop equipment in Iran for me to pick up, but even with my attention to detail, I hadn't done so, hoping for an uneventful trip, or, if worse came to worst, counting on an exfil through a maintenance tunnel.

Oh, well, to err is human…

I went back to the window. The cops were piling out of the cars. At least, judging by the uniforms, I was dealing with ordinary cops on the beat and not with the Quds Force—a special intelligence branch of the Islamic Revolutionary Guard Corps. I should be able to handle this, maybe even without killing the yokels.

I went down the hall and hid behind an old armoire. Local police here were sloppy and overly confident, anticipating an easy catch and the rich reward that would undoubtedly follow. I was about to disabuse them of that notion.

They stomped up the staircase like a herd of elephants. Once in the corridor, they took out their service pistols and started creeping along slightly hunched, guns held up in two hands, heads moving in all directions. It was comical. They were clearly reenacting their favorite action movies. Everything they did was completely wrong from a tactical perspective. They were all doing the same thing instead of moving in a staggered formation covering each other. It would have been better for them if they'd simply taken a leisurely stroll down the corridor.

As the first cop reached the armoire, I grabbed him in a lightning-quick motion and twisted his head. His neck snapped, and I was now a proud owner of a human shield and a fully-loaded sidearm. Holding his dead body in front of me, I came out from behind the armoire and shot a few of his colleagues. Three more cops fell before the rest figured out what was going on and ran away like gazelles.

Time to do a bit of math. On the one hand, I had three police cruisers with, say, four cops per car. With four down, it left me with eight bogies. On the other was my well-trained body plus the gun I'd borrowed from the dead cop. The odds looked fairly even.

Before my pursuers regrouped and called for backup, I ran in the opposite direction to the farthest window from the entrance staircase. I broke the window by throwing the body of the dead cop through it, then jumped out of the building. It was only the second floor, so I landed on my feet and started running toward my car. The cops hadn't expected me to jump out of the window, so the idiots hadn't even covered the entire perimeter of the building.

I had a good head start and my car was outside their view, so I got into it and pulled out. But I was impatient to get out and the tires screeched as I drove away. Big mistake. The tires screeching was heard as far away as the Council building and betrayed my escape plan. The cops jumped in their cruisers and followed me at high speed.

Car chases look great in the movies, but in real life, and in an unfamiliar city, local cops have all the advantages. I was trying to stick to a general southerly direction, but old Middle Eastern towns are not laid out like Washington D.C. with wide avenues and clear signage. At that point, all I was hoping for was not to turn onto a dead-end street. My luck held for a bit. I was hitting anything and everything standing in my way, smashing cars, donkey carts, and street peddlers, so my rental car soon looked like a "just married" vehicle with all kinds of jingling stuff and fluttering clothes hanging off it.

I kept turning and swerving, weaving in and out of heavy traffic. When I finally turned into a narrow street where the cop cars had to line up single file, I decided to end the circus. I pulled the hand brake and spun the car around to face my pursuers, grabbed the gun, and stuck it out the open driver's-side window, preparing to fire at the leading car. I pulled the trigger and—damn it!—my gun jammed. The dead clown of a cop I'd taken it from must have never cleaned it.

Well, if I couldn't stop them I could at least block them. I revved the rental car, jammed on the gas, and jumped out the door. It crashed into the leading cop car, wreaking havoc among my pursuers. They were so discombobulated they didn't even open fire on me as I ran down the street.

Once I got far enough away, I slowed down to catch my breath and mingled with the crowd. Just as I thought I was home-free, thinking of a suitable story for the car-rental guy, I again heard the wailing of sirens, and two Toyota Land Cruisers with flashers materialized out of thin air. Too few people were on the street at this hour, so mingling with the crowd didn't work, and my pursuers must have received my description from the cops. I was pretty sure these guys were Quds Force. They were pros, and I was unarmed and on foot.

The situation had changed for the worse.

I spotted a slightly ajar door to a three-story building on my right and ran in. I ran upstairs hoping to get to the roof. I heard the Land Cruisers stop at the entrance and the loud trudging of boots on the stairs behind me. Of course, the door to the roof was locked. I rammed it with my shoulder, and thankfully the lock gave in. I burst onto the roof and surveyed my surroundings. The space was dotted with large dish antennae—good places to hide from the bullets. The roof was too high up for a safe jump down to the street, but the adjacent building was close enough for a good leap. Just as my pursuers reached the roof, I executed my hasty plan.

Running from dish to dish dodging bullets, I reached the edge of the roof and jumped to the next building. Given how close the buildings were along the whole block, I thought I would jump from roof to roof until my pursuers ran out of steam and I could lose them for good.

I'd underestimated the Quds Force. Those guys were in good shape and no idiots.

As I jumped, three heavily armed soldiers popped up on the next roof down. They'd obviously figured out this was my only escape route and called for reinforcements.

Great…

I hid behind a dish antenna and looked around. Jumping to a building across the street wouldn't be possible, even for my perfectly made body—there are limits to human abilities and the HHS refused to equip their products with supernatural abilities, so no Incredible Hulk stunts. I was caught between the two groups of Quds guys. I decided the optimal thing was just to keep running forward. I spotted an old TV antenna barely hanging on, and pulled it out to use as a spear. Better than nothing, I figured.

Dashing through the maze of antenna dishes, I ran toward the guys on the next roof blocking my escape route. They showered me with the bullets from their AK-47s, but the heavy metal dishes obscured their line of sight, and my zigzagging made me even harder to hit. Yet, I felt a sting in my left shoulder, then another in my left hip. Bastards! Now I had to deal with Rafael and his whinnies and explain how and why I'd damaged their precious masterpiece.

I approached the gap between the roofs separating me and the Quds soldiers. There were only three of them, and while there were no doubt more downstairs, three was manageable. If I could get close enough for hand-to-hand combat, special forces or no special forces, they were no match for my "made in HHS" body, even wounded.

The bullet wounds slowed me down, but I was still capable of jumping across to the roof with the blocking team. Ignoring the pain in my hip and shoulder, I leaped. I stumbled, but was able to dive behind the nearest dish. My opponents were surprised, but quickly recovered and advanced toward me. They moved in perfect special forces formation, with covering fire from behind as the front man advanced. This was no longer a dumb circus with local cops taking their cue from movies. These guys knew what they were doing.

Still, I was too much, even for a properly-trained special forces team. As the front man reached me, I whacked his gun away using my wounded left hand and shoved my antenna spear up through his chin with my good hand. Again I could use the dead soldier as a shield, and now I had a good rifle with a few additional magazines from his Kevlar vest.

Take that, you losers!

In the heat of the fighting, I had forgotten about my original pursuers…who also knew how to jump from roof to roof. My back was exposed to their fire. One well-placed shot and I would be dead. But it didn't happen. Instead, bullets whizzed by and hit me in both legs. The bastards were trying to disable me and take me alive.

Now the situation was dire. As much as I hated using my second Reincarnation Right, my choices were limited. I sighed, stuck an AK-47 under my chin, and fired. My head exploded and the whole world went dark.

CHAPTER 2

HA Department

Still dizzy from the pursuit and hurting from my exploded head, I struggled to reorient myself in the HA's reception area. I must have been expected, as the receptionist immediately ushered me into Azazel's office. Sitting in a plush chair in a quiet office was such a welcome reprieve from all the shooting and pain. Thank goodness for Reincarnation Rights!

Azazel was speaking with someone on the phone in the Angelic language. He was clearly agitated and his face was redder than a Demon's eyes.

He finally slammed the phone and turned to me. "Second body in less than three months? You might as well do your missions in a wheelchair. Then, at least, you would have a good excuse to get yourself killed at the first opportunity. I just got chewed by Rafael for the destruction of his property."

"Oh, please. You only got into a phone altercation with

Rafael. I lost my second to last Reincarnation Right! So give me a break. What else I was supposed to do? Did you even watch the footage? I was being chased by a Quds Force team and was already badly wounded. Did you want me to get caught and interrogated?"

Azazel may have been an ass, but he obviously appreciated my sacrifice of a precious Reincarnation Right to avoid detection and possible exposure of the whole Heavenly Offices operation, so he backed down. "I understand. But still, I just hate when that grumbler Rafael bitches and moans about how precious his work is for the Creation."

I gave him a sympathetic look. I could relate. "Were there any other repercussions of the incident?"

He waved a hand. "The Iranians raised a huge stink about a U.S. clandestine team operating on their sovereign territory and pledged retaliation."

"Do we care?"

"Only insomuch as any international tension may result in more casualties. We are not in the business of pruning the monkey population.," He looked at me with disdain. "Although if you ask me, we could easily get rid of a few billion of you and spare the Earth of your harmful presence. Unfortunately, the Creator has a different view and treats you as a protected species."

I ignored his diatribe. Typical Azazel, bitter and unhappy with everything.

Once he'd vented, he took on a more serious tone. "The

bigger problem, however, is that you killed a whole bunch of cops who were acting in the line of duty. This will have to be reviewed by Samael once the mission is complete."

Seeing my indignant expression, he added calmly, "I am not trying to threaten you. You know that murder is strictly prohibited."

"Not murder. They actively interfered with my mission. Isn't that one of the exceptions?"

"But did they act maliciously? They were simply doing their normal job, not actively interfering with your mission."

"You're saying this manhunt didn't qualify as actively and maliciously interfering with a mission? You must be joking. Should I have left the manuscript to the Iranians and surrendered myself for a friendly chat somewhere in a MOIS black ops basement? I imagine I would have been happy to enlighten them about the workings of the Creation. By the way, did Abaddon deliver the manuscript to you?"

Azazel was too happy to change the subject. He didn't mind torturing me with threats, but a review by Samael worried him as much as it worried me. After all, he was in charge of the Program, and therefore responsible for all mishaps. Samael, who always viewed Azazel as a competitor whose presence at the Department threatened his cushy job, seized any excuse to stick it to him.

"Yeah, I got the manuscript. The letters it contained came from the Yousufzai tribe. They now occupy a large chunk of what's known as the Tribal Area in Pakistan, somewhere between Peshawar and the Khyber Pass. So, you are going to Afghanistan, my friend. Great vacation spot. The mountains are spectacular!"

I thought he'd misspoken. "Didn't you mean Pakistan?"

"Nope, I meant what I said. You are going to Afghanistan. In the Middle Ages, the tribe migrated to Pakistan from Kabul, and you will need to retrace their steps. A lot of them stayed in Afghanistan. No way to know who may have the Book. Even if you end up going to the Tribal Area, until recently it was not subject to Pakistani law, and while Pakistan did a lot to take control of the area, the border is still as porous as it could be, so moving between the countries should be simple."

This was not my idea of a successful completion of my stint in the Pilot Program. "Wait a minute. I thought the Pilot Program was designed so I'd only need to complete one successful mission to earn a pass out of Oblivion. Didn't I complete the mission in Moffat? In fact, didn't I go beyond the call of duty and identify the location of the Book of Remedies? Why do I now have to risk my honorable discharge, in the words of your Boss, and go to a war-torn area with only one Reincarnation Right and a high possibility of failure?"

Azazel raised his brows. "Since when do you monkeys define the mission and the objectives? Your mission in Moffat was not complete once we found out it was all about the Book of Remedies. Until the Book is destroyed, the mission is not complete. So stop whining and get on with it."

"Really nice, Azazel. You just moved the goalpost so

elegantly I couldn't even notice how you were screwing me all this time. You know what? Forget it. I am going to complain to Samael. This is not what he said, and I have my rights, be it in Heaven or on Earth!"

Azazel went pale and clenched his fists as if he was about to pound me into dust, but then he stopped and laughed. "Oh, what a specimen! Just because you heard from your half-witted Demon buddies that Samael and I don't always see eye to eye, do you think you now have leverage over me? As far as you are concerned, all Angels are in complete agreement. To begin with, none of you monkeys deserve a second chance. If you think complaining to Samael will get you somewhere, go ahead, be my guest. I can assure you of extra time in the Movie Room, and with the same outcome. Oblivion!"

He was right. Even if Samael used my complaint against him, my fate wouldn't change. No one in this establishment would tolerate a monkey whistle-blower.

I tried to take it a notch down. "Look, I am not threatening you. But with only one Reincarnation Right left, this is practically a suicide mission. What did I do to you that you want to hurt me so badly, even at the expense of your own career? You know full well that I cannot succeed without being killed a couple of times, and even then, it is a fifty-fifty proposition at best. The way I see it, it is a lose-lose situation for both of us. I go to Oblivion, and you don't get the Book, thus incurring the ire of your Boss. Shouldn't we at least try to make the mission more manageable?"

Azazel pursed his lips. "Yeah, as much I hate to admit it, I am betting on the wrong horse here. You are most likely unfit for this mission, even with all the backing of the HHS and the Maintenance Department. Yet, I have no desire to let you rest on laurels with a job half-done. I can try to get you a few more Reincarnation Rights. I am not promising I can. But either way, you will have to finish the mission if you want to dig your way out of Oblivion."

Oh yeah, Oblivion again, the favorite stick of my Heavenly handlers. What if I just stuff it to them and take Oblivion? Which could actually be preferable to a hapless existence in Heaven with no exhilaration and excitement afforded by a physical existence, anyway? I could almost see the face of this conceited bastard when I tell him to screw it and just send me back to the Movie Room. It would have been so much fun to see Azazel surprised to the core. The satisfaction of finally sticking it to him, could alone be worth a trip to the Movie Room.

Unfortunately, accepting Oblivion sounded so heretical to my genetically ingrained notion of good and bad that I didn't seriously consider it.

Besides, I still entertained the idea that maybe once I had the Book I could negotiate a second shot at life, which made the whole enterprise very much worth the risk. And, to completely kill the idea of choosing Oblivion over the seemingly impossible mission, I still hoped that in the end I would somehow be able to figure out what had happened to me in my past life…and why the Moffat encounter had felt as if I had been there before.

No, I had to take on the mission, no matter the risks. With a few more Reincarnation Rights, I might even have a chance of success. Not to mention that extorting even a small concession from an Angel gave me a sense of victory.

As I made up my mind, I looked at Azazel, who was patiently waiting for my internal struggle to end. He looked amused, as he couldn't possibly imagine a monkey standing up to him or even considering sacrificing everything out of principle. I finally told him I would take the mission if he could get me a few additional Reincarnation Rights.

He chuckled and patted me on the back. "I am glad you finally came to your senses. So, what else do you need?"

"Besides an arsenal sufficient to arm the entire U.S. Marine Corps along with an army of Demons helping me out in that paradise on Earth? It would be good to know where to start. Do I get help from the Maintenance?"

"I can get you something even better. You see, so many of you monkeys try to strike a deal, as you say, with the Devil—"

Samael would not like that reference, I mused.

"—that I have compiled an extended Rolodex of scumbags and villains all over the world. The guy you need is Haji Juma Khan, a drug dealer par excellence and a first-rate rogue. The guy was so good he was taken to the U.S., prosecuted by the Americans, and guess what? He was released ten years later without any trial and disappeared. I personally think he betrayed everybody who was anybody, and that those American hits on Taliban leaders were his handiwork. There is no love lost between him and the Taliban, not to mention that the Taliban doesn't like the drug trade. But Juma is a survivor. As far as I know, he is back in the old country, alive and well, selling anything he can, from poppy seeds to grenade launchers. You've got to love the type! A lot of tribal people are engaged in the drug trade. Juma knows them all, as well as the tricky ins and outs of the region."

"So, how do I approach him?"

"Don't you love having me do your job while you collect the credit? Don't worry, I will get you in. A few years ago, Juma was selling his merchandise through the Kyrgyz Mafia boss, Kamchi Kolbayev. Kyrgyz authorities reported that Kamchi was killed in a shootout. However, rumors in the region persisted that it was all a ruse and Kamchi was alive and well, hiding somewhere in Central Asia."

"But we are sure he was killed, right?"

Azazel raised his brows. "Really? Do you want me to show you the Movie Room records, or you will take my word for it?"

Asking a Heavenly Offices official whether they were sure of the whereabouts of any human was, indeed, absurd, and I smiled, sheepishly.

Seeing I realized the stupidity of my question, Azazel continued, "So, Kolbayev will be your reference. I will get a Maintenance ticket to Ashmodai to arrange for a call using Kamchi's voice to one of Juma's known associates asking for a meeting. You will go to Juma and tell him Kolbayev is back in business, and you are working with him on a new gig, tracking down an ancient book that could fetch the price of a tactical nuke on the open market. Given the earlier phone call and the rumors of Kamchi being still alive, Juma should believe you. On top of that, you can always count on human greed. The opportunity to make a few million bucks will get you through any door."

"But what will stop him from finding the Book for himself and killing me in the process?"

A broad smile covered Azazel's face. "Nothing, my friend. That is why you are outfitted with the best body, the toughest muscles, and the best brains. You will have to double-cross him before he double-crosses you. And if you fail, you can always use the Reincarnation ticket you so successfully extorted from me, and come back with your tail between your legs and a newly found realization of how lowly you monkeys truly are."

Bastard.

"Hey, at least wait till I fail before you insult me," I muttered. "By the way, I was wondering whether I can request a body and do a real R&R somewhere. My soul is exhausted from the past months' adventures. I am afraid I will develop PTSD and won't be fit for a mission. How about I get a vacation before I go to that charming country you are sending me to? Aren't we supposed to get vacation time?"

"Azazel winced. "Gosh, even dead you need to satisfy your carnal pleasures. All right, you have a week. And don't abuse the body. I don't want another whiney call from this wuss Rafael."

CHAPTER 3

Las Vegas, NV

Having been granted a whole week of respite, I took on my new body. Those assholes at the HHS refused to give me a brand new one, citing my previous careless treatment of HHS property, and gave me the refurbished one from the Moffat mission instead. I bitched and moaned, but truth be told, a well-repaired body of a fit forty-year-old full of muscles and brains wasn't that bad. Of course, they couldn't resist leaving the ugly bullet wound scars from Moffat. Whatever. A man is even more manly with a few scars.

After being fitted with the body, I was taken to a so-called recovery room where I was given the documentation package in a thick folder brimming with paper. Normally, I would grab the passport, driver's license, and credit cards, then throw everything else away, to the chagrin of the recovery room personnel. But this time, curiosity got the better of me. I figured since I had time I might as well look at what the bureaucrats had prepared for me.

Boy, did I regret never opening the packages before!

In addition to the U.S. passport, New York driver's license, and a wide variety of credit cards, it contained a detailed manual of body care, all broken down to the smallest detail. It even listed the recommended hypoallergenic shampoo and body wash, as well as detailed instructions on how to avoid respiratory diseases. What I took out after the manual shook me to the core. The package contained a concealed carry permit issued by the New York City Police Department, a medical insurance card accepted in all fifty states and most other countries, prescriptions for antibiotics and other drugs not available over the counter in case the body got sick, and to top it off, a pilot's license certifying the bearer for all-weather flying for all types of small planes.

Damn. If this was a standard package, what would they include in a deluxe one?

I was so impressed that I even thanked the recovery room staff, forgetting how much I hated those sticklers for the rules..

With all these accouterments, it was time to choose my R&R destination. I picked Sin City—Las Vegas. What could be better to let off steam than a week in a nice controlled environment?

Las Vegas in winter felt just right for me. Not too hot—it was only 60 degrees—and not too busy, since the Christmas season had just passed. I didn't need to be inconspicuous, so I got myself a suite at the Venetian and rented a Maserati Grand

Tourismo convertible to drive around town. Screw Azazel's expense account!

Once I'd settled in my posh suite with its assigned butler, I called the number of the city's top escort service, which I'd gotten from my Demon buddies. Demons didn't need girls, but the number of scumbags going through their hands was so vast that they knew all the perverts in the world, along with the seedy places in every town that catered to them.

While fornication was frowned upon in the Heavenly Offices, as long as you were not engaged in an adulterous affair and did not deviate from a mission, it wouldn't be considered a major rule infraction. Even the Creator recognized the weaknesses of the human race.

I didn't know why, but I wanted someone who looked like the sacrifice girl from Moffat—innocent-looking, maybe even a bit clumsy, slim with no voluptuous shape. Something about that girl had turned me on, and I couldn't let it go. I specifically repeated that I didn't want a burnt-out whore playing a high school girl with bobby sox and false braids, but I did want someone who would enjoy sex. The madam on the phone assured me she had exactly what I needed, albeit the hair color might differ a bit.

Though not exactly what I had in mind, the girl who knocked on the door of my hotel suite was a stunning young girl with suntanned skin, jet-black hair, and ravishing, dark, almond-shaped eyes. She was dressed in a tight black dress with a hem way above her knees and a plunging neckline. If I were her,

I would have chosen something less revealing on top, as her breasts were too small to fulfill the promise of cleavage, but it suited me all the same. Her long, thin legs in black pantyhose stuck out from under the dress as she tried to show as many goods as possible. She wore bright red lipstick, light eyeshadow, and black eyeliner. Her long eyelashes were covered in black mascara. She radiated sex and desire.

Yet, with all her sensuality, she did not look vulgar or horny…more like Maria from *West Side Story* trying to tame her hormones and curious about her sexuality. She was not the Moffat girl by any stretch of the imagination, but in the end, I decided the madam had gotten it right—she was exactly what the doctor ordered.

When she walked in, we didn't say much. I didn't feel like introducing myself or asking her name. She must have felt my slight disappointment and attributed it to her appearance.

"You don't like what you see? Wanna see more?" she asked in a hot whisper. Her voice was deep, guttural, and arousing, as was every bit of her body.

I gently caressed her cheek, and she lowered her head to the side inviting me to kiss her neck. Her move was natural, not horny. She definitely seemed like she was looking forward to enjoying some good sex.

I pushed her buttocks slightly. She understood and raised her legs, locking them around my waist. My lips lightly touched hers and she opened her mouth, accepting my kiss.

I took her to the bed and carefully lowered her onto the

sheets. The bed was not made up since I didn't want to be bothered by room service. She laid down and her eyes fluttered shut in anticipation, and I could feel the tantalizing thrum of life coursing through her veins. She compliantly stretched up her arms, allowing me to pull off her dress and undo her bra.

Her breasts were small but her dark-brown nipples were hard. She instinctively moved her arms to cover her breasts but I kept them in place. Moving my lips down her body, I gently bit her nipples. She took a deep breath. I gently pulled down her pantyhose and the red thong she wore underneath. She arched her body, helping me pull them down, baring herself in an inviting move.

I moved my hand to her labia, found what felt like her G-spot, and lightly massaged it with my finger. She squeezed her legs and moaned quietly. She was all wet, ready for action. I pulled my body up and gently penetrated her. She gasped softly as I filled her completely. I didn't have a chance or a need to examine the genitalia of my body before the mission and was pleasantly surprised that Rafael's guys had been so generous with my endowment. I fully expected them to attach a two-inch pencil stub between my legs just out of spite.

I didn't know much about this body's sexual prowess. It performed well in combat and had the intellectual capacity to address complex situations, but I hadn't had sex since, well, since the time I died, I guess. This was the first tryst I'd been permitted to have in the Pilot Program. While the body functioned properly, I wasn't sure whether I would finish too early. I tried to pace myself, moving slowly while kissing her breasts and arousing her more and more. Finally, she reached a crescendo, screaming loudly, and I let myself release as well.

The release made my body limp and my mind full of pleasure. I lay down on top of her for a few moments, unable and unwilling to separate. She didn't rush me either. A while later I finally got out of her, turned on my side, and gently stroked her hair. Her eyes were radiant. She smiled, grateful for me not being a total dick caring only about his own ejaculation but actually trying to share the pleasure of sex with her. The words were not necessary and we simply stretched on the bed and looked at each other.

I broke the silence first. "I was thinking about going for a drink. Care to join me, if you don't have any other engagements?"

She blushed. It was cruel of me to remind her of her occupation.

"I'm sorry, what I meant was whether you have some spare time or if you need to be somewhere else."

My excuse came out clumsy as well, but she appeared to appreciate my efforts not to offend her. "No, I'm free, and drinks sound great." Could it be that slim amateurs were no longer in demand in Sin City?

We went to the garage where my Maserati was waiting. At the sight of my ride, her eyes lit up with the excitement of a child laying her hands on a highly-coveted toy. She asked me to lower the top.

"Are you sure? It is cold out."

She nodded like a naughty child. I lowered the top and off we went. She stuck her face into the wind like a happy puppy and closed her eyes. I pulled in at what looked like a nice bar off the Strip and we went in.

We went straight to the bar. She ordered a glass of white wine, which I figured in her mind was a drink for proper ladies. I got myself a Cosmopolitan and we sat on bar stools waiting for the drinks.

"You are all blue in the face," I said. "It was silly to ride with the top down in winter." I pulled her to me and took her hands in mine, rubbing them gently.

Encouraged by my considerate behavior, she decided to make it a real date, where intimate conversation was as important as sex. She looked me straight in the eyes. "So, what do you do when you are not in Vegas?"

Maybe, I'd gotten too comfy. Yet, I didn't want to disappoint her. "Ah, you know, the art stuff," I said being deliberately vague.

She nodded. It was good enough for her. "I am actually in college," she volunteered. "Ivy league," she said proudly. "But I'm from around here, so I came back for the winter break."

I could see she desperately wanted me to ask her why she was doing what she was doing, to give her a chance to redeem herself, but I was not in the mood for listening to a confession. Having witnessed so much filth and misery lately, I was not ready for another sad story. I was living in the moment and it felt great.

"Wow, you must be a brainiac!" I said with a grin.

She giggled softly.

"So, how is your wine? I asked after the barman brought us our drinks and she took her first sip. I wanted to steer her away from the confession subject.

"I guess it's good, but I am not a wine expert," she admitted honestly.

We started chatting about wine, then moved to cars, the weather in Vegas, new casinos opening up on the Strip, anything but personal subjects. I enjoyed telling her jokes, which she seemed to love no matter how silly they were.

Suddenly an athletically-built man in his twenties stumbled over next to her and slapped her buttocks. The guy was tipsy but far from being drunk. A boyfriend? I really didn't need a jealous encounter.

But the man quickly cleared my suspicions. "Hello, darling," he said. "Servicing the community, I see."

Her face turned red.

The guy turned to me. "Hey, man, did you enjoy her? She may not be a pro, but she and her colleagues did a real performance for us. The whole modesty act really turns you on. It was a bachelor party to remember, for sure." He waved to his friends with a grin.

The girl's eyes filled with tears. The fairy tale had ended and grim reality had reared its ugly head. What a downer!

I looked over to the table the man was waving at. There were four other similarly built jocks sitting there and smiling salaciously.

Ah, what the heck. Probably not my business, but it was my fairy tale, too, and neither the girl nor I deserved this rude interruption.

I got up from my bar stool. The guy was approximately the same height as me, and while I didn't get the pleasure of looking down at him, I was spared the embarrassment of looking up.

"What I am enjoying right now is a conversation with a lady, and I would appreciate it if you take your rude comments somewhere else," I said calmly.

"A lady?" The asshole brayed like a horny donkey. "This whore really had you, man. Let me tell you—"

He didn't finish. My right hook to his chin knocked him unconscious. His friends didn't expect that, but they looked like trained athletes with good reaction times, and they all jumped to their feet. Right. Four amateurs relying on their oversized muscles and minuscule brains? Not even a fair fight.

I strode straight to their table. One of them swung at me with a wild fist. With ease, I ducked under his blow and delivered a sharp elbow to his groin. He crumpled to the floor, clutching himself in agony. His buddies realized they were in for a real fight. One of them snatched a beer bottle and smashed the neck on the table, trying to emulate a movie-style bar brawl. He lunged toward me, attempting to slash me with the jagged glass.

I was too quick. I caught his wrist in an iron grip and twisted it with such force that I could hear bone cracking. As he howled in pain, I swiftly moved to the next one and kicked his shin, causing him to lose his balance, stumble, and fall on his knees with his face nearly touching the hard surface of the table. Grabbing him by the hair, I instinctively went to smash his head into it. But in that split second I realized murdering an innocent bystander would get me in trouble with the Heavenly Offices, not to mention undue attention from the local cops. At the last moment, I softened the blow, and though the table cracked, I was pretty sure the hit was survivable.

The last member of the group grabbed a chair and swung it wildly at me. I managed to block the blow, but the rickety old chair shattered on impact, leaving a deep scratch along my arm. The sudden surge of pain and, more important, the unnecessary damage to the property of the HHS only fueled my anger. I retaliated with a fierce and brutal beating, unleashing all of my pent-up frustration and rage on the idiot who had dared to harm me. Each punch landed with satisfying thuds, accompanied by grunts and groans from my opponent. He crumpled to the floor and I continued to pummel him, nourishing my anger.

The first guy suddenly snapped out of his haze and lunged at me. I saw his impending attack in my peripheral vision and dodged him, but he was still able to slash me with a sharp object. I saw the quick gleam of a switchblade.

Seriously? He'd pulled a *knife* at me?

I spun around, knocked the blade out of his hand, and bared my teeth in a monstrous grin, winding up for another punch. He shrank backward, anticipating a deadly blow. Lucky for him, even he was considered an innocent bystander by Samael's standards, so I just delivered a proverbial slap on the wrist, or rather, on his head, knocking him unconscious for the second time.

When the fight had started, I saw the barman calling the cops, and that was another thing I didn't need. I grabbed the girl's hand and we ran outside. Her eyes were wide, with a mixture of fear and fascination. No doubt seeing me as a knight in shining armor standing up for her. She was back in her fairy tale.

What I saw, however, was a brewing problem, exacerbated by the approaching wail of sirens.

"Are you hurt?" she asked with true concern in her voice.

"Don't worry about me. Let me drive you somewhere. Where do you want to go?"

"Home?" she asked cautiously. She gave me an address and my GPS showed an hour's drive.

An hour was a long time, and if someone at the bar had seen my ride, it would be easy for cops to send out a BOLO and find us, even in this town filled with luxury toys. But I couldn't turn her down.

I dropped her off at a shabby ranch house on the outskirts of Vegas.

"Do you want to come in?" she asked timidly. "You are bleeding. Let me clean up your wound."

"Look, I would love that, but I wasn't exactly truthful with you about my job. I really don't need any trouble with the cops, and I'd rather disappear before someone sees me. I hope you understand. Have a great life."

She pursed her lips, but kept her composure and just nodded.

As I drove away, I kept thinking about her. I didn't know what she'd gotten into her head about me, but I hoped I hadn't scarred her for life with all the fairy tale nonsense.

CHAPTER 4

Tribal Area, Pakistan

I quickly checked out of the Venetian, returned Maserati to the rental company after wiping down the driver's seat to avoid leaving any blood stains, and went to a shabby motel downtown to spend my last days in Vegas tending my wounds. I didn't need to be chewed up by Rafael's cronies for hurting the body. Thankfully, considering all the scars they had adorned me with, a light knife wound and a bruise from the splintered chair just added to the collection. Hopefully, the stingy bureaucrats didn't keep track of the number of scars!

I was a bit disappointed that my steamy vacation had been cut short by a stupid bar brawl, but it was time to get ready for the Hindukush safari anyway. Having learned my lesson from my experience in Iran, I wanted to be prepared. When I got back, I made sure to order the necessary equipment in plenty of time.

When I stopped by the Requisition Room to pick it up, Uzza was ready for me. He had assembled the best weaponry ever invented by a sick human mind.

The arsenal was impressive. XM-7s with grenade launchers, Glock 19s, a couple of Kevlar vests, a bag full of magazines and grenades, a few landmines, two Patriot tactical combat knives, as well as night vision and thermal imaging goggles. Plus a few burner phones with GPS and satellite connectivity. What else could a tourist wish for?

"Nice set," I said checking the weapons. Despite all Uzza's dumb derangement, you had to give it to him—he knew how to inflict the maximum damage. "Any tactical nukes you could throw in for a good measure?"

Uzza didn't get the joke. "Don't you know WMDs are not allowed?"

I sighed. He may be an Angel but he was still a total moron. "Whatever. Just get it delivered to Kabul and text me the drop location."

Next, I stopped by the HHS. This time I requested an upgrade for Urdu, Pashto, and Dari. To the utter chagrin of the receptionist, I had a proper upgrade order, so she begrudgingly sent me to be outfitted with those additional languages.

I had to make one more stop before starting my journey. I needed to check back with Azazel. He was undoubtedly aware of my little stint in Vegas but didn't bring it up. He must have appreciated my restraint in not killing those miserable wretches at the bar, saving him an unpleasant talk in his boss's office.

He gave me a full briefing, making me memorize the location of my meeting as well as Juma's appearance.

"Just try to avoid trouble." His way of obliquely mentioning the Vegas affair.

I was thankful to him for not lecturing me and dutifully nodded.

I decided against flying to Kabul. First, flights to Kabul were few and far between, and second, any tourist to a country controlled by the rabidly anti-Western Taliban would raise a lot of suspicions. Besides, I wanted to survey the Tribal Area. If I was to succeed, in all likelihood the Tribal Area would play a big role in finding the Book. So, instead of Kabul, I flew Qatar Airlines to Peshawar, Pakistan, with a layover in Doha, playing a rich American tourist fresh out off the tour of the Gulf States and now going sightseeing in the Hindukush.

After checking into a hotel and booking the famous Khyber Pass train tour, I went for a walk. Peshawar was too modern and civilized to be of interest in my search. It was unlikely that anything as ancient as the Book of Remedies would be hidden there, amid all the modern civilization. The Khyber Pass tour held more promise for my mission.

In the morning, I boarded an old British train pulled by a steam engine with a few antique railcars in tow. The scenery around the Khyber Pass hadn't changed much since the time of the British Raj. No wonder it had such an appeal to the Western tourists who flocked to tour the Tribal Areas. They reminded me of the gullible cormorants that curiously and without fear approached the hungry sailors landing for the first time on the Galapagos, just to be butchered en masse. The only thing that separated the foolish cormorant-like tourists from bloodbath and kidnapping was a platoon of Pakistani soldiers armed to the teeth carefully watching the surroundings, all too aware of the dangers.

The landscape stretched out before us in all its spectacular glory. The towering peaks of the Hindukush loomed proudly, untouched by industrial development's polluting grasp. Amidst the rugged terrain were remnants of old forts built by British colonial forces in a futile attempt to subdue the fiercely independent inhabitants. The ruins served as a stark reminder of how little modern civilization meant in this region. As the train chugged along, locals flocked to its side, hawking their wares to the curious foreigners passing through. Children jumped up and clung to the train steps, their faces beaming with excitement as the noisy steam-spewing engine rumbled by. For many in this region, the passage of the train was a highlight of their day—a brief glimpse into an unknown world beyond their native land, offering them a taste of a strange and different way of life.

The train tour ended at Landi Kotal, the home of the legendary British Rifles, with obligatory saber dances and a walk through a museum full of pictures of British and local members of the regiment. I quietly snuck out of the show, passing through the heavily guarded gates of the garrison and into the town. I would have been stopped, as no foreigners were allowed on an unguarded trip to town, but a conveniently located souvenir shop selling local clothes, which I purchased and augmented with some dust and mud from behind the store, helped me leave unnoticed.

Landi Kotal reminded me of Port Mos Eisley in Star Wars. It was the same wretched hive of scum and villainy, minus the cantina full of adorable monsters and young Harrison Ford with his boots on the table. In all other respects, the town felt as rowdy, lawless, and dangerous as the famous Tatooine spaceport, notwithstanding consistent efforts by the Pakistani government to tame it. The streets were bustling with activity, the air thick with a palpable sense of danger. Gun shops were everywhere, the prices of their deadly wares cheaper than a new smartphone. As I cautiously made my way through the dirty, crowded streets, I wanted to get a better feel for what I was about to experience.

I decided to mingle with the locals and get a sense of what was going on, just in case. The best source of news in this kind of place was gossip rather than newspapers. A small gun shop nestled between two stalls selling spices and fabrics caught my attention. The door was wide open and an elderly Pashtun man stood at the counter. In the background, a couple of youngsters were busily assembling AK-47s with practiced efficiency. It was a stark reminder that weapons were an everyday part of life in this neck of the world.

"*Salam alaikum, sahib.* How is business going?" I said in a broken Pashto. I didn't want to pretend to be a Pashtun, to avoid getting questions about my ancestry. Everybody knew everybody in this kind of place, and getting into a discussion of kinship would quickly land me in trouble.

"Business is good, thank you for asking," responded the owner. "Are you Pashtun?" he asked.

I switched to Dari. "No, Tajik."

He looked at me suspiciously. "You don't look like a Tajik."

"Ah," I threw up my hands. "My mother was a Kurd."

"You are far from home, my friend," said the owner, no doubt testing my bona fides.

"Yeah, coming from Jalalabad to Peshawar. My cousin works in construction there and he promised to get me a good job."

"Landi Kotal is out of the way, no?"

"You know, it is not that easy to get a visa, so coming through here was much easier," I said in a hushed tone. "How are things around here?" I was eager to change the subject.

Satisfied with my credentials, the owner sighed. "Eh, business is tough. Police snoop around, and check on everyone. There is a rumor that the government will require permits for all gun shops. After the merger of the Tribal Area with Khyber Pakhtunkhwa, things went from bad to worse. You were lucky you were able to cross the border. They shut down almost all passages."

"Yes," I said sympathetically. "Is it just bad here in town or everywhere?"

"Mostly, here. It is harder for the government to control

us further up in the mountains. Up there, we can still live following our customs. You have to come down, however, to trade and get supplies. That is where they get you."

"Vah. Terrible." I shook my head.

Apparently bored of sitting in his shop alone, he ranted on for a bit and I listened carefully, trying to get a lay of the land in the Tribal Area. As he went on, I learned where the army bases were, on which days they liked to raid villages, and which crossings were still open. We also discussed the upcoming local elections and the big weddings of the most important families—all of which could be useful in my mission.

As the old man got more and more talkative, I decided to fish for more intel while I could. "I actually had a friend from Yousufzai. His name was Ghazan. Do you know him? He lived in Jalalabad but moved to the Tribal Area. If I wanted to find him, where should I look?"

Either my tone was not trustworthy or I misread the local customs, but the owner got suspicious again. "I don't know anyone named Ghazan. Yousufzai live everywhere. What was his last name?"

I gave him a bogus response, and he liked that even less. His talkativeness evaporated and he switched to the subject of business. "So, what kind of gun can I offer you?" he said curtly.

"Just need something nice. What do you have in stock?"

"Anything your soul desires, my friend. You need a rifle, a pistol? I have nice AK-47s here.

I considered. "How much for an AK?"

"If you want original Chinese-made, it would be sixty thousand but if you want local, I can sell it to you for thirty."

"That's too expensive. Can you give me a locally-made one for ten?"

"Eh, what are you saying? Where did you see these prices? You can get an old hunting rifle for ten and even that would need a repair. Anyway, why do you need a rifle if you are going to Peshawar? No one walks around there touting an AK-47." His eyes squinted and he pierced me with a probing look.

All too happy to make a hasty exit, I came up with a lousy excuse as to why I was looking for a gun, then bid my farewell and left.

My intel mission hadn't worked as well as I'd have liked, but at least I learned a little about the army, and a lot about which questions not to ask of locals.

As I was walking down the street, I saw in the window of one of the shops the reflections of the two youngsters from the gun shop. They were following me. I looked for a more or less deserted area and hid behind a corner. As they reached me, I punched the first one in the throat. As he was gasping for air, I moved to the second youngster who was trying to point his AK-47 at me. I grabbed the muzzle and pulled it forward. The kid lost his balance and fell. As he lay dazed and disoriented, I snatched the rifle from his grasp and hit him over the head with its butt. Thankfully, the few onlookers were hesitant to intervene, choosing instead to go about their business and ignore the altercation. I walked away quickly before the local police showed up.

By the time I got back to the tour, the train was boarding for a trip back. My absence had been noticed. Worried guards were shouting and looking everywhere. The last thing the Pakistani government needed was a foolish Westerner being lost in this uncontrollable place. I snuck back through the store, took off the local garb, and stepped back on the platform. Donning the expression of an unsuspecting tourist to whom the concept of danger was utterly alien, I apologized to my angry but relieved chaperons and boarded the train.

Upon my return to Peshawar, I checked out of the hotel, put on a Shalwar Kameez—an Afghan outfit composed of a long shirt hanging almost to the ankles combined with loose pants—and a traditional Pashto head covering, and walked outside to disappear from the modern world, being replaced by a forty-year-old muscular Pashtun man in local clothing.

In my guise, I approached a shady-looking auto repair shop where cash was welcomed and documents were optional. There I bought a twenty-year-old truck without doors, painted in a surreal combination of red, green, and yellow, and decorated with red fringes and beads. The shop owner assured me it ran better than a Porsche Cayenne and was equipped for off-road driving. Porsche Cayenne my ass. Still, the car started, the tire tread was not entirely worn off, and the engine pistons didn't sound like they were about to spring out of the cylinders. Good enough to cross the border.

My identity of a Pashtun man on my way to a big wedding

in Jalalabad should be acceptable to any border patrol. My passport was good, and, given that a fair number of Pashtuns were light-skinned, my appearance would hold up as well.

As it turned out, the guards on both sides of the Torkham border crossing were fairly lax and unconcerned, given my impeccable language skills, an appropriately banged-up truck, and my perfect documents.

I was on my way to Kabul and the next milestone in my trip—to meet Haji Juma Khan.

CHAPTER 5

Kabul, Afghanistan

Kabul was within a stone's throw of the Torkham border crossing. Unfortunately, the main highway was shut down and I had to use a roundabout route. I didn't mind the extra time and the bumpy country roads. The detour helped me get a better sense of my surroundings. After the Taliban takeover and with American money drying up, the countryside looked like medieval ruins amidst the forests and mountains. Electricity was sparse and villages were dark, lit mostly by campfires. I liked it, though. The less civilization, the easier it was to disappear and stay under the radar.

As I got closer to the city of Kabul, I hit a Taliban roadblock. They had an American Humvee with a fifty-caliber mount, and were checking everyone's papers. When my turn came, I showed them my passport and visa.

"What are you doing here?" asked a grim-looking soldier

dressed in military fatigues and a black turban.

"Picking up my sister in Kabul to go to a wedding in Jalalabad."

"What's the name of your sister? Where does she live?"

I politely gave him an answer.

"Wait here." He went to speak to a commander sitting in the Humvee. I could see them gesticulating, apparently discussing my story. I was beginning to get nervous. I could, of course, run out of the car and take out the entire patrol, even though I was unarmed, but that kind of ruckus would leave me without a car and exposed, and the Taliban would be searching everywhere for me. No, it was better to sit quietly and wait for further developments.

As the soldier and commander continued their lively conversation, another soldier called out to them, dragging someone from the car behind me. The entire patrol ran over to him. As they passed me, the soldier who had been checking my papers threw my passport onto my lap and yelled, "Go, go!"

I was relieved. It had been my first, although I was sure by no means the last, encounter with the Taliban. I made a few mental notes to myself. First, they would suspect you no matter what, second, they were well-armed and didn't hesitate to use force, thus third, I needed to avoid patrols as much as possible.

I made it to Kabul early in the evening and went looking for the address where I was supposed to meet Juma.

The designated meeting spot was tucked away in the depths

of a dilapidated Kabul neighborhood with cramped huts blindly staring through shattered windows stacked upon one another. The scene around me was chaotic and disheveled, with stray cats darting between piles of trash and the smell of smoke and dust hanging in the air. The streets were unmarked, making it difficult to pinpoint the exact location. It took me some time to find the specific door among the maze of rundown buildings and finally knock on it.

A husky man in an Afghan dress and obligatory AK-47 on his shoulder opened the door. I handed him a note concocted by the Maintenance Department to identify myself. The guy carefully looked at it, then patted me for weapons, looked up and down the street to make sure I didn't bring an army in tow, then ushered me inside.

The inside of the house was very different from the semi-ruinous exterior. Hidden by thick curtains to shield against the prying eyes of neighbors and the Taliban, the living room boasted a modern Sony TV and a collection of laptops surrounded by a vast array of smartphones and burners sitting on a coffee table next to a comfy couch and a Laz-Y-Boy recliner. A bunch of grizzly-looking Afghans sat on the floor and the couch, watching a Pakistani sitcom on TV, with Dari subtitles. Their AK-47s were lined up on the floor next to the coffee table. Apparently, the sitcoms sounded funny even in Afghanistan because the men laughed incessantly. Juma, whose picture Azazel had made me memorize, was not among them. I quietly sat on the recliner to wait.

A large man got up and came to the recliner, towering over me like Andre the Giant.

"Why you want see me?" he said in broken English.

"I have no business with you, my friend," I said smiling. "I am here to see Haji Juma Khan and you are not him. Why don't you go and call your boss and don't waste my time with this bullshit!"

The guy bellowed and raised his hand to slap me. I hit him in the groin in an unnoticeable hand movement, not even getting up from the recliner. He hunched forward, groaning in pain. The rest of the crew jumped up and reached for their guns. I was faster. I threw Andre the Giant toward them and in a few quick moves put a couple more on the floor. Reaching the coffee table in one leap, I picked up one of the guns, grabbed one of the men in a lock, using him as a shield, and trained the gun on the rest of the men.

"Well, well, what do we have here? Did an American cowboy join us for a party?" The voice came from behind me. "Put down the guns," it said tersely in Dari to the rest of the Afghans. They immediately complied.

I turned around. A large, middle-aged Afghan with a salt-and-pepper beard in a free-flowing white shirt, vest, and a beige Afghan hat walked into the room. If I didn't know better, I would have thought I was talking to a respectable elder graced by many years of piety.

"You are way too jumpy, my friend," the man said to me with a broad smile. "Can't you tell the difference between a joke and a real danger? My guys were just horsing with you!"

His English was perfect notwithstanding a thick Afghan accent. What could be a better ESL training program than ten years in an American federal penitentiary?

"So, what brings you here, cowboy?" He motioned me to the recliner. "Please sit, and leave the gun alone. You are among friends here."

I let the man I was holding in a lock go, put the gun down, and sat on the recliner. The other men stood up, sore from my blows, and went quietly to the back of the room, leaving the couch to their boss.

"You know what brings me here, Juma Khan. Didn't you get word from Kamchi Bei?"

Of course, of course, I did. My dear friend Kamchi, I was so happy to hear from him alive and well, praise Allah All-Merciful. I always knew this jackal could outwit all the cops in the world. So, tell me, where is he, what is he up to these days? Why didn't he come himself?"

I squinted my eyes and threw up my hands. "Come on, Juma. The guy is officially dead and you want me to tell you where he is? Given your cozy relationship with the Americans, I don't think Kamchi would thank me for giving you his whereabouts."

Juma's eyes narrowed and nostrils flared. For a moment, his ruthless nature sprang out of his pious elder routine. However, he quickly contained himself, and a broad smile returned.

"Ah, Americans, Shmamericans. A man does what he

needs to do, my friend. Besides, the Americans are gone and the Taliban is in charge even though no one here likes those self-righteous bastards who don't let people have fun." He digressed. "Screw Taliban. I wish the Americans stayed longer. DEA was much easier to deal with than the Taliban, and the food in your prison was good too. I liked all those burgers and fries with Coca-Cola."

"If you want burgers and Cola, let's try to get the deal done and avoid us being served as shish-kabob in a Taliban prison."

"Shish-kabob." Juma laughed heartily and patted me on the shoulder. "That's a good one."

His subordinates didn't quite understand English but decided to laugh, as well.

Juma stopped laughing abruptly. "So, what kind of a deal are you and Kamchi-Bei trying to make, my American friend?"

"We are looking for an ancient book."

Juma winced.

Seeing his hesitation, I quickly added, "Wait. Before you dismiss my proposal, I have an offer for this book from a dealer for ten million dollars, and if we want to do an auction ourselves, we can probably skip the dealer markup and get to at least twenty million, all in hard cash. Unlike, hash, heroin, or grenade launchers, this merchandise can be easily handled in a bag. Well, except you will need a few suitcases to collect the cash."

Juma laughed again. "I like suitcases full of cash." His face showed that he was interested if not trusting. "What kind of book can bring this much money? Even rich dumb Americans don't pay for nothing."

"The book is called the Book of Remedies and it dates back to the dawn of humanity. The last known reference to it came from the elders of the Yousufzai tribe in pre-Islamic Afghanistan. After that, nothing, but I have reason to suspect that the Yousufzai kept it here somewhere. I know, most of them are now in the Tribal Area, but they had the Book before they emigrated from Kabul, so it might make sense to retrace their steps and check on the remaining Yousufzai here in Afghanistan, then move our search to the Tribal Area if needed. I am sure with your connections on both sides of the border, that would be an easy task for you."

Juma sighed. "Oy, American, you know how hard it is for a Baluch to talk to Pashtuns? They don't trust us, especially after the Pakistanis merged a few Pashtun districts into Baluchistan."

"I am sure they will make an exception for you, Juma. Business is business, after all, and how many American Humvees with fifty-caliber mounts did you exchange for hefty sacks of heroin with Pashtuns?"

Juma scoffed. "Yes, but the book sounds weird and tribesmen don't like weird, especially when it comes to something ancient. They are very superstitious and ancient means black magic to them." He switched topics. "By the way, what's my cut? Fifty Percent?"

Now, we were talking! But I needed to bargain to be more believable. Greed was something every drug lord believed in.

"I was thinking about a finder's fee of two million, and you don't need to worry about selling it."

He looked at me indignantly. "Hey, American, I am not doing anything unless we are equal partners. I can find the Book myself and sell it through my distribution channels. I don't need you for that."

"But neither you nor your dealers have the buyers or know the merchandise."

"Still ten percent is nothing. We should go in as partners." He snapped his fingers to emphasize the point.

"Look, it is my deal and I am bringing you in. I can give you three million."

Juma kept silent for a moment considering the offer…and the chances of swindling me down the road and keeping the entire booty to himself. "Five million."

"Four. I need to assume that I must sell it through a dealer because the auction will require me to find buyers whom I don't know. So, forty-sixty is a fair split."

Juma thought for a few more minutes. "Deal. Four million cash, with two million in advance, and you can do with the Book anything you want."

"I don't have two million on me, my friend. I am not an idiot to come here with a stash of cash, just to be robbed by your associates."

"Hey, American, don't insult me and my team. Who is talking about robbing? I am an honest businessman. All I need is to cover the expenses of the search and a good-faith deposit to show the seriousness of your intentions. How do I know you are not some buffoon who is simply fishing around?"

That's fair," I said. "But, at this point, I am willing to give you one million when you have started the search and can bring me the first leads. One million should be enough to show that you are dealing with serious players. This is my best and final. If it doesn't work for you, I am going to find someone else."

I rose to leave, but Juma slapped me on my knee.

"Sit, sit. Let's have tea, talk it over."

I moved his hand off my knee. "There is nothing to talk over. One million upon the first lead, and it had better be credible."

"All right, all right." Juma sighed. "You drive a hard bargain, American, taking advantage of us poor Afghans." He sighed again. "All this bargaining has tired me. Enough of this business, already." He waved his hand as if getting rid of an annoying fly. "Let's eat and relax. I will make a few phone calls in the morning, give you some names and you will bring me the money."

I sat down. Men brought tea and sweets. I was tired from all the driving and the initial tension, and wanted to hit the pillow. Juma obliged by putting me in a nice guest bedroom with a good American mattress. The guy knew how to live life even on the shabby outskirts of the poorest country in the world.

The next morning, I woke up to the call to prayer from a nearby minaret. Juma was not around, but my hosts—or captors, one couldn't tell the difference—were exceedingly polite and served breakfast with fresh Afghan bread, cheese, fried eggs, and strong, sweetened hot tea. Nice. I felt fully rested and asked about Juma. The man who brought breakfast shrugged his shoulders, meaning either "I don't know" or "I don't understand English." I didn't want to show that I understood their language. Let them think I am an arrogant American who decided he could play on their turf and win. Besides, the dumber you looked, the more intel you got.

Juma showed up during midday. Lunch was served. To my surprise, he took out a bottle of a twenty-five-year-old single-malt Laphroaig. I looked at him, surprised.

He laughed. "Hey, I am not a Taliban, and I got to like the whiskey they would bring me in America."

"Some life you had there, Juma. Never heard of federal prisons serving whiskey."

He bared his teeth in a smile. "When you know as much as I do, you can get whiskey, girls, boys, and anything else you may desire. Your countrymen can be very generous when it comes to hard-to-come-by information."

What a character! Yet, I enjoyed the smoky taste of the exquisite whiskey. The bastard had good taste in things.

Halfway through shish-kabob and whiskey, I asked him, "So what did you find out?"

"Unfortunately, not too much. Just a few names of Yusufzai elders we can approach. We will have to go to Asadabad in Kunar Valley and meet a fellow by the name of Wadaan."

Wadaan meant prosperous in Dari. Whether it was a real name or a nom-de-guerre, it was a good name for a person who was supposed to have the right connections, I thought. I said out loud, "Who is this fellow? Some big boss at Yousufzai?"

"Nah, the guy is just, as you say, a wheeler-dealer, but he has good connections with Pashto tribes. Acts as a middleman and deals in hash, heroin, guns, the usual."

"Must be a nice chap," I said sarcastically.

Juma either ignored or didn't get my sarcasm. "Yes, he is a good fellow, very reliable, and an honest businessman. We will need to pay him well, though. I told him I have a stupid American archeologist who is willing to pay good money for some old book. Good money for him would be a hundred thousand. So, this is the first lead, my friend. Give me my one million."

"How do I know you are not lying?"

Juma looked indignant. "We Afghans don't lie. We keep our word. You offend me, American. If you were not my guest, I would slit your throat for these words!"

I shook my head. "Whatever. How do you want your money? Check, wire?"

Juma raised his brows, his face showed incredulity. "Zelle, credit card, whatever you want." He raised his voice. "Are you dumb? You are in Afghanistan. It is cash only, my friend." For a second, he got suspicious. "You don't have cash?"

Now it was my turn to play offended. I slapped his knee. "Don't say these things, Juma. I have everything I need and everything you want. You will have your million at sunup tomorrow before we go to the Kunar Valley. I just need to get to the right place to pick it up." As his eyes lit with greed, I added, "And don't try to send your cronies to spy on me or you will be a few soldiers short. There are enough guns where I am going to give them a proper welcome."

"You are a mean fellow, American. Trust is everything in our trade! If we don't trust each other, how can we do business? I trust you because you are my partner. So, why would I spy on you? Don't you need a security detail, though?"

"Oh, please." I waved my hand. "No, thank you, I don't need bodyguards. I will find my way around."

That night, I snuck out of the house. Juma kept his word—probably to lull my suspicions and catch me unaware next time—and no one was following me. I especially looked for little boys, who often act as spies, but there were no boys or even grown-ups around. I got into my truck and drove away, using a circuitous route to make sure I was not being followed. After driving for a while, I came to the drop location, where I got the weapons, put on a Kevlar vest under my tunic, stuck two Glocks at the back of my waist belt, and loaded the rest into the truck. A quick call to Abaddon, and I became one million dollars richer via a duffle bag filled with used hundred-dollar bills, just as the drug dealers prefer.

CHAPTER 6

Asadabad, Afghanistan

I got back right at dawn, but Juma and his crew were already up. A few Toyota SUVs were parked outside of the house and the team was loading them up with supplies, which in this part of the world meant everything from gas and bottled water to ammunition and warm blankets. I gave Juma his money. He didn't even bother to count it, just peeked inside the duffle bag to make sure it was filled to the brim. Once he'd checked the bag, he patted me on the back and got into the front Toyota SUV.

"Hey, couldn't you find something less conspicuous?"

"What are you talking about?" He turned to me laughing. "After your countrymen left, it is now easier to find a new Highlander than an old Russian UAZ."

I shrugged and got into my red-yellow-green monstrosity, which looked totally out of character with the rest of the rides. Our caravan moved slowly out of Kabul on our way to Asadabad, the capital of the Kunar province.

All main roads to and from Kabul were still closed, and my companions clearly didn't care much for meeting a Taliban patrol. They masterfully navigated the region, however, driving down sandy paths and staying away from roads and Taliban patrols, so all I had to do was follow them and pray that my joke of a truck wouldn't stall or blow up at the next turn. What astonished me the most was that no one among them even thought about slowing down as we plowed through the sand or followed serpentine mountainous roads, with one side perilously sliding off the cliff. Driving skills were part of the standard package included with my body but, as I was going through this rollercoaster of a drive, I thought that Rafael's people could learn a thing or two from Juma's men when they were finally brought to the Movie Room.

Once we entered the Kunar Province, the caravan returned to highways, apparently no longer worried about patrols, and I thanked the Creator for keeping my truck in one piece against all odds. From that point on, the trip became uneventful, except that we were passed by a large convoy with gun-mounted Taliban trucks at both ends, guarding a bus and a truck both bearing the red and white *Médecins Sans Frontières* emblem, and two Land Rovers with Press signs driving in the middle. I didn't think much about it at the time. The do-good feel-good Doctors Without Borders could be found risking their lives in every war-torn country in the world.

Asadabad looked like any other Afghan town—a few more or less modern buildings in the center and a maze of dusty streets packed with cars, mopeds, street peddlers, and mudbrick houses everywhere else. Our posse hit those streets with demolition derby speed. Traffic lights in Asadabad were as infrequent as the Taliban in New York. Instead of following a semblance of traffic regulations, the vehicles and pedestrians created a homogenous moving mass with drivers and walkers yelling at each other something like, "Open your eyes, you blipping moron!"

I was trying not to get lost. Notwithstanding Juma's assurances that Highlanders were just as common in Afghanistan as they were in the developed world, a bunch of new Toyota SUVs looked very distinct in the sea of banged-up cars and trucks. Thankfully, the locals took notice of the unusual convoy and gave way, correctly assuming that the SUVs were packed with dangerous men, guns, and explosives. After an hour of navigating through the town, we stopped at what would be considered an expansive villa by local standards. Juma's driver honked, and an armed guard opened the door.

Judging by the house, Wadaan was a serious player, not some street hustler. As we pulled inside the gate, he came running out of the house to meet us. Everything about him was middle—middle-aged, medium-built, and middle-class. I struggled to find any distinguishing marks other than a henna-dyed beard.

He was all smiles as he greeted Juma. When Juma got out

of the car, they embraced and kissed each other, followed by obligatory inquiries into each other's well-being. After hugs and kisses were over, Juma pointed at me quietly standing to one side. Pretending that I didn't know a word of Dari would have been unconvincing—even an ignorant American would have looked at the Afghanistan Tour Guide for Dummies before coming here. So, I successfully botched a few customary greetings, further affirming my ineptitude and foolhardiness.

Wadaan politely smiled, ignoring my linguistic failures, shook my hand, and invited us into the house. We were brought to a posh living room and seated on soft cushions around a well-made Persian rug in the middle of the room as women quickly served tea and sweets. Again, most of the conversation went in Dari, as if I weren't there, until Wadaan finally turned to me.

"So, you are here looking for some book from the Yousufzai? How do these illiterate goat herders have such a fancy book?"

"Don't judge the book by its cover." I winked, but the Afghans didn't get the joke. I changed the tone. "Their tribe belongs to an ancient culture, and even if most of it might have been lost, they still have the artifacts."

"What does this book of yours look like?"

"I don't know," I admitted.

Wadaan furrowed his brows and tilted his head, likely wondering if Juma was playing a prank on him by bringing an insane foreigner to his house.

Ignoring his looks, I continued, "It is so ancient that no

one knows exactly how it looks, but it is written in an ancient language and the script will not look like the Farsi alphabet. Also, given the time when the Book was written, I reckon it will be a parchment scroll in some fancy textile dress. Let me put it this way, I will know when I see it."

"How can I find something if I don't know what it looks like?"

"If the Book still exists, it must have been preserved in the tribal memory. Yousufzai elders should know exactly what you are talking about."

"If this book is such an important heirloom to the Yousufzai, why would they sell it? How much might it cost?"

"I don't know exactly," I lied. "Maybe, five hundred thousand dollars? That is good money for poor people, even if it means they have to give up something that could have been valuable at some point but is no longer of any use to them anyway."

Wadaan wasn't a very imaginative guy and, given that a used Humvee could probably be sold here for a hundred thousand dollars, five hundred thousand for some old book sounded like an exorbitant price. "What is in it for me?" He asked.

"How much do you want?"

"You Americans are rich. If you are willing to pay five hundred thousand to these savages, you can probably sell it for five times that much." No matter how unimaginative Wadaan was, he clearly understood the concept of arbitrage. "So, I want five hundred thousand, too."

I looked at him slack-jawed, threw back my head, and

started laughing, slapping my knees. Everyone around the table sat quietly. My behavior was unconventional, to say the least, but that was exactly the impression I needed to leave.

"You are a funny man, Wadaan," I said. I never expected to leave one million dollars in Afghanistan. It is not worth it. I can give you fifty thousand but not more than that."

Wadaan was genuinely upset. "Oy, what are you saying, American? Trying to take advantage of us poor Afghans?"

Five hundred thousand meant nothing to me, just like one million, or any other amount for that matter. Unlimited expense accounts in the Heavenly Offices really meant unlimited. However, I didn't want to give any ideas to Juma or arouse too much greed in Wadaan. I knew that offending a host was a no-no in Afghanistan, but I needed to stick to the role of a gullible Galapagos cormorant who was too confident to see the danger. As long as they were not afraid of me being too smart for them, I could easily preempt any attempt at double-crossing.

Ignoring Wadaan, I turned to Juma and said in English, knowing full well that Wadaan would understand, "Why did you bring me here? Screw him, we are leaving. These middlemen are dime a dozen." I got up.

Wadaan's eyes flashed in anger. He was already riled up by my arrogant outburst of laughter, and now I was plainly humiliating him. Juma, sensing the brewing trouble, apologized to Wadaan and asked him to give us a few minutes. He threw up his arms and opened his eyes wide as if to say, "These are the kinds of idiots I have to deal with sometimes."

He motioned me outside.

Once outside, he whispered angrily, "Are you crazy, offending the host? You have a death wish?"

I continued to play my role. "I don't like when some lowlife tries to bargain with me to extort a better deal," I whispered back.

"All right, just take my word for it, what you are doing now will get you killed. Keep your mouth shut and let me do the talking. I told you we have to give him a hundred thousand, and I will get him to agree to a hundred thousand."

We went back inside. Wadaan was still fuming. Juma hugged him again, apologizing for the foolhardy American who didn't understand or bother to learn the local customs. He gave a whole speech about how rotten the Western world was and how one could not expect any honor from those people. Everyone around nodded in agreement, sympathizing with poor Juma who had to expose himself to the ungodly infidels for the good of the nation.

I sat with pursed lips and furrowed brows, the epitome of hurt innocence. The scene was so comical that I barely contained myself from laughter, but it did the trick and pacified our host. He and Juma engaged in a heated bargain, full of polite words, mutual indignation, and hand gestures.

After a bit of bickering done in accordance with local customs, Juma turned to me. "Honorable Wadaan agreed to take one hundred thousand dollars out of respect for me, but you must apologize for your rude behavior."

I pretended to push back but eventually apologized, shook Wadaan's hand, and the deal was struck. We were invited to partake in a meal prepared in our honor, and while the women were serving meats and bread, one of the guards came in looking worried and whispered something in Wadaan's ear. Wadaan apologized and ran outside.

I looked out the window and saw two armed men in fatigues, wearing black Perahan turbans. Wadaan spoke to them for a few minutes, then took out a roll of money and stuck it into the vest of one of them. The men left, and Wadaan came back into the house smiling.

"Taliban?" asked Juma.

"Aah." Wadaan dismissively threw up his hand. "Don't worry about it. Those were local guys and I know them well. They saw that I had guests and came to warn me to keep it quiet today. Doctors without Borders from Mazar-i-Sharif came in with a mobile hospital to treat local people, accompanied by a bunch of journalists. For the Taliban it is a PR stunt, so they don't want any hiccups."

Juma nodded in approval. The rest of the visit was uneventful. We were fed lunch, drank tea and, while most of the conversation was in Dari, Juma magnanimously translated and Wadaan switched to English a few times, to honor their guest. He promised to put us in touch with the Yousufzai elders in a few days.

PART III

NORA

CHAPTER 1

Kunar Valley, Afghanistan

It was late afternoon by the time we left Wadaan's place for the trip back to Juma's safe house in Kabul. I remembered my mental note to avoid Taliban patrols at any cost and felt a bit uneasy about the earlier encounter with Taliban soldiers, sharing my concerns with Juma.

Juma waved me off. "Don't worry. Wadaan took care of it. He is no friend of the Taliban, and he and I go back a long time. Betraying me is a bad business," he added, winking. "And Wadaan is a good businessman."

I was still concerned. I was not afraid of a fight, but making too much noise was not prudent, not to mention I didn't want to spill blood unless absolutely necessary. To alleviate my fears, Juma instructed his men to send one of the trucks a couple of miles ahead of us. "That way, even if the Taliban plans to ambush us, the advance team will warn us and we will take an alternate route."

I shrugged and got into my truck, putting my weapons on the front seat just in case. Remembering my first encounter with the Taliban on the way to Kabul and the rules I had established for myself for dealing with them, I still had a bad feeling about it. Just to be doubly sure, I decided to keep my distance from the rest of Juma's trucks, to give me some extra reaction time.

My premonition proved to be true. The Taliban must have been watching the convoy of Toyota SUVs from the moment we left Asadabad, and figured out Juma's ruse of an advance car. A Taliban patrol hiding on a highway shoulder with their lights off three miles out of Asadabad let the first car through, then ambushed the rest of our convoy. They hit the first SUV with an RPG to block the road and moved one of their armored cars behind the Toyotas to prevent us from escaping. Juma's men scurried out of the SUVs into the shrubbery surrounding the highway.

I was lucky, however. The distance I had kept from the main convoy, plus apparent miscommunication between Taliban posts who had probably been advised only of a caravan of Toyota SUVs and knew nothing of a colorful truck without doors, resulted in a Taliban patrol car cutting the convoy's retreat after the last Toyota but before my truck.

When I heard an explosion and saw an armored car with high beams swerving onto the highway behind the last Toyota, I turned off my lights and stopped on the shoulder. Grabbing my arsenal, I snuck closer to the action, staying hidden in the bushes along the road.

From my vantage point, I watched a firefight that looked more like a slaughter. Juma's men were badly outgunned and outnumbered. Fifty-caliber mounts on Taliban trucks wreaked havoc among them, and the feeble attempts to return fire did little damage to the patrol. The first car was gone, and everyone from the third car blocked by the rearguard Taliban truck was either dead or dying, scattered along the highway. Juma and his three men from the middle vehicle ran for cover and made it into the bushes, then slid down the slope to the Kunar River. They shot back without even looking, mostly wasting the ammunition. Taliban fighters pursued them on foot, spraying them with bullets from an elevated position.

I carefully crept down and hid behind a boulder on the slope. Juma's men were pinned behind a group of short, crooked trees on the slope, and their pursuers steadily advanced toward them. Oblivious to my presence, they walked freely without even trying to hide. Putting on my night vision goggles, I had a perfect view of the attackers. I let my XM-7 do the work. As the clattering of my rifle started, a number of the Taliban fighters fell right away and the others ran for cover from the surprise attack. Encouraged by unexpected help, Juma's men started returning fire with more accuracy.

The Taliban patrol was in a pickle, but they were battle-hardened veterans used to fighting against superior Western forces. I could see more of them coming down from the highway. They had to cover both me and Juma's men, but they had enough fighters to split their forces and go after all of us. The situation was becoming more and more ominous, but I was not prepared to waste any Reincarnation Rights or lose the only people who could help me find the Book.

The night was cloudy, and the dim moonlight barely lit the slope. Wearing the night vision goggles, I held an advantage over the Taliban. As they were attacking the boulder where I was hiding, I moved to a different one, waited for an opportune moment, left my rifle by the boulder, took out the Glocks, and crept closer to them. The men looked like shadows in the almost moonless night, and no one could immediately see the difference between friend and foe. As I ran through their midst, I shot from both pistols simultaneously in all directions. At such close range, every shot was lethal. After strafing the road I returned to my rifle, and while they were trying to identify who was shooting, sprayed them with another burst. At this point, most of our enemies on the slopes were hit, and Juma's men dealt with them, finishing off the wounded. I climbed back up to the highway and shot a few grenades from my rifle's grenade launcher at the trucks to eliminate any potential danger from them.

After making sure all our attackers had been eliminated, I slid down the slope to check on Juma and his men. One of his fighters lay dead nearby, two others were wounded, albeit more or less functional. But Juma was badly hurt.

There was no more time to play dumb American. "Can you walk?" I asked Juma in Dari.

He nodded, apparently not even noticing that I was speaking in his native tongue.

I called on his other two companions and ordered them to pick him up and follow me. I didn't want to take any chances. The Taliban patrol had been destroyed, but there was no guarantee they hadn't radioed for help before I finished them off with the grenades. Running along the river and leaving our footprints in muddy soil was a sure way of getting caught. We had to cross the river.

While the current slowed down in winter compared to the early spring months when snow in the mountains melted and filled the waters, the Kunar River was still a formidable obstacle. It was not very deep, but the current was fast, and I could hear its deafening roar as it hit the rocks in the middle of the stream. I tried to find a place to cross. A few yards downstream, I saw a few decaying logs thrown across the water, resting on the rocks on both sides of the river. There were quite a few of that kind of makeshift crossing left by the American troops and local engineers who used them to build pontoon bridges. The logs were old but looked sturdy enough to walk on.

I glanced over at my posse. There was no way those wounded men could carry Juma across. It would be a miracle if they crossed it themselves without slipping and getting washed away by the current. I loaded Juma on my shoulders and stepped onto the first log, trying to balance like a gymnast on a flying trapeze. The other two men waited for me to cross.

The logs were indeed sturdy but slippery. As I almost reached the other bank, my foot slipped and I slid into the water, but managed to grab the log at the very last moment. Juma held fast, but he was suffocating me with his grip. Gathering all my strength not to be carried away by the current, I pulled us forward. A rock sitting next to the crossing provided good foot support so I could push myself back up onto the log. As I climbed across, I had no strength to get back on my feet, and made the rest of the way on all fours.

The other two men, seeing me slip once, decided to take no chances and crawled across all the logs. Wet and tired, we finally got to the other side and started climbing the slope. It was a laborious trip. but we made it before any more Taliban showed up.

CHAPTER 2

Doctors Without Borders Hospital, Asadabad, Afghanistan

As we reached the top of the riverbank, I saw a few shabby shacks a short distance away. The sight of a village gave all of us additional strength despite our wounds and exhaustion. As we entered the settlement, the villagers helped us into one of the mudbrick shacks. Finally, we could breathe. We had been given shelter, and were now protected by the Afghan law of hospitality... reinforced by the sight of our guns and a few wads of cash.

I looked at Juma's wounds. He had taken a bullet to the stomach, or so I thought, and was bleeding badly. I did everything to stop the bleeding, but we needed a doctor or he would die soon.

"Wadaan, stinking jackal," Juma cursed weakly.

"Save your strength. We will have time later to figure out

whose fault it was. You need a doctor, my friend. Let me try and find you one."

Finally, I hatched a plan. I went outside of the village, closer to the river and away from onlookers, and issued a maintenance ticket to Abaddon. He appeared right away, again with a loud *bang*. The idiot would never learn. Thankfully, the roar of the river was loud enough to muffle the noise.

"What do you want?" he said, looking around. "You know I cannot help you fighting. No supernatural interference, remember?"

"I know, I know. I am dealing with the situation myself. I just need an upgrade."

Abaddon tilted his head. "Such as?"

"Can you get me a woman's voice?'

"What?" Abaddon paused for a second, then hunched forward in laughter, slapping his furry thighs. "Do you also want me to sew a pussy between your legs?" he said through the laughter.

I waited for him to calm down. "Ha, ha, funny. Just get me a woman's voice upgrade, and quickly."

Abaddon rubbed his head. "You know you will have to go back to the HHS for an upgrade. They can even get you a full woman's body if you need it, but I have to get an upgrade order from Azazel and that might take a while."

"Can we go into a Pause while you are running the errands?"

"Nah, I wouldn't be able to hold the Pause for that long. You know those bureaucrats at the HHS, they will procrastinate till the second Deluge." Abaddon raised his finger. "But I can check with the Requisition Room and see if Uzza has any voice modulators. Should be much faster. The guy is not a stickler for paperwork, and I can convince him to give me the modulator on the existing order."

"Beautiful," I said. "Go, go! What are waiting for?" Before Abaddon disappeared through the maintenance tunnel, I quickly added, "And do me a favor, stop banging so loudly when you come back or the entire village will see your furry Genie face."

Abaddon waved his paw and disappeared.

He came back in a few moments carrying something in his hands. "Latest model, state of the art. Oh, and Uzza said if you want to go kinky, he has a couple of nice silicone dolls for you."

"Tell him to shove'em up his ass," I said, trying out the device.

"Angels don't have asses," answered Abaddon seriously.

What can you do with these clowns? They tried to be funny but, for the life of them, they couldn't get human wit no matter how much I tried to teach them.

The device worked fine. It produced a bit of an artificial squeaky sound, but muffled by a burqa and a good amount of surrounding noise, it should do. I went back to the village, grabbed one of the freshly laundered burqas drying on the ropes between the huts, put it on top of my *shalwar kameez*, stashed the Glocks at the back of my waist, and ran back to Asadabad along the village's side of the river, intending to use the bridge into the city.

I ran as fast as I could. It was reasonable to assume the Taliban, alerted to the loss of its patrol, was already searching for us on both sides of the river. It was just a matter of time before they found Juma and his men in the village, and while the law of hospitality was very strong among Afghans, I couldn't know how long it would hold once a troop of Taliban armed to the teeth showed up.

A three-mile run would have been easy, just a morning jog, except that I was exhausted from the prior firefight and the river crossing. Also, breathing through the burqa while carrying guns and wearing a Kevlar vest underneath made the running even harder. I was almost out of breath when I saw the lights of Asadabad. I slowed down and crossed the bridge to the city. It was already morning and I quickly melted into the sea of blue burqas walking to their daily chores. It wasn't too hard to find the mobile hospital, which was now the talk of the town.

The hospital was located on the outskirts of the city in a large field fenced off by barbed wire. It consisted of numerous tents where doctors, both local and from Doctors Without Borders, saw patients. The location must have been chosen for better crowd control as the large area provided a great vantage point for the guards surrounding the fence and manning a few makeshift wooden towers at the four corners.

Approaching the hospital, I saw two long lines—one for men and one for women—of patients trying to make it to the hospital. Cutting the line would attract too much attention, so I begrudgingly came to the end of the women's queue, cursing the poor state of healthcare in Afghanistan. To my surprise, there were no men in the women's line as all obligatory male companions were told to wait on the side to avoid excessive crowding. Good. One less thing to explain. To my further pleasant surprise, the line went fast. The guards maintained order and there was very little pushing and shoving, even though there was a lot of screaming and yelling. The guards would only let in people who claimed a serious illness. With women, they had to rely on their word, since touching a woman was *haram*, forbidden. When my turn came, I gave a typical Afghan female name and concocted a story of complications and excessive bleeding after a recent birth. For Afghan men, a woman bleeding after birth was impure, so the story assured me that the guards would try to get rid of me as soon as possible. He asked where was my husband, and I motioned vaguely toward the crowd of men standing beside the fence.

Once inside, I was led to a tent that had an examination room separated by an opaque screen, and a guard standing inside with his rifle on one shoulder. There were two or three more women in the tent waiting for a doctor.

Finally, the doctor showed up…and I froze.

The doctor was the Moffat girl!

Except she was now wearing a head scarf, a white coat with a name tag that said "Nora" in English and Dari, and dark-brown cat-eye glasses. She looked even more beautiful in her doctor outfit than when I'd seen her the first time in Colorado, naked and shivering from cold and terror.

My insides started churning with an unfamiliar feeling I'd not had since that mission. It was not a simple animal desire for a female of the species, it was something else I couldn't explain. Was I experiencing a déjà vu again? Or did this woman somehow stir feelings that dead men shouldn't be having, whether wearing a physical shell or not? Was this fate, or a simple coincidence? I didn't have time to dwell on all these questions. I had to move fast. Nora, accompanied by an interpreter wearing a hijab, moved behind the curtain.

Finally, my turn came and I walked in.

Nora, through the interpreter, asked me what was I complaining about and asked me to take off the burqa. I was lucky that one of the women behind me in the tent was moaning loudly in pain, providing a sound cover for me. I didn't want to hurt Nora, but the mission was of paramount importance. In one swift motion, I whipped off the burqa, and before anyone could react, pistol-whipped the interpreter and jammed my palm over Nora's mouth while training my nine-millimeter on her.

"If you want to live, do exactly as I say," I said in a frightening whisper. "Nod if I understand."

Disoriented and scared, she nodded.

"I will now remove my hand, but if you scream, you will get a bullet in the head. Is that understood?" I raised my voice slightly.

She energetically nodded again. Her eyes were wide open

and her pupils dilated. Which only made her even more beautiful.

"Now, take off your white coat, put on the hijab of the interpreter, and go with me quietly."

Before we left the safety of the curtained area, I took off my backpack and swept into it all available medicine and supplies from the medicine cabinet standing next to the examination table.

After I put the burqa back on, we walked out, her first, with me right after her jamming my pistol against her ribs. The guard looked at us. I quickly said, "I need to go to a specialist. The interpreter will take me. The doctor wants you to wait a few minutes until she comes back."

Surprised that it was me talking instead of the interpreter, the guard turned to Nora and asked her if this was right. She, of course, didn't understand, but the guard's intonation and a sharp nudge under her rib from my pistol made her nod convincingly. Satisfied with her response and thinking I was one of those loud-mouthed women who knew it all and always chimed in first, the guard let us pass and we walked slowly toward the fence.

She wanted to run but I held her back.

"Do not run and do not try to attract attention or you are dead," I growled.

"What do you want from me?" she whispered. "I don't have any money and they will be looking for me everywhere. We are protected by the government."

"Just shut up and walk."

She was very obedient, probably due to her experience in Moffat. I was sure this kidnapping brought back her PTSD with vengeance and, while I felt genuinely sorry for her, her submissive behavior worked fine for me. I gave us five minutes tops before the interpreter regained her consciousness and raised the alarm.

Moving behind the tents and staying out of the sightline of the crowd, we made it to the fence. I found a spot with almost no people around, took out my tactical combat knife, and using its serrated edge, quickly cut through the wire, all the while pressing Nora against it to prevent any unwise moves on her part. Once the wire was cut, I pushed her through and ducked through myself. The few bystanders looked on in amazement. I threw off the burqa and showed them my two pistols, pressing one to my lips indicating to stay quiet. They quickly understood that I was not to be trifled with and complied.

I grabbed Nora by the hand and ran across the street, quickly disappearing behind a mudbrick building situated across from the hospital. As we hid behind the building, I heard the noises and screams, indicating that my brief excursion was finally exposed. The bystanders who saw us would now undoubtedly alert the Taliban as to the direction we ran in. So we had no time to slow down.

I saw a truck parked along the street. Hitting the driver's-side window with my elbow, I broke it and opened the door, then threw Nora into the passenger seat. I hotwired the car and took off before anyone noticed the theft.

Now that I had a ride, our chances of getting out of town had improved dramatically, especially if the Taliban guards searching for us didn't see us taking off in a vehicle. My luck had held so far. Reaching the outskirts, I quickly navigated the morning rush, got out of town, and drove to the log crossing we'd used last night.

"Get out of the truck."

I dragged her out, pushed the truck into the river, and we slid down the slope to the riverbank.

Once we reached the logs, I barked, "Get on my shoulders and hold on for your life. And if you do anything stupid, I will throw you into the river and you will be swept along by the current and crack your head on one of the rocks. Do you understand me?"

She was panicking, and I couldn't tell whether she was more afraid of me or of the roaring current and the flimsy, makeshift log bridge.

I shook her by the shoulders, hoping her fear of me was stronger. "Don't worry about the river. If you do everything I say, I will carry you safely to the other bank."

She compliantly climbed onto my back and firmly grabbed my neck. Learning from last night's experience, I walked carefully, and this time made it without slipping.

On the other side of the river, I pushed her up the slope. Once we made it to the top, I sat down to catch my breath.

She sat down next to me, scared witless and not knowing what to do. Finally, she found the strength to break her silence and asked in a hushed voice. "Where are you taking me? We are here to help your people, we are doctors, we didn't do anything bad to you."

"Just keep quiet lady. I simply need your medical expertise and if you do everything I tell you, you will be returned safely."

It dawned on her that I had spoken American English. Somehow, thinking I was an American, calmed her down a bit.

"You are not an Afghan, are you? Are you CIA?" She must have felt the protection of the long arm of the American justice system. Her tone of voice became cockier.

I had to disabuse her of this sense of safety and squeezed her arm. She whimpered in pain.

"Doesn't matter who I am. Just do what you are told. Got it?"

She nodded, her fear returning to her eyes even stronger than before.

CHAPTER 3

Village in Kunar Valley, Afghanistan

After a brief respite, we continued to the village where I had left Juma and his men. As we came closer, I heard noises and gunshots. My worst fears had materialized—the Taliban found us faster than I'd hoped. Hiding behind small crooked trees with Nora in tow, I peeked at the village's main square. Juma's men were lying in a pool of blood before the shack where they had been hiding, and Juma had been dragged out with his hands tied by a rope.

Two trucks with mounted fifty-caliber machine guns stood nearby. The villagers, mostly elders, women, and children, had been lined up before the trucks with the fifty-cals trained on them. Now I had a dilemma—leave the villagers to their fate, let the Taliban take Juma and try to free him somewhere down the road, or get involved. The former didn't sit right with me. Letting the innocent villagers be slaughtered because they had helped us would be too low. And the chances of freeing Juma from the Taliban would not be that great, and I needed him for my mission. So, the last one became the only option.

I told Nora to stay put and wait for me. Somehow, I felt that she wouldn't run away, but to be on the safe side, I tied her to a tree with one of the laundry lines hanging nearby. I quietly crawled toward the trucks. They were surrounded by the Taliban fighters with guns at the ready, intently peering around at the surroundings. Judging by the lack of men of fighting age on the firing line, I assumed that most of the able-bodied men were hiding outside the village, ready to fight for the lives of their loved ones. In this neck of the woods, every man knew how to fight and handle a gun. If my assumption was correct, all I needed to do was to disable the machine guns.

I found an opening between the Taliban fighters surrounding the trucks, snuck past them, and climbed onto the closest truck. A quick slice of my knife and the first gunner was done. I took out my Glock with the suppressor and shot the second gunner in the head. Unfortunately, turning the tables and using the machine guns on the Taliban wasn't possible since they were too close to the trucks and the mounted guns wouldn't adjust low enough, so I started firing the pistols, hitting them one after the other.

They turned their full attention to me, but just as I'd expected, I heard a clutter of assault rifles from the bushes surrounding the village and the Taliban started falling like flies. The villagers hiding in the bushes advanced on the Taliban troops. I supported their advance by making sure the machine guns stayed silent, warding off any attempts by the Taliban to retake them.

After a relatively short and chaotic firefight, the villagers retook their village. I ran back to the tree where I'd left Nora. As expected, she was still there and hadn't even tried to untie the rope, simply covering her head against the blast of weapons. I brought her back to the village square where concerned elders lively discussed what to do about their conundrum. This was a mess, and repercussions would be inevitable.

The last thing I needed was to jeopardize the whole village. I spoke to the elders, and together we loaded the dead bodies on the trucks. I deputized one of the villagers to drive one of the trucks, put Juma and Nora in the other one, and grabbed a few towels, a kettle, an AK-47 with extra magazines, and some food. As we were about to leave, I saw the villagers trying to take the machine guns off the truck mounts. I tried to dissuade them because these guns would be a proverbial smoking gun should the Taliban come back, but their temptation to possess the fearsome weapons was too much for me to fight. I let it go and we drove away.

A few miles into the valley, we discarded the dead bodies into the river. I helped the other driver push his truck down the slope into the water, waved to him, and continued driving as far from that place as possible while searching for a suitable shelter.

Finally, I found what I was looking for—a nice cave in the

mountains. Juma was unconscious and couldn't walk. I asked Nora to help. At this point, the doctor in her kicked in, and she helped me bring Juma into the cave. As we pulled him out of the truck, he moaned in pain but remained unconscious. She finally understood why I had brought her in, but I thought an explanation was in order anyway.

"Nora," I said. She looked at me quizzically and I moved my eyes toward her name tag. "I need to hide the truck, but I trust you will take care of your patient. I apologize for the rough treatment, but my friend was teetering on the brink of death and I desperately needed a doctor. If I'd cut you some slack, you would have done something silly, killing both of us in the process. Once this is over, I will let you slap me as many times as you want, but for now, please, I need you to take care of the patient." I put emphasis on the word patient. "I will get rid of the truck and be right back."

She looked at me contemptuously. Of course, she would take care of the patient – she was a doctor after all. I nodded and gave her my backpack containing the medicine and her glasses, a few bottles of water from the truck, and walked out of the cave.

My first thought was to hide the truck under some branches, but even stripped of the machine gun, it was still too conspicuous with its military equipment and reinforced doors and trunk. Could I just remove the signs of its identity? I had no tools and no paint to make it resemble a civilian vehicle even remotely. In this truck we would be sitting ducks, literally. I didn't know the terrain well enough to avoid Taliban encounters, so the truck had to go. We would have to stay in the cave until Juma regained a bit of strength to walk, and then would continue on foot. I didn't have a clear plan for my next steps, but at this point, I was just trying to manage the situation one step at a time.

CHAPTER 4

Somewhere in Kunar Valley, Afghanistan

Nora was still working on Juma's wounds when I came back. She was laser-focused on her patient, oblivious to everything else. I sat down and watched silently. Yes, that was the same young woman who had captured my imagination in Moffat and whose memory had led me to my adventure in Vegas. Her iridescent blue eyes sparkled like jewels, contrasting against her dirty and matted hair. Despite the unkempt state of her appearance, her slim body exuded a natural grace and beauty. As she leaned over Juma, her swan-like neck was exposed, accentuated by the cascading locks of her hair falling to one side. The magnetic pull of her presence was irresistible, drawing me in with an almost overwhelming force. I experienced the same strange churning sensation in my stomach as in the hospital when I saw her for the first—or rather, the second—time. I didn't have a spare moment to examine my feelings at the hospital, but now, away from danger, I tried to analyze what was it that so impacted my senses. The feelings were both elusive and powerful. I couldn't make sense of them. All I knew was that it was far different from the feelings of sympathy for a helpless victim or the sensual pleasure I had experienced with the call girl in Vegas. Even remorse for having hurt Nora earlier couldn't account for my feelings. I relished looking at her and didn't want the moment to pass.

Yet, I was certainly not ready to call it love, especially since that word didn't mean much to me after I had died. The more I looked at her, the more I became convinced that somehow, something in her connected me to my past life. Was she a dead ringer for my wife or girlfriend, which would account for my feelings for her? Or, is it something else? But though I couldn't identify my emotions or their genesis, I definitely felt an overpowering desire—no, a quintessential need to feel her closeness, to touch her, embrace her, and hold her in my arms, protecting her against this dangerous and unforgiving world. To put it simply, if you brushed away all the poetic nonsense so even a Demon could understand it, I was hopelessly hooked. And without even knowing it, she was reeling me in with the dogged determination of a fisherman.

In the meantime, the day went by and the stars lit up a clear sky. I started a fire. Nora was finally done and had dozed off, exhausted by the day's events, her face illuminated by the campfire flames, adding to her gravitational pull. Juma's wounds were dressed and he was sleeping, loaded up with antibiotics and painkillers. Suddenly, he tried to move and moaned in pain. Nora woke up momentarily, checking on his wound and fixing the blanket she had covered him with.

Sensing me watching her, she said, "The fever should subside by morning once antibiotics start working. Thankfully, the wounds were not life-threatening and the bullets missed his vital organs. It was a miracle that one bullet went less than an inch from his liver. A little bit to the left and he would be dead."

"Yep," I responded. "It is amazing how little separates the dead from the living. In any event, I cannot thank you enough for everything you did for my friend. You must be exhausted. Why don't you lie down and get some more sleep? I will watch over both of you." Seeing her hesitation, I added, smiling, "I can assure you, you have nothing to fear. You are as safe as anyone could be in this country."

She didn't argue and passed out in a second, as today's ordeal had completely drained her. I covered her with a blanket, pushed another under her head as a pillow, and walked outside to check around.

Everything was quiet and the mountains under the starry sky looked shadowy and silent. The chorusing of cicadas added to the sense of security. Here I was, surrounded by enemies, with a helpless woman and a wounded man on my hands, yet somehow I felt at peace. The Angels were right, we humans are irrational creatures.

It was early afternoon the next day when I heard goats

bleating in the distance. That meant we were dangerously close to people, and I imagined the Taliban would not be stingy with the reward for finding us, properly incentivizing the poor inhabitants of the region. The only safe thing to do was to move farther into the mountains, reducing the chances of human encounters. I decided to rouse my companions.

Nora woke up right away. She looked more or less rested. Juma was still sleeping.

I gave her a serious look. "Here is the situation. We are safe for now, but I'm not sure how long we can use this hideout. Assuming the Taliban found their trucks in the river, they will start a concentric search, slowly increasing the range. We are too conspicuous and way too close to human habitation. If there is a price on our heads, the locals will sell us out in no time. So we need to get going."

"Can you let me go now?" she asked meekly. "At this point, I am just a burden for you two."

"I wish I could. Unfortunately, I cannot drive you back without getting us all killed, and alone, a good-looking woman without a chaperon will never make it through the valley in one piece. Believe it or not, I do feel responsible for you. I promise, once we reach safety I will arrange for your return to civilization."

She took my reference to her good looks as a flimsy attempt to dupe her into staying with us. Now that she realized I had no desire to hurt her, her fear of me was replaced with anger. "You kidnap me and beat the daylight out of me, but now you worry about my safety? You shouldn't have kidnapped me in the first place!" Her voice was ringing.

Arguing with her would have been futile. I decided to go for shock therapy. Without saying a word, I took out my gun and racked the slide.

Her eyes filled with horror.

Instead of firing at her, I flipped it and handed it to her. "The gun is locked and loaded. If you want to avenge my mistreatment of you, and if you believe you can make it back on your own, just squeeze the trigger." I raised my hands in the air. "There is no point in me trying to convince you of the honesty of my intentions…although truth be told, I never lied to you, even when I kidnapped you."

This was not very fair on my part, as I knew she would never shoot me, but as said, I'd decided to go for shock therapy. Guns are very good for that, whether you are facing the muzzle or stroking the trigger.

She stood for a moment, then indignantly threw the gun on the ground. "I am not a murderer like you. I don't kill people, I give them life." She obviously felt very proud of her moral convictions.

I smiled as kindly as I could. "I know, and that is why I feel responsible for you. I assure you, you are not a hostage and are free to go at any time. But please, let me take you to safety. You have done so much for me—my tongue had slipped but I quickly corrected myself—for *us*, that I owe you a life debt, and I fully intend to repay it." I felt like a pompous ass saying something so pathetic, but the earnest tone of my voice calmed her down. She was still angry— either at me or at herself for not shooting me when she had a chance—but now I knew she wouldn't go anywhere.

She pursed her lips. "All right, I will go with you, but only because you put me in this untenable position. Fair warning: once we are back to civilization I will leave you, and I will tell my story to the first journalist I can find. Let the whole world know of lawless Americans kidnapping doctors who came here to treat poor sick people."

I gave her a thumbs-up. "Deal. Can we shake on it?" I extended my hand, but she demonstratively turned her back to me. Her behavior was so childish that I felt even more endeared to this cute and innocent young woman. I took back my hand.

"If Juma can walk, we will be moving out at dusk. It may be too dangerous to walk in the sunlight."

By the time the sun set, Juma had woken up. He was dizzy, but the danger to his life had passed. He was a true survivor. "Where am I?" he asked, glancing around with a frown.

"In some God-forsaken cave somewhere in the valley. By the way, meet your savior, Dr. Nora. I brought her from Asadabad to save your sorry ass."

Juma looked incredulous. "Did *you* save my life, American?" He spoke Dari, meaning that notwithstanding his pain and delirium, it had registered in his mind that I knew the language and that my being a dumb Western tourist was simply a clever disguise.

"I guess I did. Didn't you say we're partners?"

He jeered. "I underestimated you, American. Well, you are now my blood brother. Your life is my life, and your fight is my fight."

"Oh, please. Don't be so pompous, Juma. You will sell me out at the first opportunity, but that's okay. I never had any doubts about your prowess and intelligence. That's why I saved you and want to continue working with you."

He laughed so hard that he started choking in pain. Nora quickly came to him and asked him to lie still. She hadn't understood a word of our conversation, but laughter was not good for her patient at the moment.

Juma caught his breath. "Well, let's pray an opportunity to betray you will never arise. That way we can remain blood brothers no matter what." He turned to Nora and switched to English, "The words fail me, doctor. You saved my life and it is yours for the taking."

Nora didn't know what to say, but smiled bashfully and replied, "I am glad you are feeling better."

"Haji, Juma Khan at your service, ma'am, and many people in this country would die to have my gratitude."

This didn't impress her, clearly not thinking much of either of us, but she said nothing.

Juma lay there with a scow. As his memory came back to him, he smacked his lips, "Did that bastard Wadaan sell us out?"

"Looks that way."

"Dumb asshole," he said in English.

"Hey, easy brother. You are in the presence of a lady.

Juma apologized profusely. "I beg your forgiveness, ma'am. We Afghans are simple people, but we cannot tolerate a betrayal. I was referring to the traitor who sold us out."

Again Nora said nothing, but I noticed a smirk of indignation in her eyes. She surely understood that we were not friends of the Taliban, and we didn't care to encounter other people either. Which, I guessed, in her mind clearly put us in the category of filthy drug dealers or heartless spies—not much different in her book.

"So, what's next, American?" asked Juma.

"Well, we don't have a car, and I reckon the Taliban is on our heels. We should move farther into the mountains where there are fewer people, then try to contact your colleagues who may be able to drag us out of here. I have a satellite phone, but we are too deep in the valley so no reception. Are you strong enough to walk?"

Juma realized my proposal made sense. "If you can help me walk, I can do it. Once we get satellite reception I will contact my people in Jalalabad and have them pick us up. When I am in touch with my crew, we will have food, money, and a small army."

"Okay, let's go then." I gathered our belongings and weapons, and put most of them on my back. Using a sturdy branch, I fashioned a cane for Juma. As much as I hated it, I had to ask Nora to carry some of our stuff. She didn't object.

Before we moved out, I handed her one of my Glocks.

She pushed it back, but I insisted. "Look, it is a dangerous trip, and your moral convictions may not bode well for you in this place. Here is how you get it ready for action." I racked Glock's slide. "If we are in danger and you have to choose between your life and someone else's, I suggest you squeeze this trigger. Besides, won't you feel safer having a gun, as you are traveling in the company of rogues and wretches?"

She scoffed, but took the gun.

We started walking slowly toward the mountains. It was a bizarre sight—a wounded man barely walking with a cane and leaning on me, a fragile woman loaded with a ton of stuff as a beast of burden, and one able-bodied man who was responsible for this company of invalids and girl scouts. As we came closer to the mountains, the path went uphill and became harder and harder to climb. We had to take a break, and then another, and another, making me feel less and less safe. There was no cover anywhere, and we were completely exposed. After a few hours of the grueling journey, I finally spotted a small cavern in the mountainside.

"We will rest here. I'll try my phone to see if we are high enough to get reception."

We unloaded our belongings and unwound the blankets, and I started a fire—inside the cave to avoid being spotted. Juma was exhausted. His wound had started bleeding, so Nora changed his dressing and loaded him up with another dose of antibiotics and painkillers.

Once Juma was asleep, Nora and I sat next to the fire watching its flames.

I broke the silence. "You should have thanked him."

"Who?"

"Juma. A man in this country, especially one as important as Juma, offering his gratitude to a woman is no small thing."

Her eyes bulged and her brows furrowed. "Are you out of your mind? Just because I agreed to go with you doesn't mean I like or respect you. Now you want me to thank my captors who happen to be shady drug lords, as it's clear to me that's who you are? I haven't developed the Stockholm syndrome yet, you know."

Her outburst upset me. I desperately wanted her to like me and had done everything in my power to make as good an impression as possible, given the circumstances. But she just gave me the cold shoulder and called me names.

"First, I am not a drug dealer, and while Juma might be one, he is here because he is helping me with a search. Second, you are not such a saint either, working for the Taliban."

"I don't work for the Taliban, I medically treat Afghan people who were robbed by your government for some stupid political reasons."

"Treat? Why? So they would hang better on the cranes? And, speaking of my government—not that I give two hoots about it—Americans tried to give them some semblance of freedom. It just didn't work."

"Killing thousands in the process?"

"Yes, which was a small percentage of the deaths caused by the Taliban. At least be fair in your criticism."

Not having anything to say in response, she pursed her lips like a child denied her favorite toy and ordered to go to sleep before her bedtime.

I was pissed, as well…although there was no reason for it. I didn't even know if I was an American. I could have been a Taliban fighter before I died, for all I knew. Yet, somehow, everything about this woman stirred my feelings.

We sat quietly for a while, then curiosity got the better of Nora. "So, if you are not a drug dealer, what are you doing in this country? CIA?"

"No," I said sarcastically. "I already told you I'm not CIA, and I'm not a servant of your much-hated imperialists. I am an archeologist." For some reason, the designation given to me by Juma when we visited Wadaan sounded like a good wedge into winning her heart.

"What?" she looked truly incredulous.

"Yes, believe it or not, the world consists not just of heartless scoundrels and self-righteous do-gooders. Some of us are interested in the past more than we are interested in the present or the future."

She let the do-gooder's reference slide. "So, are you looking for some artifacts?"

"Yep, I am. I am trying to find an ancient book, which presumably was brought to Afghanistan from the Middle East by the Yousufzai tribe, who claim to be the descendants of Israel's lost tribes." I caught myself. I'd gotten so excited by my mission that I sounded like Professor Khoshaba.

She was definitely curious, but couldn't resist sending another vengeful missive. "So, you are going to steal a national treasure from this poor country and put it in some museum for the enjoyment of wealthy Westerners? Or, better yet, sell it to some filthy rich guy who will keep it in his private collection?"

Now, that was too much. "I am not stealing anything. Did you forget when these crazy fanatics defaced the Buddha statues listed in UNESCO's World Heritage List, despite the very feeble protests from your do-gooder friends?"

Again she had nothing to say, but she was not willing to concede, either, so she retreated to the safety of pursed lips. We spent a few more minutes in silence, with both of us absolutely convinced that we hated each other, at least on ideological grounds.

"I'm tired, I am going to bed," she finally said. "Please don't kill me when I'm asleep. At least, have the courage to wake me up before you shoot me."

I squinted. "Don't worry. You are perfectly safe. I am a man of my word. Besides, I am not going to waste a perfectly good bullet on you."

She gasped, prepared to answer something particularly offensive, but not finding anything that would hurt me sufficiently, grabbed her blanket and went to sleep.

I sat there dumbfounded, trying to understand why I had picked a fight with a woman who engendered such tender feelings within me. Finding no answer, I decided to let this thought go unanswered.

CHAPTER 5

Hindukush Crossing, Afghanistan

I woke up from the sunrays gently rolling over my face through the entrance to the cavern. I went outside to try my luck with the satellite phone. After walking around the cave, I finally got a couple of bars. I pulled Juma out of his sleep to break the happy news. He got up immediately, notwithstanding his wounds, and limped outside with my sat phone. Nora was still sleeping, and I started working on the breakfast.

I could hear Juma screaming on the phone, though it was hard to make out what he was saying. After a few minutes, he walked back in, looking gloomy.

"What happened? Couldn't get a team to pick us up?"

"No, my men are eager to fetch us back. The problem is, after your stint at the hospital and a few corpses showing up downstream, the valley is teeming with Taliban fighters scouring every nook and cranny around here. I don't have enough men to fight the entire army. We have to get out of this valley. They can pick us up southeast of here, but we will have to walk a lot and cross the Hindukush."

"Cross what?"

Juma pointed to the cloud-covered mountains with snow caps barely visible through the clouds. "We don't have to go all the way to the summit, but we will have to go through some high-altitude passes. That is our best option."

I gazed wide-eyed at the huge mountains. "How long will it take?"

"I don't know. With me limping and the woman, probably, three, four days. Maybe five."

The idea of spending a few days climbing mountains in subzero temperatures sounded insane.

Seeing disbelief on my face, Juma asked, "Do you have any other ideas?"

I sat thinking, but all other options were just as lousy, if not more so.

"Maybe, we should leave the woman?" he suggested. "The two of us should be able to make it a lot faster."

"No," I bellowed so loudly that he pulled back and Nora woke up.

"What's going on?" she asked, rubbing her sleepy eyes.

"Let's talk over breakfast. It's almost done."

Once we sat down to eat, I explained the situation to Nora. She couldn't understand the danger. To her it sounded like an exciting adventure, similar to what she'd seen in documentaries and movies about mountain climbers. Explaining the dangers better and giving her the choice of staying behind and taking her chances with the Taliban and locals would have been a responsible thing to do. But selfishly, I didn't want to part ways with her. Staying alone here would mean certain capture, rape, and possibly death for her, I told myself to justify my selfishness.

Juma was as surprised by her positive disposition, as well, but he had his own agenda. He needed me, and knew there was no way I was leaving the woman behind. Besides, having a doctor in the tow wouldn't be bad for a wounded man. "All right, it is done then," he said happily. "We move out as soon as we finish eating."

We gathered our belongings and went on our way.

At the beginning of our hike, the only challenges were the steep incline, falling rocks, and tough terrain, but those were manageable. By nightfall, we made it to the higher and colder altitude. We searched for shelter and eventually found a small depression in one of the cliffs, just big enough for us to squeeze into for the night. The wind howled relentlessly while we huddled together under our blankets, bracing ourselves against the blizzard that raged outside.

In the morning, the weather got even worse. The wind and snow made walking very tough, but we wrapped ourselves in blankets and continued. I took Nora's load from her since she was struggling to walk. Every step felt like an uphill battle, but we persevered, determined to reach our destination.

The fierce, swirling whiteout made it nearly impossible to

see more than a few feet in front of us. We trudged forward, hunched against the biting wind that seemed to penetrate even our warmest layers. Our only guide was the faint glow of my phone's GPS, its battery dangerously low from constant use. The cold seeped into our bones, draining our energy with every step. We could only manage short bursts of walking before needing to rest, our bodies growing weaker by the hour. As darkness descended upon us, we had likely traveled a few miles but it felt like we were no closer to our destination than when we started out. Thankfully, luck was on our side once again when I stumbled upon another cavern nestled within the rocks. We huddled close to our fire, grateful for its warmth and light in this treacherous storm.

The third day was hellish. The blizzard had stopped, but it was bitterly cold and blankets did little to warm us up. Nora's face was almost unrecognizable beneath the layers of frost that clung to her cheeks and nose. Despite my best efforts to keep warm, I, too, was suffering from frostbite and could feel the numbing pain creeping up my extremities. Juma, on the other hand, seemed immune to the harsh weather as he trudged on without complaint. The cold had actually helped his wound by freezing it solid.

Sacrifices had to be made in order to survive this journey. So, I made the difficult decision to leave behind any non-essential supplies to lighten my load and help Nora navigate through the knee-deep snow. But as we continued, I could no longer ignore Nora's increasing limp and her labored breathing.

We stopped for a break.

"Show me your feet."

She shook her head.

"Stop screwing around. Show me your feet, damn it," I demanded.

She reluctantly complied. At the hospital where I took her, she had been wearing sneakers with no socks. Before we left, I had wrapped her feet and legs with cloth to make her them warmer and her steps more cushioned. Now my makeshift solution was in tatters and her feet were both frozen and bleeding. The tips of her toes had slowly started darkening, and I was worried about gangrene. I offered to carry her.

She indignantly refused.

I rubbed her feet with the rubbing alcohol from her medicine bag to increase circulation, applied a generous amount of anti-inflammatory ointment, and replaced the rags on her feet with new makeshift moccasins out of spare cloth bandages. They looked flimsy and weak compared to proper footwear, but I hoped they would hold up for at least a few more days of our relentless journey.

As the sun slowly descended below the horizon casting the snow-covered landscape in a golden glow, we finally came to a stop. Our group was exhausted and there was no place to take shelter. I quickly scraped away at the frozen ground, creating a hollow for us to huddle in. The snow provided some insulation from the bitter cold, but it was far from comfortable. We pressed our shivering bodies together, trying to share what little warmth we had left between us. My hands were numb and raw from digging in the icy ground. I desperately searched for any kind of fuel to start a fire, but all I could find was snow and ice. Both Juma and Nora's breathing became slow and steady, indicating they had drifted off into unconsciousness. I knew that we wouldn't survive much longer in these conditions and something supernatural, if not miraculous, was in order. I climbed out of our shelter and sent a maintenance call to Abaddon.

To my surprise, he showed up quietly with almost no smell of sulfur. Looking around curiously, he asked, "What do you want?

"I need help. We are not going to make it out of here alive."

"You know I cannot help you in a way that alerts humans of supernatural help." He thought for a second and his face brightened. "Why don't you kill the woman, drink her blood, and eat her? That should give you enough calories to make it out alive."

I had no strength to argue and simply waved him off. What was the point of explaining to a Demon that cannibalism, especially when it involved eating a woman for whom you have strong feelings, was not in the cards?

"No, we are not eating anyone."

Abaddon's face showed his disappointment. He obviously loved the idea of a human monkey eating another human monkey.

"All I need from you is a snow-covered tent less than a

mile east of here, full of supplies and a half-frozen dead man. Make it look like he was mortally wounded and succumbed to his wounds. There is nothing supernatural about a climber carrying contraband and dying in the mountains, is there?"

Abaddon scratched his head. "I suppose not. Let me confirm with Ashmodai, though. He knows the manual better than I do and I don't want to take the responsibility upon myself."

"Fuck you, Abaddon," I said in a menacing undertone. "And fuck your boss. We are dying here, and if I die, I will be back to Azazel's office in no time and will report to him that you refused to help me when it was well within your authority. Care for Oblivion, Demon?"

Abaddon growled. "All right, I'll do it. But I will put in the minimum amount of supplies, not more than one person could carry."

"Whatever. Can you also throw in a donkey tied to a post, next to the tent?"

"Hey, now you are getting greedy. I doubt it, but let me check if pack donkeys can climb this high."

Abaddon disappeared and I went back to our shelter, warmed by a new hope.

As we woke up the next morning, my posse was depressed and weak, and I had to drag them out, urging them to move.

Abaddon didn't let me down. In less than a mile, I saw an orange snow-covered tent. I yelled to my companions. When they saw the tent, their spirits rose and we all started to run.

The dead man in the tent was duly frozen and looked like he

had bled to death. I took off his boots for Nora, then we threw him outside without any compunction. No one cared where he came from or how he'd ended up here. All we cared about was the lifeline, and the hand that threw it was of no concern to any of us.

The tent featured a tiny portable stove with a little bit of coal in it, blankets, and some food. For my companions, this was a treasure trove, but I cursed Abaddon's stinginess under my breath. What, did he actually Google to see how much a single person could carry? Was it really necessary to be so literal? And what was wrong with leaving us a donkey? Damn coward!

The tent was heavenly, though. We lit up the stove, took off our outer layer of clothes, and stretched our legs. Both Juma and Nora were so happy they couldn't stop laughing and joking around. I cooked hot food, the first in days. For the final kicker, there was a half-empty bottle of whiskey. Nice touch, Abaddon!

We ate, drank, and laughed. Nora's laugh was so contagious that I couldn't help but join in. She was drunk, and needed to go outside. I offered to accompany her. She winked, smiled, and shook her finger. She stumbled outside, then came back shivering, and I hugged her to warm her up. She didn't object, only mumbled something about me being a wily coyote, after which she pushed me aside and happily fell asleep.

The tent definitely helped, although we were not out of the woods, not just yet. Nora's legs were still in bad shape, Juma was exhausted from straining his wound, and I could carry only so much. But the respite did miracles. Our rested bodies along with our newly-acquired hope drove us forward. Nora had gotten new boots and clean, warm socks to prevent sores. The tent and the stove were state of the art—light and durable, but as expected, no one had any qualms about how this super-duper high-tech gear had so conveniently ended up out here in the middle of nowhere. I packed the tent and the stove, stashed some food, and begrudgingly left the rest, including the weapons and the Kevlar vest. It was too heavy for me to carry everything.

The next day we walked much faster, and when we stopped to rest we had shelter and fire. The day after that, we started our descent and finally left the freezing alpine region. Walking downhill was less taxing than climbing uphill, and the lively greenery around us kept our spirits up. It took us one more day before we finally made it to the rendezvous point. At the sight of a couple of Toyota SUVs surrounded by armed men, our joy had no bounds. We must have presented a really sorry sight, because even Juma's hardened henchmen looked at us with sympathy and compassion.

But thankfully, Juma was back in the saddle, in charge, and in full control of the situation.

We arrived in Jalalabad after a few hours, during which all of us happily enjoyed the comfortable seats of a climate-controlled SUV.

CHAPTER 6

Jalalabad, Afghanistan

The safe house was large and comfortable, and we were assured there would be no Taliban around. Juma disappeared to deal with Wadaan's betrayal and other business, so Nora and I were left to our own devices. Our hosts were very polite, probably instructed by Juma to give us their best service and plenty of privacy.

The first day we got there, Nora demonstratively locked herself in her room. Once the danger had passed, she'd remembered how much she hated me and didn't hesitate to show it. We were back to being enemies, or more likely, a man and a woman having strong feelings for each other but unable to understand or too afraid to express them.

We spent a few days recuperating and treating our sores and frostbite. I saw her examining her toes, clearly concerned with the possibility of gangrene. I asked her how they were, but she gave me the cold shoulder again, tersely answering, "They are fine, thank you."

The signs of possible gangrene made her even more upset with me for not telling her about the real dangers of the hike and giving her the choice of not going with us. "You should have told me what lay ahead before we started out. It was unfair of you to give me no choice."

As the grown-up between us two, I responsibly decided to patch things up with her. Knowing her adventurous spirit, sightseeing sounded like a good idea. When I told our bodyguards we wanted to walk around the city, they conferred and said it would be fine, but they would accompany us, just in case.

I carefully knocked on Nora's door.

"Who is there?"

"Can I come in?"

"Go away. I am busy."

"Don't you want to hear what I have to say?"

"No." She sounded confident but I could hear a note of curiosity in her voice.

Staying at the closed door, I continued, "I just thought maybe we could go to town, sightseeing. We have plenty of time and nothing to do. Don't tell me you've liked being locked in your room all this time."

Curiosity got the better of her. I heard some shuffling by the door, and she opened it. She must have just showered because her body was wrapped in a long towel and her hair was still wet.

Gosh, she was stunning. Her free-flowing hair was shiny and her blue eyes resembled a cloudless sky.

She wrinkled her nose and squinted, trying to look cold. "All right, I will go, but it doesn't mean I've forgotten everything you did to me."

"Of course, not," I said, barely managing to keep a serious face. "This is just a temporary truce, nothing more."

"Right," she said. "Let me get dressed." She shut the door on my nose.

When she came out of her room moments later, she was wearing a traditional Pashtun dress of bright colors. The traditional *monisto* highlighted her beautiful neck adorned by her wavy hair. She noticed my admiration, and despite her professed animosity to me and my ilk, she flirtatiously pirouetted in front of me.

"You are so beautiful. I really hate that you have to wear a burqa, but safety first."

She sighed and nodded. After a last look in the mirror and being satisfied with her appearance, she put on a *chadari*, the Afghan version of a burqa, and we went out.

We took a colorful yellow-orange three-wheeled cab with an open cabin and a soft leather top over the back seats. Once in town, she forgot about everything else and was running around like a child, sticking her nose everywhere. Our chaperons knew the city well and were only too happy to guide us through the mixture of the ancient and the modern. I translated, and she peppered me and them with questions, wanting to know everything.

The city was teeming with street peddlers, passersby, and cars. The sounds of honking, street vendor calls inviting people to try their fare, and loud music, all interspersed by muezzins' calls to prayer from countless minarets, added to the city's Eastern ambiance. We walked through Siraj-ul Emarat Park surrounding the imposing King Amanullah Mausoleum, enjoying beautiful flowers and the spacious but crowded meadows. She wanted to try every local food, and thoroughly enjoyed drinking *dough*, the local yogurt drink. Our chaperons took us to one of the famous Jalalabad papermills, where paper was still made the way it was hundreds of years ago. She loved it, and we had to keep her away from striking up conversations with the workers. No need to attract attention to a foreigner strolling the streets of Jalalabad.

On our way back to the house in the open cab, she snuggled next to me, as if by accident. I held my breath, afraid of breaking the contact.

"This was great," she said. "Today was the first sightseeing tour in Afghanistan I've had," she admitted. "I came here in early January for the spring semester with Doctors Without Borders, was driven straight to Mazar-i-Sharif, and a few days later was sent to Asadabad." She paused. "Where you kidnapped me and cut short my trip." She furrowed her brows in fake anger, but I could tell she was not upset.

After we got back home, in the evening I suggested having

dinner together and she agreed. Our hosts prepared it, set it up in her room, and left us alone. They even got us a decent bottle of wine. You've got to give it to these drug dealers who know how to find things despite government regulations. Claiming we had to save electricity, I lit a kerosene lamp.

The food was great, the wine was good, and the dim light of the lamp projected dancing shadows on the walls. The table filled with Eastern delicacies and colorful copper utensils added to the ambiance of the room, resembling a scene from the Arabian Nights. She was still in her Afghan dress but without the *chadari*, and I could barely contain myself.

We talked and talked and talked. She didn't tell me anything about Moffat—it was clearly too traumatic for her to remember—but her naked body covered in goose bumps still haunted me. Dead or not, I really wanted her.

She talked about her joining Doctors Without Borders for the medical school internship, and how she wanted to become a pediatrician to help children in underprivileged countries. The talk of underprivileged countries somehow reminded her that we were still enemies. "And everything went as planned until you kidnapped me and cut my internship short. How am I supposed to get back, and what I am supposed to say at school? That I spent a good part of my internship tending to known criminals and becoming an accomplice in the process?" Unlike her mention of kidnapping in the cab, now she was serious, upset over the need to explain everything at school and a failed internship.

I felt as if a sharp knife had hit me in the groin. Why did she have to bring it up? "Hey, you had the chance to shoot me but you didn't. What's your problem now?"

"Some choice you gave me—either to become a murderer or a drug dealer." She curled her lips.

Instead of diffusing the tension, I wanted to hit back, unable to cope with my feelings. "Don't fool yourself. The only reason you are here is not to save children but to enjoy the journey to an exotic country, and I only spiced it up. That was why you didn't run away regardless of your many chances. So, if anything, you should be thankful to me for tickling your sense of adventure."

She jumped up, her eyes flashing, her fists clenched, and her chin jutted. Even in her anger, she was stunningly beautiful. "You know what? You are an asshole, and I regret the day I walked into that tent thinking I was helping a poor ailing woman. Get the hell out and take your stupid lamp with you." Her eyes were teary as she pushed me out of the room.

Why was I such an idiot? I hated myself for doing this. Everything had been going so well. Why couldn't I have let her remarks slide?

I was ready to bang my head against the wall as I went to bed. I couldn't sleep. No matter how much I tried to convince myself I was just a bodiless soul and all of this was just part of the mission, I couldn't get her out of my head. Her beautiful laughter and equally beautiful angry outbursts, as well as the image of her pirouetting in a colorful Afghan dress were firmly imprinted in my brain.

Ah, screw it!

I knocked on her door. She wasn't sleeping, either. "Go away, you bastard." She sounded like a child whose favorite doll had been taken away from her.

"Please."

"I said go away!"

"Not a chance." I pushed at the door. It was locked. I easily kicked out the lock and walked inside.

She was sitting on her bed wearing pajamas, holding her knees up to her chin. Her watery eyes were full of indignation. Without raising her head, she cried, "What, are you going to rape me now? Sure, go ahead, use your brute strength. How could I be so stupid thinking that you were actually a decent man?" She started sobbing.

I came closer, got on my knees next to her bed, and tipped up her head. Even on my knees, we on the same level.

She angrily turned away. "Don't touch me or I will scream."

"Scream all you like." I tugged her head a touch closer to mine.

She clenched her fists and started beating me on my chest, weeping. Her blows were lighter than mosquito bites. I pulled her even closer and kissed her on the mouth.

She continued pushing and punching me for a bit longer, then suddenly stopped, passionately hugging me and opening her mouth, responding to my kiss. Her kiss was hungry, carnivorous, craving sex. I felt as if I was fusing with her tender body.

We couldn't get enough of each other.

Our lips parted, and I started kissing her body. Tracing a path from her neck over her bare shoulders, following the delicate ridge of her collar bone, I slowly moved down toward the soft valleys that lay below. I maneuvered gently to her navel, where I took a moment, teasingly swirling my tongue around its shallow dip. As I reached her genitals, she flinched as if she'd been jolted by a tantalizing current, and moaned softly. She pulled me up and locked her legs around my waist. I rose on my elbows to make sure the weight of my body didn't crush her, and slowly slid inside her. She let out a hushed grunt and squeezed her legs. I slowly continued farther in. She pulled toward me as if making sure she got as much of me as she could. I was within her domain now, treading in uncharted territory where my swollen member met her cavity, wet with anticipation and pleasure.

Without disengaging, I turned around and sat on the bed to let her ride me. She did so in a frenzy of desire. She was insatiable, kissing me on the lips and biting my neck, all while thrusting herself onto me over and over again. I could barely restrain myself, trying to let her finish first. I didn't have to wait long. She climaxed, screaming in a high pitch of satisfied pleasure. I exploded right away and fell on the bed, releasing her legs. She leaned on me, unwilling to separate until I gently pushed her onto her side.

She put her head on my shoulder. "I am so confused. Sometimes I think I hate you, and sometimes I think I love you, and when I think that, I hate myself for not hating you. Why can't it be simpler?"

I chuckled softly. "Nothing is simple in life, darling. Except at this very moment."

She nodded quietly. "Anyway, it was a good fuck." She looked up at me coyly and quickly added, "Probably because I haven't been with a man for a while."

I lightly smacked her on her lips. "Admit it, you have never had sex like this."

Her mouth twisted into a grimace and her nose scrunched up as if to block out a foul smell. "Don't flatter yourself." She pushed me away. "Anyway, I am tired. Get out of here."

I stroked her hair. "Don't you want me to sing you a lullaby?"

"No, I don't. I would be much better off without your presence. Besides, how do I know you are not going to rape me while I sleep?"

Still, instead of pushing me out of bed, she giggled and cuddled in my arms, quietly falling asleep, a beautiful being entrusted to my care by the Creator. I slowly dozed, holding her in my arms.

The next morning, she woke up early and saw I was sitting next to her. Happy to see me, she stretched out her hands, looking happy. "I had such a wonderful dream, cuddling in your arms," she said yawning. Then she suddenly stopped and looked down at her body. She was still naked and her pajamas lay crumpled on the bed. "What happened last night?" she asked cautiously.

"Nothing much," I said making a serious face. "I raped you mercilessly, and you loved it, then you fell asleep and snored all night like an elephant."

She jokingly hit me on the chest. "You are a liar. I don't snore."

I squinted. "Not entirely. I don't think I lied about the first part. You enjoyed having sex with me."

She crinkled her nose and pretended to roar, although it sounded more like the purr of a housecat. She kissed me on the cheek. "Now, get out of here and let me take a shower. I want to get all your stink off my body, you burly bear!"

"What a coincidence. I was about to take a shower myself. Given how precious water is in this country, I think we should be environmentally conscious and share the shower."

She frowned, but then looked naughtily at me, took my hand, and walked us into the shower.

As the hot water cascaded down our bodies, a sultry mist permeated the air around us. Her body, dewy and glistening under the warm rivulets, sent my pulse racing. I squeezed body wash onto my hands and began to lather her supple form. As I massaged the silky suds into her skin, she purred quietly, enjoying my gentle strokes. After a while, she looked like a cute little ghost covered in foam, trying not to swallow the body wash as I teasingly rubbed the bubbly foam onto her face. Her nose crinkled adorably in response. She wiped the froth off her lips and rubbed her eyes.

Unable to restrain myself, I kissed her mouth, and she responded passionately, as if she'd been waiting for me to make the first move. I could feel how our bodies yearned for more intimate contact. My skin tingled where she touched me, and I could tell hers did, too—a clear indication that this encounter was far from over. Gently lubricated by hot water, our bodies merged in another bout of insatiable ecstasy.

After we came out of the shower a long time later, she wrapped herself in a fluffy towel and turned to me as if seeing me for the first time. I was drowning in her bottomless blue eyes, unable to hide her powerful sway over me.

She asked coyly, "We are going to town again, aren't we?"

I bowed. "Of course, my lady. Anything your heart desires."

As we walked down the streets of Jalalabad continuing our tour, I couldn't contain the urge to take her hand. She surreptitiously touched my butt when no one was watching and giggled naughtily under the *chadari*. We cherished every moment together. The world stopped existing for me— I was all-consumed by this beautiful woman.

That night, we had our meal under the kerosene lamp again…although this time the meal was shorter and the lovemaking was longer. When we finally exhausted all our energy, she fell asleep again cuddling in my arms, her face lit with a satisfied smile.

I stayed up for a while, lying motionlessly so as not to disturb her. I was no longer puzzled by the mystery of my attraction to her. After all, whether I had been close to her in my past life or met her for the first time after my death, I enjoyed being with Nora, and that was enough for now.

PART IV

THE BOOK

CHAPTER 1

Tribal Area, Pakistan

Juma came back to the safe house after three days, and I reluctantly had to get back to reality and the mission.

"So, what's the news?" I asked

"I spoke to Wadaan. He swore on his father's memory that he didn't betray us and that the Taliban was simply trying to clean up the neighborhood for their publicity stunt with the hospital."

"And you believe him?"

"What I believe is that he gave a solemn oath, and even a scumbag like him wouldn't use an oath in vain. If he was lying, he would burn in Hell for all eternity, which is more than I could ever do to him. Besides, it doesn't matter. I have my men here, and Wadaan will think twice before double-crossing me."

I didn't believe in the oaths of drug dealers and hustlers but it was not my place to argue. I cared more about my mission.

"Did he give you anything else besides his solemn oath?"

"In fact, he did. He found us a contact. Kuza Bandar Khan, one of the Yousufzai chieftains, has agreed to meet with us in his village not far from Landi Kotal."

"Good news! So, we are going back to Pakistan?'

"We are, indeed. We will have to cross the border on foot through the mountains, though. Do you want to take your girlfriend with us, or did she lose all appetite for mountain-climbing during our last crossing?"

I didn't like his reference to Nora as my girlfriend, though I should have expected his men would give him a detailed report of the past few days.

He patted me on the back. "Hey, don't take offense American. I meant it in a good sense."

"None taken. You may be right, it may be a good idea to leave her here. I assume her security will be assured?"

Juma shrugged in indignation. "How could you possibly think your blood brother would let anything happen to your woman?"

The conversation with Nora was much harder. No matter how much I pleaded, trying to convince her to stay and explaining the dangers of the Tribal Area, she would have none of it. She was excited about a new adventure, and she knew she held sway over me. All she needed to do was to purse her lips and make puppy eyes, and I was had. The rational part of my mind told me to hold fast and leave her in Jalalabad. Alas, her insistence combined with my desire to keep her close won the day.

I told Juma that Nora was coming with us.

He jeered, threw up his arms, and said, "You know she will be your responsibility?"

"Of course. Don't worry about her. She is a trooper and will not jeopardize the mission."

"As you wish, my friend, as you wish. I am sure you know what you are doing."

Though he didn't look at all convinced.

We were soon back at the Khyber Pass, but this time we didn't go through any of the border crossings. We got out of the cars, loaded our stuff onto the donkeys ordered by Juma in advance, and moved out through the Hindukush. Like a true gentleman, Juma got an extra donkey for Nora to ride.

We walked almost the entire day, but the hike was not tiring. Nora was continually looking around, awestruck by the view of the mountains. Unlike our last miserable crossing, she was comfortably seated on a donkey, so she had a chance to enjoy the scenery. The rest of us were primarily focused on security, making sure we avoided any unpleasant encounters.

We crossed the border in the middle of the night. The scenery was exactly the same and I would not have known we were in Pakistan if Juma hadn't told me.

I thought of the countless conquerors who had sliced and diced this region according to their ambitions with utter disregard for local people. Was I becoming a do-gooder like

Nora? I guess compassion was contagious, after all.

Once we were on the Pakistani side, we were met by SUVs also ordered by Juma, and we enjoyed a much more comfortable ride. Our safe house in Landi Kotal was spacious enough to accommodate everyone, with even a separate room for Nora. As much as I wanted to join her there, I resisted the temptation. She winked at me playfully as she went to her room, and I sent her a secret air kiss.

The next day we drove to the village of Kuza Bandar. Again, I tried to convince Nora to stay at the safe house in Landi Kotal, trying to cajole her with promises of sightseeing once we came back, and again I lost. Notwithstanding her youthful appearance, she had the determination of an iron lady for not taking no for an answer.

The ride through the mountainous passes was bumpy, suited more for walking or horseback than for driving. As I looked out the window of the SUV, I saw how our side wheels barely missed slipping off the edge of the cliffs. We caught up with Kuza and his tribesmen on one of the mountainous pastures. The tribe was on the move out of their village, tending to their herds. Their mobile settlement looked every bit the nomadic encampment, with tents and colorfully-dressed tribesmen. For me, it was just a bunch of hostiles ready to take us out at any moment, but for Nora it looked like a movie scene, and she greedily savored every bit of the exotic.

We were taken to the palatial tent of Kuza Bandar. Before we entered, the guards patted us down and took away our weapons.

Other than Juma and me, our retinue was not allowed in, and had to stay outside. But Nora wanted to come in with us. To Juma, that was absolute madness, and I agreed with him. But again and again I showed my weakness in the presence of this woman. To make matters worse, she wore a *hijab* instead of a burqa, revealing her Western appearance in tight jeans and a white blouse.

Kuza sat on the cushions surrounded by his tribal elders. He was a big man with a copper beard dyed by henna and wore traditional Pashto garb. The white turban and a richly decorated robe highlighted his importance. Armed men stood by his sides.

Nora's presence at our meeting raised the tribesmen's eyebrows, but Juma explained that she was our American doctor, hired for the expedition in case someone got hurt. How this explanation made her appearance any more appropriate was beyond me, but the tribesmen nodded in approval, praising Juma's foresight.

Juma started with obligatory praises to Kuza and his kin, and inquired into their welfare. I was back in my role of an arrogant American who didn't understand anything, sitting next to Nora. Two gullible cormorants willingly walking into the midst of a tribe of hungry sailors.

We were served a sumptuous meal followed by tea and sweets. The tribe's women brought everything quietly and disappeared as silently as they had appeared, which made Nora's presence even less appropriate. We'd been seated at the far end of the table, closest to the entrance and farthest from Kuza, which made me feel a bit more secure. I wasn't sure I was so nervous because Nora was here or because the tribesmen made me uncomfortable, but I was anticipating trouble. I am sure the tribesmen noticed my skittishness, which, while adding to my assumed role of an ignorant foreigner, made me more vulnerable in their eyes. Juma, with his reputation as a powerful drug lord and his armed men outside, was the only thing that separated me and Nora from an immediate assault.

Once the meal was over, it was time to get down to business. However, it was impolite to start a business conversation ourselves, so we had to wait until Kuza finally inquired as to the purpose of our visit. Juma explained what we were looking for. When Juma mentioned the Book, he was at a loss how to explain what it was, but to our surprise, Kuza stopped him.

"You don't need to explain it to me, Juma Khan. I know exactly what you are talking about. There was a book treasured by our people since time immemorial. No one knows exactly where it is hidden, but as part of our inauguration into tribal leadership, every chieftain in our tribe is given one of these amulets." He pointed to a richly decorated glass vial incrusted in gems and gold hanging around his neck. "It is said to contain the way to find the Book. Many have tried to figure out how it works, but no one has been able to unlock its secret."

Wow, this was definitely a breakthrough! I had to contain myself so as not to betray my language skills.

Juma was also excited, but he quickly put on a mask of indifference. "Interesting story, Kuza Khan. Maybe we will have better luck with your amulet? Not the same as the Book, of course, but we would be willing to buy it from you. It is of no use to you anyway, and the American—" He pointed at me "—is willing to pay a good price."

Kuza thought for a few minutes, and no one dared to break the silence. He finally spoke. "This is a family heirloom, whether the legend is true or not, and it is not for sale."

He was clearly testing our interest, trying to see how much we would insist on buying his trinket. It was hard to decide whether it was better to thank him for his hospitality and leave, hoping that he would hasten to sell his amulet, or to start bargaining.

Juma decided to bargain. "Oh, honorable Kuza Khan, the American will pay a lot of money. Think about how much good it will do for your people. You can even buy yourself a doctor." He laughed.

The tribesmen laughed, as well.

Kuza abruptly stopped laughing, and his tribesmen followed suit. "So, how much is the American willing to pay?"

Juma turned and inclined his ear to me.

I decided to go for the kill. "Tell him one million American dollars, and it is not negotiable," I whispered..

Juma shook his head, disapproving of my decision to go VA Banque. "Are you sure you don't want to start lower?"

I shook my head.

"All right, it is your money, American," he whispered back.

Juma turned to Kuza. "Our American guest is willing to pay one million American dollars and this is everything he has," he said.

Upon hearing the number, the tribesmen looked at each other and an intense murmur went through the room.

Kuza raised his hand motioning his people to keep silent. "Not enough," he said.

I guess the concept of non-negotiable was not known in this part of the world. I decided to repeat the ignorant-American routine I had pulled on Wadaan.

I got to my feet. "Please thank Kuza Khan for his hospitality, but we have a long ride back home. Ask him to excuse us for our hasty departure." This was half-insult half-threat, but Kuza struck me as a rational person. One million dollars could easily outweigh my insolence. Besides, once on my feet, even unarmed I could have taken down most of Kuza's retinue before they raised the alarm.

Juma's eyes went wide. By now he knew I was playing a role, but unlike me, he appreciated the difference between Wadaan and the tribesmen, and was certain that I had miscalculated.

Yet, my gamble worked… Or so I thought.

Kuza politely extended his hand, motioning for me to sit back down. I pretended to hesitate, but then sat down, keeping a disappointed expression.

Kuza went silent for a few moments, then spoke slowly as if checking every word. "We all know this is a priceless artifact, and no matter how much you offer, it would be low for me to part with such a precious heirloom." He paused for greater effect. "However, you are my guests, and I cannot deny your request. If you add your doctor to the price, I will give you the amulet."

A lightning strike would have had less of an effect on me. The sly fox had outwitted me, and I hadn't even seen it coming! All my missteps—from the moment I'd agreed to take Nora with me to the Tribal Area, to bringing her into Kuza's tent, to Juma's joking about Kuza buying himself a doctor—raced through my mind. I couldn't keep a poker face, no matter how much I tried.

Nora, of course, was clueless, gazing around at what she thought were friendly faces around her.

Seeing the storm of emotions on my face, and either remembering his blood debt to me or fearing I would do something unseemly and get us all killed in the process, Juma decided to buy us some time. "Would Honorable Kuza Khan allow us a moment to discuss? Please excuse our stepping out of your tent."

Kuza magnanimously nodded.

We went outside and Nora followed. "Can you give us room, darling?" I asked her.

As she stepped aside, becoming nervous seeing my distress but still not understanding anything, I turned to Juma. "This is madness," I whispered to him. "I will double, triple, the price."

"Too late, my friend," he responded, sighing. "Kuza will never lose face in front of his tribesmen, and any additional price instead of your girlfriend would be viewed as a refusal. Under the circumstances, it would mean we would have to fight our way out. I don't have enough men to take on the entire tribe. You shouldn't have brought her here," he added with a genuine sadness in his voice.

"This is not happening," I whispered menacingly. "I will kill this whole tribe and turn the entire Tribal Area into a barren desert before I allow him to take Nora."

Juma smiled softly, as if trying to reason with a child. "Come on, be real, American. I know you fight well, maybe even too well, but you are up against at least a hundred armed fighters. I am ready to stand by your side, but what can ten men do against an army? It would be suicide, and they would still take Nora."

"Can't we just run to the cars and drive away?"

"It took us half an hour to climb up here from where we left our cars. They will catch up to us on horses in no time."

"Well, let's go back to the tent, then, and I will take Kuza hostage. They will have no choice but to let us go." I was desperate.

Juma shrugged. "You know as well as I do that your plan won't work. They are watching us and are already suspicious, seeing your agitation. They won't let you anywhere near Kuza.

"Then, do something!" For the first time in our relationship

I pleaded with him, in the futile hope that he could come up with something. Anything.

He touched my shoulder. "Even I have my limits. We are on Kuza's turf, and he holds all the cards. Just accept it for what it is."

The world closed in on me, and I couldn't think straight. This was not happening. No! This was *not* happening. *Think, think, there has got to be a way out.*

Thoughts raced through my head. Maybe if I called Abaddon he could help me. But I knew full well it wouldn't happen. First, the girl was not part of my mission. Second, it was an absolute no-no to make a maintenance call in the presence of humans, and I didn't have authorization to break the rule. Even Beelzebub, who owed me for concealing his association with Long, would not respond. Besides, he would not get the maintenance ticket because he was not assigned to me. All I had left was to plead with the Creator, but we all knew how that worked. The Creator did not respond to pleas from scoundrels like me.

My body went limp. I felt complete resignation and nodded.

Juma went back to the tent to complete the bargain.

Once Juma left, Nora came over to me. She mistook my desperation for disappointment at not being able to complete the bargain. "What is it? Kuza can't help you, can he? Don't be so upset, we will find another way." She gently patted me on my arm.

If only she knew!

I stood silently with my head down, unable to form words.

Juma finally stepped out of the tent. "They will take the girl now, and you will bring one million dollars to Landi Kotal tomorrow, at which point you will receive the amulet," he said matter-of-factly and gave a signal to two tribesmen who'd come out with him.

They came closer and grabbed Nora by her arms.

"Hey, get your hands off me!" She tried unsuccessfully to pry off the hands of the tribesmen. "What's going on?" She looked at me searching for help, still confident I would not let the filthy men touch her.

I turned away, unable to look her in the eyes.

She suddenly understood. "So, I am the price?" she said.

Juma couldn't look at her, either, and turned his body in another direction.

Abandoned and sold like chattel, Nora's expression said she couldn't fully process what was going on. Her legs gave way, and the tribesmen had to drag her into Kuza's tent.

If she'd yelled and cursed, I would have felt better, but she was completely silent.

Why wouldn't the Creator send a bolt of lightning, killing everyone, including me, to end this nightmare?

CHAPTER 2

Road to Landi Kotal, Pakistan

The tribesmen walked us all the way back to our cars, at which point they returned our guns. Juma grabbed my pistols before I could unload them into the tribesmen, and pushed me into the car.

As we drove back to Landi Kotal, I sat wordlessly next to Juma in the back seat.

Nora's dead, expressionless eyes, their light extinguished by my betrayal, burned in my soul. Yes, the mission was the mission, and I was dead anyway, but how much of a lowlife was I to betray her like that? I felt as though I was back in the Movie Room, replaying over and over the moment I'd left her in the hands of Kuza Bandar.

Juma felt my anguish. "Don't fret, American. You did what you had to do. You have a goal you need to achieve, and she stood in the way."

"Would you have done this to your wife? Daughter?"

His eyes squinted. "Now you talking honor, my friend. No, I would not, because no amount of money is worth losing honor."

"So, you think you are honorable, and I am just a greedy piece of garbage?"

"No, I think you are an idiot for taking your woman into a lion's den. I would never have exposed my wives or my daughters to this kind of danger, but you did. That is the difference between us. I don't know who you are, or why you need the Book, or where you acquired your abundant fighting skills and your money, but you are still a dumbass. You don't tempt fate by provoking it."

I grabbed my face in my hands, stifling a groan.

Juma softened his tone. "But it is not my business to judge you. It is between you and Allah. Only He can judge a man. Or…" He paused. "A man can judge himself."

I sat silently, listening to the hum of the car's engine, until I couldn't take it anymore. "Oh, the hell with it. Stop the car!"

Juma was instantly alarmed. "Hey, hey, don't do anything rash. We had a deal with Kuza, and you cannot go back on it. No amount of money will save you from the revenge of the tribe. Not to mention that going back on your word is just as dishonorable as selling your girl."

"Don't worry about my honor. I lost it a long time ago. But I will not lose my girl. Go back home, Juma. I release you from your blood oath. This is something I have to do myself."

"And what about our deal?"

"What about it? I gave you your million. That should more than cover your expenses, and if you want to go after the Book, be my guest. Now you know where to look for it, and I am no longer interested. I will give you the names of dealers who can help you sell it."

Juma shook his head. "I don't need your dealers. I will figure out how to live my life, because I am certain you have just forfeited yours." He gave me a puzzled look." You are a strange man, American. You came on the recommendation of a murderous scumbag, and he was probably not the only scumbag you've dealt with. I assumed you were one of them, and that you were in this for the money. But now I cannot understand you." He held up his hands. "Yet, I respect your decision. I will not help you, but I won't interfere, either. Peace be upon you, my friend."

He extended his hand and I shook it.

I was thankful to Juma for his lecture about honor, no matter how funny it sounded on the lips of a rogue. It was all I'd needed.

I took the guns, stashed them into my belt, put on the Kevlar vest, stuffed the rest of my gear into a backpack, and got out of the car. I waited a few moments as the vehicles sped away, then turned back to the tribal encampment.

But as I was just about to start walking to go after Nora, an unexpected and powerful force pulled me back. Everything went black, and I found myself standing next to Azazel. He must have been watching the mission and hit the Pause.

"What the fuck are you doing, monkey? Did you forget your mission? Can't keep your dick in your pants?"

I lunged at him in rage, forgetting I was dealing with an Angel, and was instantly punished, lying on my back with Azazel squeezing the life out of my soul.

His nostrils flared, "You insolent wretch! You dare to raise a hand against an Angel? I will send you straight to Oblivion!"

"Go ahead, be my guest," I wheezed out, struggling to stay conscious in his iron grip. "Better Oblivion than being forced to watch this betrayal in the Movie Room over and over again."

As I was about to happily drift into unconsciousness, Azazel loosened up his hold. "Get up, you stupid animal. You are lucky I need you to finish the job. So go and finish it!" he bellowed.

"Fuck you, Azazel," I said in a scratchy voice, trying to catch my breath. "Do it yourself. You can do anything you want with me, but you cannot take away my free will. Either kill me now, or let me go to save the girl!"

"Oh, sure," Azazel replied sarcastically. "So easy to be a hero when you have Reincarnation Rights, isn't it? Especially now, after I got you three additional ones."

"Shove 'em all up your ass. I don't need your stinking Reincarnation Rights, or any other favors from you, for that matter. Do you think I am going to beg for my life? You didn't figure us out over the past six thousand years, my friend, did you?"

Azazel looked at me curiously. "Well, if that is what you wish. You can go and try to save your girlfriend, but your

Reincarnation Rights are hereby suspended. This time, you will die for real. Good luck with your feelings, monkey. I hope she was worth it."

"You bet she was. But how could a cold creature like you, devoid of life, understand that? Go back to your miserable Angelic existence."

"See you in the Movie Room, monkey," said Azazel with a smirk.

"Yeah, yeah, you bastard. I am done being afraid of your threats. Let me out of the Pause. Now!"

Azazel shrugged and disappeared, leaving me where I stood. I felt a *whoosh* go through my body. So, this was how the suspension of Reincarnation Rights felt.

Well, the choice had been made. Nothing to do about it now.

CHAPTER 3

Somewhere near Kuza Encampment, Tribal Area, Pakistan

I reached the tribe's encampment in the middle of the night. Most of the tribesmen were asleep, save for a few sentries warming themselves by a fire. The scene reminded me of the Moffat mission—the same kind of chilly night in the mountains—except that here I was on my own, with no Reincarnation Rights, and a burning desire to take revenge on everyone in this accursed place.

I snuck past the guards and went to Kuza's tent, hoping Nora was still there. Even if she wasn't, I figured I would grab the bastard and beat her location out of him.

Kuza's tent was guarded by two big tribesmen. I quietly went behind the back of one of them, slashed his throat, then lunged at the second guard, shoving my knife into his Adam's apple. Neither had a chance to raise the alarm, gurgling and drowning in their own blood.

I went into the tent. Kuza must have been sleeping in a

separate compartment behind the room where we'd had our meeting. Nora was sitting on cushions in the middle of the tent, pale as marble, not moving a muscle, blindly staring at the wall. Two women were sleeping next to her, one on her right and the other on her left. Were they actively and maliciously interfering with my mission? What about the guards whose throats I had just slashed? Who gives a shit? I was no longer on a mission, and Samael could roast me in the hottest furnace of Hell for all I cared.

Still, killing innocent, defenseless women was not right. Nora would not approve. It would have been easy to smother them both with a pillow, but at this point, all that mattered was what Nora would think of my actions.

I approached the one who looked like a lighter sleeper, gagged her, covered the gag with tape, and tied her hands and legs with zip ties before she could scream. Her companion didn't hear anything. I gagged and cuffed her, too. They looked at me with bulging eyes, moaning in fear, but the gags efficiently muffled any sound.

Nora was in too much shock to understand what was going on. She might have fainted, but I didn't have time to check her vitals. I grabbed her, threw her over my shoulder, and snuck out of the tent.

I thought of running with her on my shoulder, but that would have been difficult…and slow. Instead, I went to the stable and grabbed the largest and meanest stallion I could find. I should have checked first whether my body was capable of horseback riding, but I assumed it was part of a standard package at the HHS, since they'd even thought of equipping me with airplane pilot skills. I saddled up the beast and grabbed the reigns. The horse nickered, but complied with my silent orders. I threw Nora's motionless body across the saddle, jumped up behind her, and rode away, pushing the horse to a gallop. I was right about the HHS package—I felt like a born rider.

The horse's nickering and the hoofbeats alarmed the sentries, but it was too late. Let them chase me, if they can!

After a couple of hours of a mad gallop through the shallow ravines and mountain creeks of the Hindukush, my adrenaline level finally subsided. I thought I was far enough from the tribe to be safe. Footprints didn't stick well to mountainous terrain, plus I had ridden down multiple creeks to avoid being tracked. Now it was time to take care of my treasure.

I stopped the foam-covered horse, tied it to a small tree, and lowered Nora from the saddle. She was still unconscious, either from the original ordeal or because of the insane ride. I gently slapped her cheek.

She woke up and retched. When she saw me, her eyes blazed with loathing.

She was too weak to yell, but her tone reflected a steely resolve mixed with burning hatred. "What the hell are you doing here?" she wheezed in an angry whisper. "Get lost. You sold me, you bastard, and now you want to make it right?"

She clenched her fist and gathered the last of her strength to hit me. There was nothing playful about her blows, and I realized a forced kiss wouldn't pacify her this time. I let her go.

Suddenly, she took a small kitchen knife from under her dress and started walking toward me. I couldn't figure out where she had found it, but that didn't really matter.

She read my mind. "I thought I would use it on him, or on myself, but you are a much better target." She sucked in a heavy breath and tried to slash me. I easily avoided her blade. Finally, she lost her footing, fell, and cried. No, she howled like a wounded animal.

I tried to reach out and caress her hair, but she pushed me away with such force that I didn't dare try anymore.

I had to do something. I tried to explain myself, although I struggled to say anything coherent. "I don't expect you to understand, or to approve of what I did, nor do I expect you ever to forgive me. All I can tell you is, yes, for one fleeting moment my prize felt more important than you. But it was just one fleeting moment, and I will regret it for the rest of my life. You cannot punish me because I am punishing myself more than any bloodthirsty sadist could ever imagine. You can only save me from this torture by taking my life, and I will not interfere." I took her hand holding the knife and put it to my throat. "Like this." I showed her a slicing motion.

"Just like with the gun in the cave," she said bitterly, swallowing her tears.

"No, not like that. There, I'd hoped—no, I'd known you wouldn't do it. Here, I want you to do it. I refuse to live the life of a scumbag who betrayed his woman. If you cannot do it, I will gladly do it for you." I grabbed the knife from her hand.

She took my hand gently and said, "Don't. I don't need your blood on my hands. I just don't want to see you anymore. One betrayal is one too many." She rose to her feet and started walking slowly, stumbling like a drunkard. Her *hijab* fell off her head and dragged behind her.

"Nora, please wait!"

She waved me off without turning, walking as far away from me as she could.

I just stood there like a pillar of salt, unable to move. I wanted to cry, but I couldn't. There were no tears left in me, just emptiness. For the first time, I welcomed Oblivion and was ready to do anything to hasten it…even going through the Movie Room, as long as this episode of my life would be erased.

Suddenly, I felt the earth tremble. Putting my ear to the ground, I heard the faint beating of hoofs. The tribesmen must have tracked us down. The new danger brought me back to reality.

I chased Nora and grabbed her hand, dragging her back to the horse.

She gave me a hateful look. "What, didn't you have enough fun with me?"

"Get into the saddle," I barked, pushed her up, mounted the horse, and gave it a violent kick. Having had a bit of rest, the horse neighed and started to run. As we got out of the ravine and onto a plain, I heard my pursuers closing in. Bullets whizzed by. I didn't care if they hit me, I just needed to protect Nora.

The tribesmen were gaining on us. There was no way the horse with two people would be able to outrun them. I pulled up and dismounted. "Grab the horse's neck and hold on for your life," I yelled.

For once, she complied. I slapped the horse's butt and the beast galloped away.

"Forgive me if you can, my love, and live a happy life," I called after her under my breath, and took my final stand behind one of the short trees dotting the plain. There was no hope for escape. I had fought enough battles to understand when I was outmanned and outgunned. This had always been a suicide mission, so it was appropriate it should end as such.

Screw them all. I was ready to die—again—no matter the consequences.

But dying was too easy. I needed to buy Nora as much time as I could.

I took cover behind a rock, pulled my weapons and night vision goggles out of the backpack, and aimed. With a couple of well-placed shots, I hit the first two. Their falls tripped a couple of the horses and slowed down the rest.

The tribesmen realized that fighting me on horseback was a disadvantage. I was not running anywhere, and they presented perfect targets, while shooting from a moving horse was tricky. They dismounted and started flanking me. The firefight started.

Soon, I ran out of ammo. My pursuers were coming closer.

Now it was down to hand-to-hand combat. Bullets could only do so much. Unfortunately, the moon was full, illuminating the entire plain, so my NVGs didn't give me any advantage. I threw them aside, crawled toward the first group of the tribesmen, and lunged at them with my knife. They hadn't expected that move, and they couldn't shoot at me for the fear of hitting one of their own. However, they quickly regained their composure and took out their own daggers.

This was a fight to the death, with no quarter to be asked or given by either side.

The sound of fighting alerted the rest of my pursuers, who converged on us from all directions. I lost all sense of self-preservation and didn't feel any pain. For me, it was as simple as slash-and-move, pierce-and-move, kill as many as you can, and most important, take as much time as possible to keep them occupied.

Suddenly, the familiar clatter of a fifty-caliber shook me out of my hypnotic state. The approaching tribesmen scurried in all directions, cut down as easily as blades of grass. The group that had engaged with me also ran for cover. A machine gun mercilessly thinned their ranks. A few more seconds and their entire posse was either dead or dying.

With my peripheral vision, I saw a couple of approaching SUVs with fifty-calibers sticking out of their moonroofs, killing everyone in sight.

As one of them approached, the door opened and a familiar voice said, "You are still alive, you dumbass! Is there even a way to kill you?" Juma came out of the SUV, laughing.

"How did you…?"

He laughed even louder. "Never heard of GPS? Did you think I would let my partner escape with the prize without me knowing it? You have to be more careful with your equipment, American!"

I slowly regained my composure and my sense of humor. "Didn't I release you from your blood oath? Who is a dumbass now?"

Juma stopped laughing. "Only Allah can release a man from his oath. But my debt is paid in full now, American. A life for a life. I don't owe you anything anymore."

"So, you incurred the wrath of the whole Yousufzai tribe just to keep your oath?"

"Nah." He waved contemptuously. "Don't be so naïve. Kuza Bandar is not the whole tribe. He had plenty of enemies who would love to see him dead…which, by the way, we most likely achieved, as I saw him among the riders. I did lose a good customer, but I still have plenty. As for his men wanting my head, this is just one village of dumb goat herders. Anyway, they will have to stand in line. There are plenty more contenders for my head ahead of them."

I shook his hand. "I guess I misjudged you, too, Juma. Thank you, and no, we are not even. I now owe you, and you will not be able to release me from my oath. But if you will forgive me, I have to go and find Nora."

"Where are going to go? You are bleeding like a lamb

slaughtered for shish kabob. Come on, let me drive you to the hospital. We will find her later."

I looked down at myself for the first time. I was dotted with bullet holes and knife wounds, losing blood a pint at a time. But I hadn't come back to worry about my life. "Just help me bandage myself so I can walk."

"All right, all right. Just get in the car and try not to bleed all over my upholstery."

He opened the door, and I saw those familiar huge blue eyes, now full of terror and tears, staring at me from the back seat. I sighed and finally let my conciseness slip away.

CHAPTER 4

Mountainous Retreat
near Jalalabad, Afghanistan

I woke up warmed by the sun's rays. I was in a tidy room in our Landi Kotal safe house, lying on a clean bed. My whole body was aching, but I was still alive. I turned my head and moaned in pain, but what I saw made me forget my condition. Nora was napping in the chair next to my bed. Forcing to move my arm, I touched her to make sure I was not dreaming.

She woke up right away and carefully looked at me. "Oh, you are finally awake. No, no, keep still or the stitches will open. Drink."

She gave me a glass of water. I drank it greedily even though my throat was sore and I almost drowned. Nora took the glass away and carefully eased my head back down on the pillow.

"How long I was out?"

"A couple of days, give or take. You lost a lot of blood, but I brought you back to life," she said proudly. "It is going to hurt, but you will live."

The whole scene felt surreal. Was I living through a fairy tale with a happy ending that I knew didn't exist in real life? Or was this just a mirage…? She didn't look like a damsel in distress madly in love with her savior, but I was still hopeful.

I opened my mouth, but was afraid to ask the question.

She saw my puzzled look. "Are you trying to figure out if I forgave you? No, I didn't. What you did was unforgivable." She paused for effect, and I waited with bated breath for the "but".

"But," she said in a flat voice, looking straight into my eyes, "when you were lying there bleeding and dying, the doctor in me took pity on you. I wish you were a chivalrous knight in shining armor, but that was not meant to be. Sometimes one gets involved with scoundrels, but it doesn't mean one doesn't feel compassion for them. You are, of course, a rogue and a scoundrel, but to my misfortune, as a future doctor, I couldn't let you die."

This was not the "but" I'd expected or wanted. I broke eye contact and stared up at the ceiling. "I don't want your pity. You should have left me to die out there." Despite knowing it was unreasonable to hope for her to welcome me back with open arms after being sold to a native warlord, I couldn't help feeling disappointed by her nonchalant tone and mention of pity. I suddenly wanted to get back at her, to cause her pain, even though I had no right to demand anything of her. "If you only stayed because you thought of me as a patient, Juma could easily have found a real doctor instead of a future doctor who hasn't even finished her first-year internship."

It was a low blow and I was aware of that, but her self-righteous behavior and constant reminders that she was morally superior to me, had been too much.

Her face drained of color and her lips tightened into a thin line. Tears welled up in her eyes, but she quickly blinked them away and said in a cold tone, "You know what? Maybe you're right. I should have left you there to die, you ungrateful bastard. Taking pity on you was my mistake."

She stood up abruptly. Her body language clearly showed that she had been torn between wanting to help her patient, even though that patient had hurt her so badly, and feeling resentment towards me. "I'll ask Juma to find you a real doctor, but until then, you'll just have to make do with me. Now, rest." Her tone was laced with bitterness and resentment. "I will do everything to ensure your speedy recovery for one reason and one reason only—so I can get you out of my life for good." She stormed out of the room in a fit of anger.

The next few days went by with me going in and out of consciousness. True to her word, Nora nursed and mothered me back to health, albeit for all the wrong reasons as far as I was concerned. I didn't remember much of it. My body was well-made, so in a couple of days I was able to get up and start walking, leaning on a cane. She watched my stitches like a hawk, changing the dressing every day.

Juma arranged for us to spend time in his mountain

retreat, a secluded villa north of Jalalabad on the Kabul River overlooking the Hindukush. His men took us there from Landi Kotal once I recovered enough to endure the drive back to Afghanistan. I couldn't help but ask Nora caustically whether a real doctor would be waiting for me at the villa, but she simply ignored my obnoxious question.

This time we went over the Torkham crossing to avoid another grueling mountain hike. It must have cost Juma an arm and a leg to pay the guards on both sides of the border, but thankfully we had a relatively short and comfortable drive all the way to Jalalabad. I was glad to get out of the Tribal Area. Danger was everywhere, and us having killed a powerful tribal chieftain was not a trifling matter. Juma apparently thought the same, and gladly returned to his home turf.

The Kabul River villa was opulent even by the American standards. It was a large two-story mansion with a couple of acres of surrounding property, and featured a gym, a sauna, a steam room, a large pool, and other amenities that defied the description of Afghanistan as one of the world's poorest countries where most of the population could not even afford food. For the first time I realized how powerful Haji Juma Khan was, that, despite the long-standing animosity between the Taliban and drug lords, they didn't dare confiscate it from him.

There was, indeed, an uneasy truce between the Taliban on one side, and the warlords and powerful drug dealers on the other. The Taliban, saddled with infighting and opposition from other religious groups such as ICIS-K, didn't want an open rebellion on the part of criminals whose private armies rivaled that of the government. Those living outside the law, satisfied with their untouchable positions, didn't stir the pot too much, content to benefit from their illegal trade and kept a low profile. Juma may not have been the most powerful among them, but due to its hidden location, his retreat didn't rub the Taliban's fur the wrong way enough to do anything about it.

For my part, I simply enjoyed the luxury without giving a second thought to internal Afghan politics. Even Nora, with her desire to help the poor and underprivileged, and her obvious dislike for shady characters like Juma, relished the respite from her ordeal.

By the end of the week, she was satisfied with my healing progress and removed some of the bandages. I took full advantage of the amenities to speed up my recovery. While still limping and needing a cane, I took long walks through the fenced property, swam in the pool every morning, and religiously exercised in the gym—to Nora's disapproval, as she thought too much exertion could open my wounds.

But in spite of her meticulous nursing, our hostility toward each other continued. I hated her for feeling only pity while I wanted her desire, and she hated me for being ungrateful and generally obnoxious. What neither of us wanted to admit was that the intense feelings we had for each other went much deeper than hurt pride or lack of gratitude. And I didn't have to wait long to see proof of that.

One night after I went to bed and dozed off, she suddenly

stormed into my room. Still hazy from slumber but using this golden opportunity to stick it to her, I said sarcastically, "What's going on? I thought doctor's rounds were supposed to be in the morning?"

Without a word, she slapped my face with a sharp, stinging *smack*. It caught me by surprise and I recoiled. But she didn't stop. She continued, one slap after another, until I'd had enough and grabbed her arms, twisting them behind her back. She let out a piercing scream, but instead of backing down, she pushed herself onto me and began biting at my face.

I managed to throw her off and pinned her down on the bed. She struggled beneath me, not wiggling her way out but trying to lock me tighter in her embrace. Her legs wrapped tight around my waist as she rubbed her body against mine. The friction sent a surge of arousal through my whole body, and I started tearing off her clothes.

She didn't resist. Instead, she clawed at my back with her nails and literally skewered herself on my swollen member, spearing it into her. Our bodies were tangled together, and she kept biting me just like a praying mantis female trying to bite off the head of her mate. Her face was contorted with anger and passion, and her eyes glinted with hatred and desire. I assumed my own reflected the same feelings. We were locked in a twisted dance of lust and brutality.

She finished as violently as she'd started, convulsing and groaning in a bizarre mix of pleasure and pain. I exploded, as well, but neither of us was willing to separate. For a few moments we lay in silence broken only by our heavy breathing, still fused to each other.

She finally pushed me away, got up, and clenched her fists, snarling like a rabid dog. I was preparing for another violent attack when she grabbed her torn clothes and walked away repeating over and over, "Bastard, Fucking bastard," in a hot, angry whisper.

She slammed the door behind her, and I sat down, dumbfounded and discombobulated. What the hell was that all about?

The next morning, she politely walked into my room and started carefully—maybe too carefully—examining my bandages. As she was about to change one of them, I grabbed her hand.

"Stop, please. Are you trying to pretend last night didn't happen? Well, it did. Shouldn't we try to deal with it as grownups?"

She threw my hand off hers. "No. I don't want to talk about it. I felt horny last night, masturbation didn't help, and you were the only dick around."

Just yesterday this offensive line would have lit me like a match and we would have ended up pissing off each other. Today, however, I looked carefully into her eyes and saw endless pain and angst.

She didn't hate me for selling her out. She hated herself for still wanting me.

I stroked her hair. She jerked her head as if bitten by a spider.

I didn't let her go and moved my face closer to hers. "Look, I know I'm a scumbag."

She nodded in agreement.

"And an ungrateful bastard and a lowlife."

She met every epithet with another nod.

"But I have one redeeming quality. I am crazy about you, and I proved it when I went on a suicide mission just to get you back."

Her pupils dilated and she opened her mouth to say something, but I put my finger to her lips.. "I know what you are going to say. I came back because I was just another man thinking through his dick who would mindlessly risk everything just to get laid. Be that as it may, and whatever my motives, I am here with you, and every fiber of my being wants to keep you near me. Just give me a chance to prove that I am worthy of forgiveness, and if I fail, you are free to go. Besides, my offer has an added benefit."

She raised her brows and looked at me quizzically.

"Next time you feel horny, you will have a dick readily available at a moment's notice."

She opened her mouth, no doubt to say something offensive, then stopped and laughed. "You are such a conceited lowlife. Can't you understand that certain actions do not deserve a second chance?"

If only she knew how well I was aware of that! I sat wordlessly on the bed.

She also kept silent for a few moments, then said matter-of-factly, "I will probably regret it for the rest of my life, but the added benefit does have a certain appeal, being stuck in this wilderness."

I chuckled. "Whatever keeps you next to me. Beggars cannot be choosers, and any reason that will keep you here is good enough for me."

She pressed her lips together, probably thinking about the whirlpool of events that had gotten her into this predicament, and wondering what the future had in store for both of us. Then she kissed me on the forehead and walked away.

The ice was broken, and her feelings for me had proven too strong for her to simply walk away.

I, however, felt rotten. Yes, I won the battle, but where would this affair lead us? I was dead, existing on borrowed time with suspended Reincarnation Rights and enough transgressions to be dragged into the Movie Room at any moment…which would undoubtedly be a prelude to Oblivion. In the end, I would have to abandon her and fail her trust again.

I didn't worry about myself, but the thought of failing her once again was unbearable. I took a deep breath. Maybe if the mission succeeded I could manage to negotiate a second lifetime in exchange for the Book. Then I would be able to grow old together with her. After all, no one knew what future the Creator had planned for any of us. Even though I would have to live that second lifetime with full knowledge of the eventual outcome, it would still be worth it…if for no other reason but to prove to this beautiful woman that she hadn't made a completely wrong choice.

Thinking about the future gave me a headache, and I waved off my thoughts. For now, I simply wanted to selfishly enjoy to the fullest extent the time I had left in the World of The Living.

I got up, took a shower, and went to her room. She was looking out the window, lost in her own thoughts.

I softly knocked on the door. "I was wondering if I could offer you to use the added benefit now," I said meekly.

She smiled. "You know what? It actually might be a good idea." She came closer to me, moved her head back, and closed her eyes.

I gently kissed her and picked her up in my arms.

She gave me a disapproving doctor's look. "You cannot lift heavy things yet, so put me down, please."

"Heavy? You are the lightest thing I've ever held in my arms."

I carried her all the way to the bed.

After we finished and lay there satisfied, she suddenly rose up as if a lightbulb had gone off in her head. "Oh, damn, I completely forgot! I have something for you. Wait here." She turned my head to the side. "Close your eyes and don't peek."

She jumped out of bed, becoming again a naughty child anticipating an exciting trick.

I dutifully closed my eyes. I heard her putting on a robe and running out of the room. In a few moments, she came back.

"Okay, now you can open."

I opened my eyes. She had a mysterious expression on her

face and held a small object wrapped in a piece of cloth in her hand.

"What is it?"

"Open it." She was full of anticipation.

I carefully untied the cloth. Inside it was Kuza Bandar's amulet. The one he claimed held the directions to the Book of Remedies.

"Holy moley! How did you get that?"

Satisfied with my extreme excitement, she gave me a conspiratorial look. "I am not telling you."

"*P-lea-se!*"

"All right, you nosy fellow. After the fight, Juma's people went through the battlefield gathering trophies. They found Kuza Bandar dead and brought this amulet back to Juma. He gave it to me to give it to you before we left to come to the villa, but I still hated you so much that I completely forgot about it."

I was elated. "You cannot even imagine. This is our ticket to freedom, happiness, everything!"

She frowned, not understanding how an amulet could buy us happiness, but her eyes appeared cautiously optimistic that it might change her life for the better. "So, what's inside it?"

"Let's see." I looked closer at the delicate amulet. I didn't have a chance to take a good look at it in Kuza's tent. Up close, I could see it had been exquisitely made—a blue glass vial with a golden snake spiraling along its length, with large red gems on the top and the bottom of the vial. The snake's head was raised above the glass and its eyes were made of diamond dust. The amulet itself was probably worth millions, although I cared far more about what was inside.

"How do you open the darn thing?" I said, rotating it in my fingers.

"Let me see," she said impatiently and pulled it out of my fingers.

"Hey, careful, don't break it!"

"Don't worry, I know what I am doing," she said confidently, and put her glasses on her nose. This was a very different, nerdy-looking Nora, a medical doctor examining a specimen, not the insatiable lover who had drained me a few minutes earlier. She crinkled her nose and stuck out her tongue in intense focus. After a couple of minutes peering intently at the amulet, she shouted victoriously, "Look! There is a tiny cut in here."

Indeed, there was a tiny groove in the middle of the vial, a sure sign of a thread by which the two parts of the amulet had been screwed together.

I tried to delicately twist it, but the glass was too fragile to apply force without breaking, and the thread had probably gotten stuck over the ages. No, we needed a professional help.

I ran to the villa guards and asked them to contact Juma immediately. In no time, they brought me a mobile phone with Juma on the line. I explained the situation to him, and he said he would send a car to bring us back to Jalalabad, where we could find a good jeweler.

While we were waiting for the car to pick us up, Nora gave me one of her conspiratorial looks. "Can we do it again? After all, you didn't say anything about a limit on the number of times I can use the added benefit," she said naughtily. Her eyes were wide and her parted lips showed her brilliantly white teeth.

I shook my head with a grin. "You are a nymphomaniac, you know that?"

She happily nodded and dropped her robe.

I didn't need to be asked twice. I took her hand and we went—no, we ran back to bed. .

CHAPTER 5

Jalalabad, Afghanistan

When we finally rushed out of the villa, the car and driver were already patiently waiting for us. Juma met us in Jalalabad, as excited as we were by this new development. He had already made a few calls, and when we arrived at his safe house, a small, bald, bespectacled man was sitting at a table. He wore dress pants and a long-sleeve shirt, a surprising outfit for post-Taliban Afghanistan. As I'd assumed, the man was a jeweler hired by Juma to open the amulet. He had his goldsmith toolbox sitting on the table next to him.

The jeweler took the amulet and examined it under a magnified glass, profusely admiring the mastery of the ancient goldsmiths. He tried to twist it apart, but the amulet wouldn't give in. He rubbed a generous amount of oil on the groove, hoping that greasing the thread would move the parts, but to no avail.

He finally shook his head. "I cannot open it. It must have fused over the years."

"So, break it," said Juma waving his hand.

The jeweler looked at him, horrified by this sacrilege. "I am sorry, *sahib*, but this is a priceless piece of jewelry. Do you really want me to break it?" he asked carefully, mindful of the ruthless reputation of his employer.

Juma shrugged. "I need what's inside. If you can preserve the outside, I will pay you more, but opening it should be your goal."

The jeweler nodded. He took out a fine glass cutter and a mallet, and lightly tapped on the glass. It wouldn't budge. He sighed and prepared to tap it again, but then something caught his attention about the gem that crowned the amulet. It was sitting in a gold pronged setting.

The jeweler's eyes lit up. "Excuse me, *sahib*. What if I remove the gem from its prongs and drill a hole into the amulet? We can try to take out whatever is inside. If that doesn't work, then I will break the glass."

"Whatever," said Juma indifferently.

I was somewhat surprised he was willing to break a priceless artifact in order to find something that may or may not be inside. Something that, based on the price I had given him, wasn't worth much more than the artifact. Was it just the excitement of the chase? Or had he figured out the real value of the Book? I couldn't tell. Since we were all focused on opening the amulet, I decided to let it go for now.

In the meantime, the jeweler had carefully loosened the golden prongs and removed the stone. He took out a small tool and drilled a hole in the glass. He worked very carefully. Once he'd pierced the glass he stopped, so as not to damage the contents. He looked inside the amulet and, using his tweezers, slowly took out a fragile piece of parchment.

I licked my lips, staring intently at the parchment as he handed it to Juma.

The jeweler's job was done. Before we examined the parchment, he paid the man and told his people to usher him out. After he'd gone, I thought I heard a muffled shot. I wouldn't be surprised if Juma had ordered his people to shoot the man to keep our secret safe, but I couldn't say for sure.

I looked at Nora to make sure she hadn't heard anything. I didn't want her to be exposed to harsh reality. For now she was living an Indiana Jones adventure, and I wanted to keep it that way.

Juma carefully unrolled the tiny parchment and looked at it through a magnifying glass. After a few moments, he handed it to me. "See what you can make of it, American. This is not a Farsi script, so I cannot read it."

I took the parchment and magnifying glass. The text was written in either Mandaean or Aramaic, I couldn't tell since the letters were the same in both alphabets. Having experience with the scrolls in the Mandaean library in Ahwaz, I could try and decipher this one, but the miniature letters and the parchment's great antiquity made my job much tougher. I couldn't deal with the crowd breathing down my neck, and asked everyone to move away from the table.

After long and laborious study, I finally figured out at least part of the text.

"I cannot make out all of it, but it appears to say that the Yousufzai entrust their precious Book to their brothers from the Lewani tribe."

Juma was visibly disappointed. "Lewani tribe? They don't even exist anymore. Is there anything else?"

I shook my head. I was just as disappointed as he was. We stared morosely at the parchment.

All of a sudden, Nora shrieked in excitement.

We turned to her. "What?"

"Wait." She lit up like an LED display. "When I went from Mazar-i-Sharif to Asadabad with Doctors Without Borders, another group was going farther south. I heard them working on the route, and they discussed stopping for a day at a small village called Lewani, not far from Kabul. Could that be the place?"

It was a long shot, but much better than nothing. At least we had a lead we could pursue. Not to mention it was Nora who had come up with the idea.

She was standing there waiting to be praised and admired.

"You know what, Sherlock Holmes?" I said, "It very well could be."

She was so proud of figuring out the clue that she couldn't wait another minute to go to the village. "All right, let's go!

What are we waiting for?" she demanded impatiently.

All the men around the table, even those who didn't know English, smiled.

"Woah, there! Not so fast, Doc," said Juma. "Let's eat first, plan the trip, and only then we will move. You can spend the night anticipating the next chapter of your great adventure."

Nora was visibly disappointed, but then I whispered to her, "We can stay in the same room and you can continue enjoying your unlimited account with me."

She blushed and gave me an angry look. "Are you out of your mind? What if someone hears us?" she whispered back.

"I will deal with that," I said, took her hand, and walked her to our room.

CHAPTER 6

Lewani Village, Afghanistan

The next morning we overslept, exhausted from a sleepless night of lovemaking and talking. She had finally dropped the pretense of hating me and let her feelings run free. She now wanted to know everything about me. I dodged her question spree, as I couldn't tell her much other than that I was dead. Yeah, not very good news for a sex partner. So, I had to wing it, but she appeared to be satisfied with my vague answers. As long as she could cuddle in my arms, she would buy all my tall tales without flinching.

When Juma finally knocked on our door, it was late morning. When I opened it a crack, he winked at me and quipped, "Enjoying life, I see. Don't forget, we still have business to attend to."

I waved him off. "Just give us an hour and we will be ready."

He threw up his hands and walked away.

When we finally went outside, we were treated to a formidable scene. In addition to the obligatory SUVs full of armed men, our convoy included two Humvees with fifty-cals sticking out of their roofs.

"Where is the air support?" I quipped.

Juma, on the other hand, didn't share my flippant attitude. "I wouldn't mind a couple of F-16s accompanying us. We are going straight into a Taliban stronghold and it is not my turf there. It may get really ugly."

"Don't be such a worrywart, Juma," I said, giving him a fist bump to the shoulder. "I feel good about our mission, and my intuition rarely deceives me."

He snickered. "Oh, yeah, just like your intuition told you how to deal with Kuza Bandar."

I shrugged. Point taken.

Before we left, however, one of Juma's men came running to us and handed Nora a bag. She thanked him and extended her hand to shake his, but he shrank away and simply bowed. I remembered that before we went to our room, she whispered something to one of the men who'd appeared to understand English.

Juma's eyes widened. "What is it?" he asked the man in Dari.

"Forgive me, *sahib*," said the man sheepishly, "but *khanoum* asked me to bring her some medical supplies. She said she may need them to help the villagers."

Juma was livid, and the man fully expected to be shot on the spot.

I touched Juma's hand, calming him down. "It might not be a bad idea. Bringing a doctor to the village will score quite a few brownie points with the villagers."

As I was saying it, he was thinking the same thing. "You are right, my friend, but your woman has no right to go over my head. You should beat her sometimes," he added with a scowl.

"Of course. I was planning to, but decided to do it when we get back to the States. That way, I will have plenty of time to beat her in the comfort of my own home." My expression was dead serious.

Juma was taken aback, not knowing whether I was joking or truly becoming a real Afghan man. In a few seconds, he understood it was sarcasm and laughed. "You Westerners will never learn how to handle your women. That is why your divorce rates are so high."

Nora didn't understand a word of our conversation, but seeing the first man's fear and Juma's anger, she realized she must have done something wrong. After her ordeal with Kuza's tribe, she understood the danger of a high-toned conversation in a language she didn't understand. "What is it?" she whispered cautiously. "I am a doctor, and I'm certain these villagers do not have access to healthcare. Why was Juma so angry?"

"Oh, nothing, my love. He thought I should beat you for talking to a strange man without my permission. So get ready to be spanked tonight. Oh, and get yourself a cushion because you won't be able to sit after the beating." I was again proud of my poker face.

For a second, Nora thought I was being serious. She opened her mouth in disbelief.

It was so much fun to tease her, but I couldn't help it, I started laughing. I gave her a light slap on the butt. "Just to give you a taste of things to come."

She realized she'd been had, pursed her lips, and punched me in the ribs. "Bastard," she mouthed.

The banter added to my good mood. I was certain of the success of our mission, and having Nora next to me made everything look brighter.

The distance between Jalalabad and Lewani village was about three hundred kilometers, but we couldn't use the direct route through Kabul and had to go via backroads. Adding a few pitstops to the driving time, we arrived at the village by sunrise the following day.

It was a small, shabby village of barely 200 inhabitants, and it looked nothing like the repository of a priceless artifact. The arrival of an armed convoy flanked by Humvees frightened the villagers. Concerned elders came out to meet us.

Juma explained the purpose of our visit and asked for hospitality. I couldn't hear the conversation, but I saw multiple bowings, chest-beating, and smiles, then shaking of heads, followed by more bowings, chest-beating, and smiles, after which Juma motioned us to disembark from our motorized armada and set up camp in the village.

While our men were carrying supplies to the guest shacks identified by the elders, I approached Juma. "So, what's the story? I could see all the gestures but couldn't hear a word."

"They offered us hospitality as they are supposed to, but when I told them about an ancient book, they got kind of cagy and pled ignorance. Their denials didn't strike me as genuine, though."

"Did you tell them about the doctor who came with us?"

"Oh, yeah. That was when they bowed and smiled."

"What was the chest beating and head shaking all about?"

"That was when they swore they had never heard of any ancient places or artifacts around here."

"Do you think they will report us to the Taliban?"

"I hope not. They gave us their hospitality, and hurting a guest is a *haram*."

I creased my brows and twisted my mouth. "I am skeptical about old traditions, especially when at risk of losing one's head."

"Yeah, but we have an army with us. Whether the Taliban's army is larger is of no concern to them because we will cut them down before the Taliban even engages. I may be in the minority in my country, but I am also skeptical about ancient traditions. I do, however, believe in the convincing power of a fifty-caliber machine gun. Besides, my men will be watching the villagers. If someone tries to leave, I will know."

I smiled and high-fived Juma. "All right, then. Let's unpack, set up a medical tent to show them the carrot, and let them think about the stick."

My love story with Nora may have made me mellow, but I was good at compartmentalizing. If someone thought I had lost my fangs to a lover's touch, they would be making a huge mistake. I was on a mission, albeit unsanctioned, and on a mission I could be as ruthless as anyone.

The next morning, we set up a doctor's tent where Nora got ready to see villagers with health issues. They all decided to take full advantage of the free healthcare, which hadn't quite taken hold in Afghanistan, and the opportunity to complain of everything from headache to malaria. Judging by the line at Nora's makeshift office, I was shocked any of the villagers were still alive and hadn't succumbed to the multiple maladies they all claimed to be afflicted by.

Juma and I decided to have a closer chat with the elders about any ancient sites around here. I warned Juma that Nora should not know about anything, and that everything had to be done in a subtle way. Juma was disappointed but begrudgingly nodded.

We started with the village headman, asking him to come to our shack for a talk. When he came in, he was immediately tied to a chair and Juma's men were about to do a number on him. They were brutes, and I expected that any man coming out of their hands would be in need of urgent care…and that Nora would have tons of unwanted questions.

The headman was scared and looked at us with bulging eyes,

preparing for the worst. One of Juma's men grabbed a club and was about to beat him when I stopped him.

"Let me try it my way first."

Juma's men looked skeptical. They knew full well that Westerners frowned on enhanced interrogation techniques. Well, they were up for surprise.

The predator in me woke up.

I came closer to the headman. "Let me introduce myself, my friend. I am a treasure hunter and I have every reason to believe that the treasure I am looking for is somewhere near here. You may not know about the treasure, but you sure as hell know about any ancient sites around. Do you want to tell me where I can find them?"

My voice reflected no emotion, and Juma's men were smiling at a naïve American trying to get information from this sly village headman in such a silly way.

The man energetically shook his head. "No, *sahib*, there are no ancient sites around here or I would know about them. We are a poor village and have no treasure."

I sighed, came up behind him, and struck him on the crown of his head. The blow was light, and the man shrank down, but clearly didn't feel pain.

"Please, *sahib*, don't hurt me! I am telling you the truth!"

I didn't say anything and hit him again. After a series of carefully measured blows with the right intervals, each of which caused a mini concussion, the man's eyes went blank, foam covered his mouth, and he started retching. The advantage of this enhanced interrogation method was a complete absence of any visible signs of violence. Even if he went to Nora, she wouldn't know what happened to him.

Juma's men were no longer smiling but were curious. I asked them to bring a bucket of water and splashed it on the man.

"Again, my friend, let me repeat my question," I said. "Are there ancient sites around here that may interest me? And, by the way, if I hear the word no from you, I will repeat the beating."

The man was barely conscious, and he sure as hell didn't want to go through it all again, but he still shook his head. Now, that was interesting. Either there were no ancient sites around here, which was impossible given we were in the middle of the ancient Median and Achaemenid Empires and within a stone's throw from the first capital of the Mughals, or he was hiding something even at the risk of being killed. Which definitely piqued my interest.

"All right, let's try again," I said.

"Please, no, *sahib*, don't do it. I know nothing," the man pleaded, scared out of his wits.

I stopped him in the middle of his plea by delivering another blow to his head. This time, the concussions occurred much faster and he went into a delirious state pretty quickly. After another cold shower, he was ready to talk.

"Yes, yes, I remember now, *sahib*," he whined.

"Great. Do tell me."

"There are some ancient ruins outside the village," the headman said shakily.

"I am sure there are many ancient ruins around here," I said in the same emotionless tone. "Something tells me you know exactly the ruins I am looking for."

His face reflected genuine surprise, but at this point I knew he was hiding something. Otherwise, why would he not just tell me about some pile of rubble outside of the village if there was nothing there?

I smiled menacingly and raised my hand.

"Please, don't do it, *sahib*. I will tell you everything. But you have to protect me. My people will kill me if they find out I gave up the location."

"Location of what?"

The man lowered his voice to a whisper. "An ancient legend says there is a place outside the village where a mausoleum stood even before the Prophet—Peace be on Him—brought us his Holy Word. That mausoleum was not a burial place of a man, but of some ancient evil so powerful that anyone who dug it up would bring a curse upon all of us. This legend is always told in a whisper, and every generation has been forbidden from going there or divulging its location to strangers. Many impetuous men have tried over the years, and they all died. Pestilence and famine always followed those attempts." He looked frightened, even more so than when I was beating the crap out of him. "Please, *sahib*, do not go there. It will doom us all!"

I patted his head, not so much to calm him down but to

remind him of the very real danger—as opposed to an ancient spooky tale—of my fist crashing down on him. He cowered in fear, preparing for another blow.

"Don't worry, my friend, I have ways of dealing with this ancient evil. Show me where this place is."

The man shook his head in terror. I was tired of his recalcitrance, and hit him on the head without warning.

He groaned and cringed in pain. "All right, all right. I will take you there, but we have to be careful. The villagers should not see us."

We went outside the hut using the backdoor, and the man took us to a barely noticeable mound right outside of the village.

"Is this it?" I asked, unimpressed.

The man nodded with resignation.

I turned to Juma. "Have your people start digging."

Juma frowned and pointed. "Look at them. They won't touch this place."

His men, indeed, looked scared. Superstitious dumbasses!

"We need to dig up the place, and the villagers are not going to help us. You heard the man and saw how much pain he was willing to take before he broke."

"We can break them the same way," Juma said with a grin.

"And bring Nora into this mess? No way!"

Juma got upset. "Hey, you deal with your woman," he said tersely. "We need to get this place opened up and see what's inside."

I wanted to punch him in the face, but deep down I knew he

was right. We needed to get in and find what we were looking for, or the past month's ordeal had been all for naught.

I pressed my lips together and sighed. "All right. Let me deal with Nora tonight." I turned to the headman, who was still standing silently by our side. "You! Go to the doctor and tell her you fell and hurt your head. If she finds out what happened, the pain you experienced in the shack would feel pleasant compared to what you will go through!"

I didn't need to threaten him twice. He nodded and ran back to the village.

That night, Nora came to bed tired but happy. She told me about all the grateful villagers, and how she'd helped them with various cures.

I barely listened. I was trying to devise a plan for how to prepare her for what would come next.

"By the way," she said, "the village headman came in almost at the end of the day. He said he had fallen and hurt his head. I couldn't do any tests, but all signs pointed to a heavy concussion. Surprisingly, he had no bruises on his head, and he wouldn't tell me the whole story. I gave him some painkillers and told him to stay in bed for a couple of days, but I am worried the damage is much more serious and he may need to be hospitalized. Can we take him to a hospital in Kabul?"

I hugged her. "Of course we can, but before we do that, I need to discuss something with you."

She looked at me quizzically.

"We found the location," I said.

"You did? Oh, wonderful!" She clapped her hands in excitement. "Did you see the Book?"

"No, unfortunately not. It needs to be dug up and therein lies the problem. This place has gotten a bad reputation through the ages, and the villagers won't help us for the fear of ancient curses."

Nora laughed. "I am sure we can convince them they are just fairy tales."

"I don't think so. These are illiterate folks steeped in superstitions, and I am afraid we'll have to use more persuasive methods."

She raised her brows. "Such as?"

"We may need to scare them a bit." Seeing her disapproval, I quickly added, "Don't worry, we won't hurt them, simply play to their superstitions and tell them we'll bring much worse curses down on their heads if they don't help us."

Nora looked suspicious. She had seen a lot of things over the past month, but me claiming I could hoodwink the villagers into believing in our ability to curse them sounded really lame.

I took her head in my hands and gave her a kiss. "Do you trust me?" I said using the most powerful argument I had.

She sighed and nodded. "Okay, do what you must, but please don't scare the children. They are so impressionable."

Phew. This had been a tough one to win. I was a bit surprised how quickly she'd bought into my bullshit, but I attributed it to her feelings for me. "Of course, we won't scare children. We plan to call a village meeting tomorrow morning."

"Can I go with you?"

"No, it would be better if you stayed home or at your clinic tent. People may start crying, and you are even more impressionable than the children. I don't want you to be upset."

She crinkled her nose, not knowing whether I was lying to her or being honest.

In the end, she decided to trust me and cuddled in my arms.

CHAPTER 7

Dig outside of Lewani, Afghanistan

The next morning just before dawn, I left a happily sleeping Nora and joined Juma's men to coral the villagers. By the time I joined them, they were already shaking the sleepy locals awake and pushing them outside with the butts of their rifles. We gathered them far enough from the shack where Nora and I were staying, just to be sure she wouldn't be awakened by their screams.

Our Humvees stood by the side of the crowd, the machine guns trained on them. The villagers were visibly scared. I was not looking forward to what I was about to do but I thought my methods might at least be less bloody than those of Juma and his men. Now was the time to tell them about our powerful curses.

I climbed onto one of the Humvees. "Listen carefully. I know all about the ancient mausoleum outside the village."

A murmur went through the crowd and I raised my hand quieting them down.

"I need you to dig it up. I know you are afraid of the ancient curse, but let me explain something. The ancient curse may or may not be true but, if you don't help us, we *will* rape all your women and carve out their bellies, gouge out the eyes of your children, and kill all the men. Just so you do not doubt my intentions, let me demonstrate."

I got down from the Humvee, grabbed the nearest baby from his mother's hands, took out my knife, and pressed it against his cheekbone right under its eye. A few drops of blood trickled down my knife. The child was wiggling and crying, and the mother was on her knees pleading for his life.

I looked at the villagers. "Is it yes or no?"

The crowd was frozen in fear. Seeing no movement, I turned my head back to the child and applied more pressure to the knife.

The village headman recovered first. He came closer and grabbed my arm. "Please, *sahib*, do not hurt the child. We gave you our hospitality and this is how you repay us?"

I pulled my arm out of his hands and hit him in the face with the knife's handle. "The only words I want to hear from your mouth are 'Yes, *sahib*, we will go and dig, and we will do it now.' Anything else and this child will be the first of many victims. I will drown your village in blood and sorrow, creating a new legend to frighten the children with."

The headman wiped the blood from his face and said, "We

will help you, but please, don't hurt us anymore."

"Good," I said, giving the child back to his mother. "All men should grab shovels and go the ancient mound. The women will remain locked in a shack, in case you get any unwise ideas."

I was pleased with the outcome. While I wouldn't hesitate to kill and maim every villager who stood between me and my shot at finding the Book and redeeming myself, I preferred not to kill innocent people, particularly children. Even wolves had their moral code.

We corralled the women into a shack and posted a couple of Juma's henchmen to guard them. Once the village men came back with shovels and other digging implements, we led them to the ancient mausoleum, where they reluctantly started digging. Juma's men yelled and occasionally hit them with the butts of their rifles to make them work faster.

I went back to Nora.

She had just woken up and was getting ready to go to her medical tent. I stopped her, saying everyone was at the dig, and they would call us if and when they found something.

"Don't you want to spend this morning with me, since there is no one around anyway?" I asked hopefully.

She nodded happily, and I dragged her back to bed. We spent a wonderful morning together, which quickly became an afternoon, and then an evening. We didn't hear from anyone, so once darkness fell and I heard villagers coming back, I offered to take her to the dig site. Anything to keep her away from the frightened villagers.

When we got to the dig site, the mound was gone and the roof of the mausoleum was visible. There was still a lot to dig out, but the work had progressed nicely. Nora and I sat on a wheelbarrow left by the workers and I hugged her.

She put her head on my shoulder and looked up at the starry sky. "It is so beautiful and peaceful," she said. "When you look up at the heavens, you cannot imagine there is so much pain and sorrow in this world."

I nodded in agreement, stroking her hair.

She suddenly changed the subject. "So, what's in this old book that makes it so valuable?" she asked without raising her head from my shoulder.

"Oh, it is very ancient. It is called The Book of Remedies and was supposedly written by Noah's son, Shem. It is said to contain remedies against all diseases in the world."

Nora was awed. "Are you saying we will be able to rid the world of all sickness?"

"That is what they say."

"Will you let me read it and use it? I will be a doctor, after all."

"Of course, my love, you will be the most famous physician in the world and they will erect a statue of you in front of the World Health Organization."

She giggled. "I can live without a statue, but being able to rid the world of all the diseases sounds incredible!"

She sat silently thinking about a wonderful future world of happy and healthy people, while I thought about how much of a scoundrel I was by lying to her. There was no way Azazel or the Heavenly Offices would permit the Book to exist, and it would quickly be destroyed once we found it.

The next morning, she and I continued our leisurely existence, interspersed with bouts of passionate sex. Nora couldn't wait to see the Book, but I convinced her to be patient. We took one of the SUVs and went for a ride through the desert around the village, keeping her as far away from the dig as possible. When we came back to the village at sunset, we found one of Juma's men standing in front of our shack waiting for us.

"*Sahib*, you must come with me. The diggers uncovered the entrance to the mausoleum."

Nora grabbed my hand. "You have to take me with you!" she pleaded.

"Okay, okay. Don't be so impatient, my dear."

We hopped into the car and drove to the site.

The mausoleum looked nothing like one of those opulent shrines I had seen around the world. It was a simple cubic building made of stone, with a heavy metal door covered in Aramaic inscriptions. I took a flashlight and examined them. They were all ancient curses promising bad things would befall anyone who entered.

"Open it," I ordered the diggers.

They shrank away in fear. Juma's men were about to start hitting them with their rifle butts, but I raised my hand. Nora was here, and violence was out of the question.

I approached the village headman, narrowed my eyes, and

said quietly, "Tell your men to pry open the door. Your women and children are still locked up, and I will send a few men there to start bringing you their bodies one by one until you do as you are told."

The headman nodded and went back to the villagers. They argued and gesticulated for a few moments, doubtless trying to assess where the greater danger lay—inside the mausoleum or in the shack where their loved ones were locked up. They must have decided that I presented a more tangible danger, and went to the mausoleum door, attempting to pry it open.

The massive door wouldn't give.

I asked Juma to bring explosives. Soon, his men came back carrying a bag full of grenades. We attached them to the hinges and what looked like a lock, tied long cords to the grenade pins, and ducked behind a mound of freshly excavated earth. I yanked the cords, pulling out the pins, and a deafening blast reverberated through the cool night air.

The door wobbled, then fell to the ground with a loud *thud*.

Juma and Nora were excited, but his men looked uneasy.

The village headman came to me. "*Sahib*, we did everything you asked. Can you now release our women and let us go?"

"Not yet, my friend. But stay outside with my men. They will guard you from any evil that might emerge from the ruins."

I told Juma's men to stay with the villagers. They were only too happy to oblige—anything to avoid entering the accursed place.

Juma, Nora, and I went inside, switching on our headband lights.

The mausoleum consisted of a large room with a stone sarcophagus placed in the middle. The sarcophagus was decorated with a worn-out and half-destroyed mosaic depicting all kinds of scary creatures and Aramaic curses spelling doom and gloom to anyone who opened it.

I tried to move the stone cover, but the passage of time had fused the heavy lid to the main body of the sarcophagus.

"Should we use grenades?" suggested Juma.

"No!" screamed Nora. "The blast could damage the Book!"

I tended to agree with her. Even though the Book was destined to be destroyed, I needed to see it to make sure it was, in fact, what I'd been searching for.

"Right. Let's bring in the diggers from outside with crowbars. Wait here."

I went outside and grabbed a few villagers. Since Nora was still inside and out of view, I wasn't shy about having Juma's men give them some rough encouragement. They reluctantly went in and started pushing at the cover stone with the crowbars. After a few minutes of grunting and puffing that felt like an eternity, the heavy stone shifted, and the inside of the sarcophagus was now reachable. I sent the diggers back outside and peeked into the stone enclosure.

The only thing inside was a fragile parcel wrapped in a dilapidated cloth. Even without opening it, I knew this was it.

The Book.

I gingerly lifted the parcel and carefully unwrapped the cloth. I could have sworn I heard drumbeats in the distance. As I slowly unwrapped it, an ancient scroll dressed in a richly decorated material emerged. The Aramaic writing on the cover said *The Book of Remedies*, followed by the same curses as were on the sarcophagus.

Surprisingly, the cover was in almost mint condition. I cautiously removed it. The scroll was covered in weird symbols that looked like letters, but none that I recognized.

The script of the First Man.

Success! I had finally done it! Mission accomplished.

An air of excitement filled the room. Nora ran up and kissed me, clapping her hands. Juma's face was lit with exhilaration.

At last, we all calmed down. I put the scroll back into its cover and said "All right, let's take it and get out of here before the village elders call the Taliban."

The mood in the room instantly changed, and Juma's expression got very serious. He pulled his gun and pointed it at me. "Please give me the Book, American." His eyes had narrowed and his whole posture showed he wasn't kidding.

Well, hell.

I could hear Azazel's voice ringing in my ears. *Double-cross him before he double-crosses you.*

Okay, first things first. I needed to defuse the tension before he pulled the trigger. Yes, I was faster, but his men were outside and I needed to soften his vigilance.

I snickered. "So much for the life's debt, eh?"

He didn't even crack a smile. "I paid my debt to you when I saved your sorry ass in that field near Kuza Bandar's village, didn't I? Besides, I am not killing you, I am just asking you nicely."

I sighed. "I hate to disappoint you, my friend, but the only way you will get the Book from me is by killing me. Fair warning—subduing me using your brutes will never work. You will simply lose a lot of your men, and will still have to kill me in the end."

Juma chuckled. "That's a conundrum, my friend, isn't it?"

"It is, indeed."

"But I have a solution," he said.

"I am all ears."

"You are not the only one I owe a debt of gratitude. I also owe her." He pointed to Nora, who stood behind me. "And I'd rather repay her than you. You wouldn't mind, would you?"

I heard the distinct *click* of a nine-millimeter behind my back.

Nora's voice said, "Of course, he wouldn't mind. Would you, my love? Please, hand the Book to Juma."

PART V

REDEMPTION

CHAPTER 1

Mausoleum outside of Lewani, Afghanistan

"What the fuck, Nora?" I turned to her and saw a pistol muzzle trained at me.

The woman before me looked like my Nora, but her eyes were very different. Her glasses were gone, and I could swear that even her eye color had changed to a dark blue, almost indigo.

"Is that my Glock?" I asked in disbelief.

"Yes, I borrowed it this morning. I hope you don't mind." She spoke in a calm, emotionless voice. "Please don't do anything silly, my love. I would hate to damage your perfect body. It has given me so much pleasure. However, I am well aware of that body's capabilities. Please note that both I and Juma are standing outside of its leap zone."

I was dumbfounded.

Wait. What had just happened? And why was she referring to my body in the third person?

One thing was clear, both Juma and Nora were indeed standing at a safe distance to avoid me jumping them and breaking their necks.

Juma took out a walkie-talkie and called his men. They came in, rifles at the ready, taking up careful positions far from me and out of each other's line of fire.

This had definitely been rehearsed.

I tried to regain my composure. "You will still have to subdue me. I am not giving you the Book."

Nora laughed. "You are right, we don't want to kill you, and these monkeys cannot subdue you."

Did she just say *monkeys*?

"I do, however, know someone who can help us resolve this standoff," she said.

Before I could respond, I smelled a familiar whiff of sulfur. The next instant I was on the floor, hogtied and staring at a pair of impeccable dress shoes.

"Hello, monkey. So nice to see you." The owner of the voice raised me from the floor in a split second and set me down on one of the stones surrounding the sarcophagus.

How could I not immediately recognize this well-dressed creature with combed fur, glowing red eyes, and well-groomed horns?

"Ashmodai. How the *fuck*—"

Ashmodai raised his hand. "I know, I know. You have many

questions, but let's start with introductions. You already know Juma, so let me introduce to you my mother, Naama, whom you know as Nora." He laughed heartily.

I was shell-shocked. How could that be? "Are you saying the Moffat ritual—"

"Worked?" Was that the shadow of a grin? "Yes, it worked just as intended to bring her back. The rest of the stuff was just a performance by those dumb Satanists, all staged for you. Anyway, Mom can answer all your questions. I have to go. I need to raise an army, awaken the Demons," he said in a fake spooky voice. "You know, Hell on Earth, and all that stuff. So much to do, so little time." He shivered in excitement. "I will leave you two lovebirds alone. He turned back to me one last time before disappearing in a *poof.* "And treat my Mom with respect, will you?"

The few seconds of silence that followed felt like an eternity.

Then Nora—Naama—came closer and caressed my cheek. I instinctively pulled away from her. Was she kidding?

"Please, my love, don't be shy. I am not here to hurt you. I have to admit, you have been one of the better lovers in my six thousand years on this Earth. On the scale of one to ten, one being child-making with the prude Noah and ten being a drug-fueled idolatrous orgy in the temple of Baal, you occupy a respectable seven."

I looked at her indignantly. "So, this—we—were all a lie?"

"No, no! How can you think that? You have to understand the nature of possession. My possessing Nora doesn't mean she has disappeared completely—it is simply two souls coexisting in one body, one controlling and the other subordinate. I possess her, but I haven't subdued her feelings or desires. I only used my control when I needed to. It was Nora who was attracted to you, and she who gave herself to you so willingly. I just enjoyed the feelings and that tingling sensation between my—our—legs every time we saw you." Her eyes turned dreamy. "As much as I hate to admit it, it was Nora you fell in love with, and it was Nora who reciprocated. She has never been able to understand the nature of her feelings for you, yet those feelings are so strong it took a lot of effort on my part to keep her under control when she was with you. Even now, I can feel how she yearns for you, and how she shares your pain. I would hate to do it, but I may have to excise her when this is all over."

"Don't you dare!" I tried to get up but couldn't.

"Or what?" She lifted a brow. "You will kill me? Unless you are an Angel who can squeeze my soul out of this body, the only way to do that would be to kill both of us." She paused with a finger to her chin. "Besides, why would you need to kill me? You can have your Nora, and I promise I will release my control when you want to make love to her. On the other hand, whenever you want to hurt innocent children or massacre a defenseless village—" She smirked, reminding me of my less-than-gentle treatment of the Lewani inhabitants "—I can take over and relieve you of those pangs of conscience. You get the best of both worlds. Two beautiful women for the price of one!" She reached out and caressed my cheek again.

I flinched.

"You are only alive," she insisted with flashing eyes, "because I have feelings for you. Don't turn away from me so hastily."

I snorted. "Wow. A heartless bitch professing love. That's a new all-time low."

"Please, my love, it is not you talking, it is your anger. You are a kind and gentle soul, despite your murderous tantrums, and saying these awful things doesn't suit you. Why do you think I am a heartless bitch? What do you truly know about me?"

I could feel she wanted to tell her story, to redeem herself in my eyes, just as that chick in Las Vegas had wanted to convince me she was not a whore but a victim of circumstance. The Las Vegas woman was much more believable. Yet, I didn't want to stop Naama. I was too curious about how she and Ashmodai had concocted this whole clusterfuck.

"I was always a sensual creature, a nymphomaniac, if you will," Naama began. "No wonder the Greeks called their female deities after me. Nymph is how they bastardized my name, unable to speak the language of the First Man. All I wanted was to love and be loved, but all my chosen partners were star-crossed. What a cruel irony!" She sighed. "I truly fell in love with Azazel. He was so handsome, so heroic. What a difference from all those lowly earthly beings!"

"Wait," I interrupted. "Aren't the Angels—"

"Dickless?" She laughed.

I winced. "Asexual was the word I was looking for."

She waved her hand. "Whatever. If you are an up-and-coming star among Angels, firmly on your way to becoming an Archangel, growing genitals is the least of your concerns. Azazel had such a brilliant career ahead of him—standing by the Throne of Glory, the only Angel entitled to receive a sacrifice other than the Creator. Remember the two goats in the Book of Leviticus? One goat to Azazel!" She sounded genuinely proud.

This time I rolled my eyes.

Thankfully Naama didn't notice as she dreamily reminisced. "But Azazel was an adventurer, keen on exploring the temptations of the flesh. We fell in love at first sight. I was so young then. Unfortunately, our affair didn't sit well with the Heavenly Offices. He lost his career, allowing the pedantic Samael to hopscotch him, and they took away my baby, Ashmodai, before I was able to see him, turning him into a hideous Demon first. I was inconsolable for eons. You say I'm a heartless bitch, but how could I feel anything ever again, after what was done to me? On top that, I was forced to marry Noah, a killjoy who could think of nothing other than building his precious ark. I still don't understand how he made all his sons with me!"

"So you did have kids with him, didn't you?"

"What would you want me to do, stay childless for all eternity? I sincerely loved all three. Not as much as my first-born, Ashmodai, but I did love them. That is why I prevailed upon Azazel to give Shem the Book. It was such a scary time. There were only eight of us humans and a bunch of animals on the whole Earth. Noah did the only thing he could do—became an alcoholic. I couldn't snap him out of it. My kids were pissed at their constantly drunk father, until one day Ham finally had it and did a number on him. Didn't go well for Ham, but I appreciated him standing up for the family. No, the Book was the only thing that could save us back then, and Azazel understood my worries."

"So, did the Book help?"

"Oh, yes. Noah quit drinking, my sons procreated at an amazing speed, and the expansion of humanity surpassed all expectations. We multiplied and were fruitful, and the seven billion people living today is testament to my foresight."

Her pathos sounded a bit phony, but she was clearly convinced that without her there would be no human beings alive today. Some Mother of Humanity!

I couldn't help but drawl, "So, without you, the Earth would now be desolate and lifeless, eh? The Creator couldn't have done it without your assistance, I suppose."

She ignored my sarcasm. "I don't presume to understand the ways of the Creator. I am sure He would have done everything right, but ultimately I did what I did, and the results were good. Why would He blame me for anything?"

"Remind me… What was your reward for being such a dedicated mother to all of us? Shouldn't you now be spending eternity in the Heavens, basking in the glory of the Creator?"

She smiled bitterly. "Maybe. But I was not prepared to give up my material existence and the pleasures that went with it.

And Azazel wasn't ready to give up our relationship. He kept me with him in the Netherworld, constantly looking for new beautiful bodies. I was jealous at first, always waiting for him, always suspecting he was attracted to the fresh human flesh more than to my soul. But eventually I came to terms with my fate."

I felt a spike of anger. "So, Nora was just another in a long line of bodies you used."

"No, this time it was different. After Azazel lost his promotion, he became bitter and blamed me for getting him in trouble. He was afraid if he continued our affair, he would end up another Fallen Angel, demoted to some shitty job like Uzza. Our relationship cooled, and I had to satisfy myself with the occasional sexual trysts of the bodies I inhabited. In the end, he betrayed me."

"How so?"

"Oh, one day, he offered me the body of Marie-Antoinette, queen of France. I was flattered and thought our relationship was finally rekindling. At first I enjoyed her lavish lifestyle, her many bisexual liaisons, and the life of luxury, waiting for Azazel to come to me. The bastard never warned me the French Revolution was coming—which he knew—and that my body would be beheaded. At the very last moment, as the guillotine separated her head and I was sinking into Oblivion, he snatched me and put me permanently into the Netherworld, saying I would never see him again." She closed her eyes. "You know how terrible it was to be imprisoned in the Netherworld?

Neither dead nor alive, my memories the only things left for me to experience. Oh, how I hated him, hated the humans, the Heavenly Offices, and the entire Creation! Until my Ashmodai was able to free me and give me Nora in Moffat."

Something didn't compute.

I narrowed my eyes and creased my brows. "Um, I am a bit hazy with world history, but didn't the French Revolution happen a few hundred years ago? What took your precious son so long to rescue you?"

She laughed. "Oh, please. Angels and Demons are all selfish creatures who don't care about anybody unless doing so suits their goals. Do you think I have any doubts about Ashmodai's true feelings? He found me when he needed me. It was a pact of convenience, not an expression of filial love. Beelzebub, who was dealing with the Satanists and occultists, found out about the Book of Remedies excerpt from that half-brained junkie, Anton Long. Ashmodai saw his opportunity and dragged me out of the Netherworld. I saw my opportunity, too, and negotiated for the best body I could get. It took me forever to find what I wanted—a woman who looked like me." She glanced at me meaningfully. "Now do you understand why I think we could be lovers?"

The sound of approaching footsteps interrupted her confession. Ashmodai walked in, accompanied by the Beelzebub.

Seeing me, Beelzebub grinned. "Oh, it's my favorite monkey! Care for a game of Texas hold'em? Oh, wait. It's hard to play with your hands tied." He was clearly enjoying my predicament and feeling avenged for me threatening him at Long's office.

"Stop it," barked Ashmodai.

Beelzebub obsequiously bowed to his boss.

"Take him to the car. We are leaving," Ashmodai ordered. "And, no," he added, answering Beelzebub's silent question, "I don't want you to use the maintenance tunnels. I don't want even a whisper of our undertaking getting to the Heavenly Offices."

Beelzebub nodded, grabbed me, and took me to one of Juma's SUVs waiting outside. As he dragged me past the dig site, I saw all the villagers lying dead and Juma's henchmen walking around finishing off the wounded. Right. Not a whisper.

"Well played, my friend," I quipped sarcastically, passing Juma.

"Hey, American, don't be so narrow-minded. What could I do when one of your furry friends—" He pointed to Beelzebub "—showed up at my door and told me to expect a dumbass American with a bullshit story about working with a dead mafia boss and an outlandish request to help him find some ancient book?"

Another unfortunate mistake. When Azazel issued a maintenance ticket for a phone call to Juma from Kamchi Kolbayev, he inadvertently gave Ashmodai the ability to contact Juma directly. One would think that Angels capable of time travel could avoid such an obvious screwup! Apparently, lack of foresight was something the Creator had built into the

Creation to ensure we didn't get too comfy…

Seeing my hesitation, Juma added, "Don't take it the wrong way, my friend. I truly like you, and when you saved my life, we became even closer. But hey, these are Demons we are talking about. No hard feelings, eh?"

"None whatsoever."

Ignoring my sarcasm, Juma gave me a thumbs up and continued his gruesome task of supervising the slaughter of innocent villagers.

Naama, who followed us to the car, wrinkled her nose at the sight of the dead bodies and turned to Juma. "Couldn't you have waited until we left? The sight and the smell is unseemly."

Juma threw up his hands, nodding toward Ashmodai.

Naama waved him off. "Bloodthirsty bastards," she said under her breath.

Beelzebub packed me into the SUV, climbed in next to me, and put a cloth bag over my head. I heard the engines start and the convoy move out, but I couldn't figure out in which direction or the purpose of the journey. I stopped trying after a while. Why would it matter where or why Ashmodai did what he was about to do?

Which, by the way, was a good question.

What, exactly, *did* he want to do with me and the Book?

CHAPTER 2

Somewhere in the Hindukush

The drive was long, and at some point I fell asleep and lost track of time. I had no idea how much time had passed when they woke me up and dragged me outside. When they removed the bag from my head, my eyes were blinded by the high noon sun. Nearby, a small village of mudbrick huts nested in the cliffs covered by meager vegetation. We could have been in the Kunar Valley or in the Tribal Area—the landscape didn't tell me much. It was somewhere in the Hindukush, between Afghanistan, Pakistan, and India. But where? I didn't really care.

Beelzebub dragged me to a place that would become my prison, accompanied by Ashmodai and Naama. For some reason, she wouldn't leave me alone. Maybe it was true that she cared about me and I was still alive only thanks to her. But even the thought of her protecting my life didn't elicit any sense of gratitude. She had possessed my Nora, pretty much killing her inside the body that I treasured so much.

We walked into a hut, and Beelzebub threw me into a wooden cage and put a metal ring around my neck. The ring was attached to the wall of the hut by a thick metal chain. He growled happily as he checked my restraints. Not fully trusting him, Ashmodai came and yanked the chain to make sure it held me properly. I winced in pain.

"Hey, easy!" shouted Naama. "He is mine, and I don't want him damaged."

Ashmodai bowed in fake subservience. "Whatever you wish, Mother, As your obedient son, I will make sure all your wishes are fulfilled."

She twisted her lips. She wanted to stay something, but Ashmodai showed her to the exit.

"Come on, Mother, let's go. I assure you I will watch over your precious new toy. For now, however, let's leave him alone and give him a chance to get used to his new accommodations. You will have plenty of time to spend with him, I promise."

Naama reluctantly walked out, and Ashmodai followed.

I wanted to ask one more question that was bothering me. "Hey, Ashmodai!"

He turned to me. "What?"

"Why do you need the Book? Was it really worth all this bruhaha to you?"

He stared at me. "Of course, it was. Do you think it is only human maladies that the Book can heal? The remedies contained in it should free us from the threat of excision every time humans worship us. Being safe from excision, I can finally assume rulership of the world."

"So, you decided to use the Book to ensure you and your buddies against the excision and safely rebel against the order established by the Heavenly Offices?"

"If you want to call it a rebellion, be my guest. I was thinking more along the lines of an orderly transition from one set of rules to another."

"Oh, right," I said mockingly. "Hell on Earth. What else would you aspire to?"

Ashmodai became incensed. "What's wrong with that? It is Earth on Earth that you should be concerned about. All this murder, war, pollution, sexual deviancy, and whatnot. Is there any mortal sin that your fellow humans are incapable of? No, my friend, Hell on Earth means a much greater degree of morality than what you have here now."

"And the Creator would undoubtedly allow this so-called transition of yours, yes?" I knew I'd hit Ashmodai's soft spot. He could deal with humans, maybe even with Angels, given the size of his army and the element of surprise, but the Creator could stop his rebellion with the blink of an eye.

"Let me worry about the Creator, monkey. So far, he hasn't stopped us, has he?" Ashmodai was probably trying to convince himself, as any mention of the Creator clearly scared him, and he wanted to wave off his fears.

I shrugged. "Well, you are the hotshot Demon. I'm sure you

know what you are doing." Sarcasm oozed from my words.

"You bet, I am," he bellowed angrily. "Besides, it is not your concern. Be thankful to my mother you are still alive." He turned to make sure Naama was not still in the hut. "But once she is tired of you, I will happily send you to Oblivion!" He laughed menacingly and walked away, leaving me with my thoughts.

Ashmodai was true to his word to his mother. I was left alone in my restraints, except for the times when Juma's men brought me food. I needed time to calm down and think, but my thoughts were confused and I couldn't come up with a decent plan, for escape or anything else.

Time stood still in my prison, the only sense of its passage was from the food deliveries. Once when the door opened, instead of my usual human handlers, a furry paw stuck my bowl into the cage.

I raised my eyes. "Abaddon, my friend. So nice of you to drop by without even a maintenance ticket. Are you here to smother me while no one is watching?"

Abaddon looked sheepish. "Hey, don't blame me for everything. I don't need this stuff. I was happy doing my job at Maintenance. It's Ashmodai and Beelzebub who love human worship and can't be satisfied with their lot." He sighed. "I am telling you, man, this rebellion is bad news." He was so distraught that he had called me man instead of monkey. "Ashmodai must be dreaming. Either the Angels will decimate us or the Creator will send us all to Oblivion."

"Then, why are you doing it ? Just go ahead and report the whole thing to Samael, and he will deal with these clowns before they create even a bigger mess."

Abaddon shrugged his shoulders. "I wish it was that easy. Even if Samael quashes the rebellion, there is no guarantee that Ashmodai won't negotiate a deal for himself and I will be branded a snitch and used as a scapegoat. No, I will play along, hoping things will work out."

"Suit yourself, but as you said, it is simple Demons like you who always get the short end of the stick."

Abaddon sniffled sadly with a nod.

I decided to probe further, to get more information, if nothing else. "Can you at least tell me why they needed this whole charade with Nora, and why they needed me?"

"Simple. Demons are not allowed to operate freely on the human plane of existence, so we needed a human to run point. The best choice would be someone from the Pilot Program who had the support of the Heavenly Offices and could still operate among the humans. By creating the ritual at Moffat, Ashmodai made sure Azazel would find out about someone looking for the Book, and he would send you, his best guy, to investigate. You picked up the scent like a bloodhound and doggedly stuck to the pursuit. The final problem was your Reincarnation Rights. If you got a whiff of Ashmodai's plot, you could have killed yourself and reported the whole affair back to Azazel. But then, Naama came up with the plan."

"What plan?"

"The best, most elaborate plan. You've got to give to her. After six thousand years of fornication, no one knows men better than she does. That was why she insisted on accompanying you to the meeting with the Yousufzai. Predictably, Kuza Bandar wanted to have Nora, who purposefully dressed provocatively. Juma conveniently suggested to Kuza he should acquire a doctor. Done deal. We were watching the live feed in Ashmodai's office, and everything was perfectly choreographed. It was like you were all following a script. I bet she loosened her control and allowed Nora's soul to take over the body after you betrayed her, because everything had to look absolutely natural. No wonder you fell into Naama's trap and relinquished your Reincarnation Rights. After that, everything went on autopilot. Azazel canceled the recording of your missions and practically wrote you off. From that point on, there was no one watching."

My mouth dropped open in surprise.

He looked at me with sympathy. "I kind of hoped you would figure things out and report to Azazel. Would have made everyone's life much easier."

I felt sorry for Abaddon in return. He truly hated this rebellion, but his paws were tied.

"Hey, don't sweat it," I said. "Maybe things will work out and the Creator will make things right."

He shook his head and walked away. "From your lips…"

"By the way," I said as he was walking out. "Thank you for

that bottle of whiskey in the tent at the Hindukush crossing. Came in handy."

He gave me a thumbs-up without turning, and closed the door behind him.

As the days passed, Naama came by a couple of times trying to recruit me to their cause. I kept my mouth shut and she took my silence for thinking over her proposal.

"Look, let me be frank with you," she said. "You know by now that Ashmodai doesn't need you anymore, and if it were up to him you would be dead, especially now you've lost your Reincarnation Rights. The only thing keeping you alive right now is me, my love, and only because I have genuine feelings for you. I want to have you by my side, to enjoy your touch and your chivalry. You can call me Nora if you want. I am okay with that."

She was actually pleading. She must have been very lonely during all those years in the Netherworld, and desperate to feel alive again. Or…maybe my déjà vu feelings at Moffat were not for nothing. Was it possible it was not Nora but Naama who was somehow connected to me?

As I contemplated this intriguing possibility, her voice brought me back to reality.

"But even I have my limits. If you don't join the cause, I will have to look for someone else. If there is one thing I've learned in the past six thousand years, it is that no one is irreplaceable. Let me leave you with that thought. I truly hope you will say yes." She turned to the door to leave.

Frankly, I was tired of this full-court press. First Abaddon bitching about this rebellion, and now she was trying to enlist me into her love life. Enough was enough.

"You know what, Naama? Leave me alone. You played with my feelings, hoodwinked me into saving you when you didn't need to be saved, and for what? To build the world's most sophisticated mouse trap. Ashmodai should have just found the records of the Book in the Records Room. I am sure he had something to do with their disappearance."

Naama looked at me quizzically, then laughed. "Oh, you have not figured it out, yet, have you? I thought you would be smarter. That's the fun part. Knowing I would try to find it, Azazel expunged all records of the Book. We needed a monkey with free will and determination to find the real thing. Nora was just an added incentive. I have to tell you, my love, you performed beyond all our expectations." She gave me an air kiss and walked out the door.

Her condescending tone and calling me a monkey left me even more convinced that I was no more than a toy to her, albeit a favorite one for the time being.

CHAPTER 3

Prison House in the Hindukush Village

The realization that I had to fend for myself amidst a Demon plot that threatened the very existence of humanity gave me added strength.

Whatever the Creator may do was not for me to ponder. However, I had been inducted into the Pilot Program to prevent exactly this kind of occurrence, and I would for damn sure see my mission through to the end.

Not to mention that I still hoped to negotiate a second life before going to the Heavens. Now my mission had transformed into stopping the Demon rebellion. My bargaining position had just improved substantially, if I could do something to foil this rebellion.

But to do that I needed to free myself.

I examined the thick metal chain and my restraints. The chain was super strong...but the mudbrick wall was not. Neither was the door to the wooden cage where they kept me imprisoned. Pulling the chain from the wall and knocking out the door was doable. Removing the ropes that tied my hands and feet wouldn't be easy without a knife, but next time a human guard walked in with food and his weapons, I could try to overpower him and cut off the restraints.

How to overpower a human with my hands and feet tied didn't worry me, nor did I think about the steps after that. First things first.

Laser-focused on escaping, I hoped my next visitor would be a human and not a Demon.

Though the Demons didn't visit me, and Ashmodai didn't deign me with his presence, another unexpected guest did pop by. Uzza, Fallen Angel, Movie Room supervisor, and sadist par excellence.

Just what I needed.

Laughing happily, he poked me a couple of times with his finger. "Hey, monkey, how does it feel to be hogtied and powerless? Let me give you a taste of the torture you will enjoy in the Movie Room!"

He dragged me out of the cage and started torturing me, twisting and stretching every bone in my body. His sadistic tricks were so painful I screamed.

Naama heard the screams and ran in. "Uzza? What the hell are you doing? Leave him alone!"

Uzza bellowed, "Don't tell me what to do, bitch. You are just as much of a monkey as he is. You are not to talk to an Angel in this manner!"

Naama clenched her fists. She knew his ilk too well to be afraid of a Fallen Angel, but she also knew she was no match for an Angel, no matter how fallen.

Disturbed by the commotion, Ashmodai arrived quietly and put his hand on Uzza's shoulder. "No need to get so angry, my friend. You need this rebellion as much as I do, so you can change your Fallen Angel status and end your demotion. We are allies and it is not in your interest to piss me off, but when you talk like this to my mom, I get really upset." Ashmodai's eyes flashed.

Uzza had no reason to be afraid of Ashmodai, but, as Naama told me, Ashmodai was gathering an army of Demons for a final standoff and the army of Demons was too much even for an Angel. Besides, he did need Ashmodai and his army.

He growled and let me go. "All right, fine. Enjoy life while you can, monkey. I will get to you later." He threw me back into the cage and angrily walked away.

Naama came up to the cage and looked at me in concern. For a moment, her eyes looked like Nora's when she was being a doctor, nursing my wounds. "Are you hurt?"

I looked closer, but Nora's eyes were gone. This was still Naama, scheming and conniving, trying to get everything she wanted at any cost.

I mimicked her tone. "Not as much as I was by your betrayal, my love."

She was not in the mood to fight. She probably still hoped I would see the light. Or maybe Nora's soul was fighting her inside the body, so every time she was close to me, Naama had difficulty controlling Nora's overwhelming feelings for me.

She stepped away from the cage and looked at Ashmodai. "Why did you bring that moron, Uzza?"

"He may be a moron but he is still an Angel, and I need all the help I can get in case we have to fight the Angelic army." They walked out arguing, and I was left with a few painful bruises, a sense of even more urgency to do something, and, thanks to Uzza, looser restraints. From which, to my satisfaction, I could now wiggle free.

I gritted my teeth, summoned all my strength, and pulled back on my left thumb with a *snap* that broke the CMC joint. Sharp pain shot through my hand and up my arm, but I managed not to scream. With my thumb now tucked inside my palm, I could work my left arm out past the knot that had been loosened by Uzza's stretching and twisting my body. The bracket holding the chain to the wall was next, and the flimsy cage door soon followed.

I was now ready for someone to walk in, praying it would be a human.

My prayers were answered. Two of Juma's henchmen walked in. One was supposed to hand me a bowl while the other stood at the doorway and aimed his rifle at me. That was the theory. In practice, however, they both knew me and allowed themselves to be sloppy, not appreciating the danger. Their AK-47s hung on their shoulders and they both came close to the cage.

As one of them approached with the food, I kicked the door into his unsuspected face and with a burst of energy, leaped up and grabbed onto the upper bar of the cage, using it as a swing to jump on the guard lying under the cage door, trampling him into unconsciousness. Then, using the cage door as a trampoline, I propelled myself toward the second guard, twisting his neck in a quick motion. Once he was dead, I carefully lowered him to the floor.

Other than the *thud* of the first body and the rumbling of the chain still attached to my neck, everything was quiet.

I finished taking off the restraints using the guard's knife, dragged one of them into a dark corner of the room away from the light, and put the other man into the cage, turning him to the wall and covering his body with rags. Even if someone walked in, it would look like I was sleeping in the cage. Unfortunately, the chain was still attached to my neck, and a search of the bodies produced no key. Well, the chain would have to wait.

I put on the guard's tunic and the Kevlar vest he was wearing over the tunic, loaded spare AK magazines into its pockets, and carefully tucked the telltale chain into the vest. A large Afghan hat kept my face hidden.

To my surprise, there were no other guards at the entrance of the prison house, and no Demons were anywhere to be seen. The village looked peaceful and quiet, just another morning with people going about their business.

Ashmodai's human helpers were indeed sloppy and lax.

A few men were playing soccer close by, their rifles leaning comfortably against the wall of a hut. Seeing me, they asked where my companion was and invited me to join the game. I waved in the direction of the prison house and gave a thumbs up to a man who just scored a goal. I slowly walked past them, heading for the mountainous terrain surrounding the village. No one bothered to check where I was going.

CHAPTER 4

Cliffs Outside of the Village

Once I got up behind the rocks and out of sight, I sat down to catch my breath and started thinking about my next steps. I couldn't possibly take on the army of Demons alone and I had no way to contact the Heavenly Offices. After they were off the mission, Azazel and his subordinates no longer received footage of my progress. Issuing a maintenance ticket to Demons would be, well, counterproductive, even if it was Abaddon who received it. I could try and alert humans in other villages or towns nearby, but they would be no match for Demons—if they even believed me. Most likely, I would quickly end up in the nearest insane asylum in a straightjacket, while Ashmodai took over the world.

No, none of that would work.

I was running out of ideas when I heard some goats bleating nearby. A couple of boys were taking the village herd up to the pasture among the rocks. As I watched them pass by, it hit me like a lightning strike. Naama's words rang in my ears. "The only Angel entitled to receive a sacrifice other than the Creator."

Of course! A goat sacrifice to Azazel!

Unfortunately, my knowledge of the Scriptures was skimpy at best, but it was worth a try.

I couldn't remember when the sacrifice was supposed to be done or what kind of goat should be sent to Azazel, but I was out of options and had to try something.

I snuck behind the shepherd boys and knocked them unconscious. Quickly inspecting the herd, I chose the largest, meanest, and blackest goat among them. The bigger the better, I figured. I pulled the chain still tucked under my Kevlar and lassoed it around the goat's neck. It bleated incessantly and tried to wiggle its way out, but I forcefully yanked the chain and he dropped to the ground. Pinning his head to the dirt with my knee, I inscribed "Azazel" on the goat's forehead in Aramaic script using my knife.

Why Aramaic? Why not? I had no idea how the goat should be identified.

Once the writing was done, I started pulling him toward the nearby cliff. The loud bleating and the screams of the shepherd boys who had regained consciousness attracted the attention of the soccer players down in the village. They saw me pulling the goat up the cliff and the boys running after me. The scene must have appeared comical and they shouted at us, some rooting for me and some for the boys. I wouldn't be surprised if they actually placed bets on who would reach the top of the cliff first.

The noise, however, also attracted Ashmodai and his Demons. Unlike humans, he quickly understood what was going on. He barked orders, and the men who had just been enjoying the silly race grabbed their guns and chased after me.

"Oh, someone must have remembered the Book of Leviticus," shouted Ashmodai. "Goat to Azazel, eh? Good move, monkey!" Notwithstanding his lighthearted tone, I could see he was not amused.

My human pursuers were too far behind, so he called on Beelzebub, who scaled the entire cliff in a couple of giant leaps. I was halfway to the top when I saw his furry face grinning in front of me.

"Come to Papa, monkey!"

"Fuck you, Beelzebub, you fucking loser!"

My choices were limited. Beelzebub blocked the way to the top, and the men approaching from behind were within shooting distance of me and the goat. They started shooting. The goat was more important, so I covered him with my body.

There was no time to think. I jumped off the cliff, and the weight of my body combined with the weight of the chain dragged the goat down along with me. Both of us fell, bouncing off the rocks and plummeting toward certain death.

Just as I closed my eyes, imagining myself back in the Movie Room with a sure ticket to Oblivion, I heard the *whoosh* of wings. Something—or someone—grabbed me and flew me over to the next cliff.

I opened my eyes. Azazel was standing in front of me, except he was no longer wearing his usual impeccable suit. Dressed in Angelic armor—which didn't look to me like Medieval armor but more like *Star Wars* imperial trooper armor—with his wings spread above me, he looked damn impressive. I understood why Naama was so in love with him.

In a single move, Azazel released the chain from my neck and pushed the dead goat aside. "I have to give it to you monkeys. When things get hot, your resourcefulness is next to none. A report of some moron trying to perform a sacrifice to me for the first time in three thousand years naturally piqued my curiosity." He winked. " Well, let's see. What do we have here?"

"Not much," I said in a ragged voice. "Just a Demon rebellion and Ashmodai trying to take over the world."

"That's it?" Azazel scoffed. "And you bothered me because of such a trifle?"

We both laughed. It was a much-needed comic relief to all the tension. However, the laughter didn't last long.

Ashmodai appeared on top of the cliff from which I had just jumped. "Hello, Father. Doing the bidding of monkeys these days, eh? Are things that bad for you in the Department?"

"Nah, things were just dandy until you decided to stick your horns in where they didn't belong." Azazel's tone turned serious. "What is wrong with you, Ashmodai? I got you everything you could ever dream of and the cushiest job for a Demon."

"Not enough, Father. I want to have what you have and

more. Why don't you help me? We are kin, after all!"

"Stop calling me father, you half-breed! Just because I spawned you doesn't entitle you to claim a special relationship with an Angel."

"I am so hurt. An Angel disclaiming his paternity." Ashmodai laughed. "Why am I not surprised? You conceited creatures have no sense of family or kinship. Although, speaking of surprises, I have someone here I'm sure you would love to see."

"Hello, my love."

Naama-Nora's voice jolted Azazel and me like an electric shock, and we both flinched.

She was dressed in a light blue *bedlah*, with a fitted bra and hip belt adorned with gold mesh. A gold chain headband with a transparent blue veil covered the lower half of her face, highlighting her wavy, free-flowing hair and piercing blue eyes. I assumed they were the festive clothes worn by pre-Diluvian women, but to me, she looked like a provocative belly dancer. I couldn't drag my gaze from her. She had deliberately exposed every part of the body that had given me so much pleasure. I was pretty sure Azazel was feeling the same way. His eyes had gone as wide as mine.

"Or should I say my loves," Naama-Nora teased.

Azazel recovered first. "Kudos, Ashmodai. You brought a belly dancer to entertain us. I think, however, you would have been better off bringing an army to defend yourself."

"Come on, Azi," cooed Naama, using the nickname she must have used when they were together. "Don't pretend seeing me doesn't bring back memories."

"Oh, yeah. Memories of pain and betrayal. How many more creatures, Angels and monkeys alike, have you screwed over in the past six thousand years? Just because I was an idiot once doesn't mean I am still as stupid as when I first met you."

Naama slowly walked up the cliff, closer to us. "You are being unfair, Azi. You were my first and you know it. Everything I knew of the art of seduction I learned from you. You, who shamelessly took advantage of an innocent girl swept off her feet by a beautiful Angel." Her voice rang louder and louder, filled with genuine anger. "I bore your child, my firstborn, and my favorite child because he reminded me of you. But even that was taken from me."

She clenched her fists. "He should have looked exactly like you and me—beautiful and angelic—and you allowed those turds in Rafael's department to turn him into a Demon, without as much as saying a word? And what about the lovely guillotine for Marie Antoinette you arranged just to be rid of me? So, who is the real traitor, eh?"

"I didn't know anything about the guillotine. I simply wanted to give you the best body available and let you enjoy the life of sin and luxury you are so fond of. And didn't I snatch you from Oblivion?"

She kept walking. "Right, a powerful Angel didn't know about a revolution that was coming soon. And thank you very much for kidnapping me and imprisoning me in the Netherworld for all eternity. Such chivalry!"

She reached us and stood in front of Azazel. Looking into his eyes, she stroked his cheek and lowered her voice. "You haven't aged a bit, my love. Just as beautiful as when I saw you the first time. This armor looks much better on you than that bureaucratic suit of yours. My loins are still shaking in response, even after all these years."

Azazel pushed her hand from his face. "Just go away. We are through, and you know it, Naama. I will not make the same mistake again."

"So it was to you who made a mistake? Why don't you just use your Angelic powers and send me straight to Oblivion? Or do you need a guillotine to do your dirty work?" She was burning with passion, anger, hatred, and love, all in one seething ball of emotion that would drive anyone mad. No doubt, she was winning this repartee.

Azazel slowly backed off and lowered his head. "What do you want from me? An apology? You have it. Didn't I pay you back with interest? You got the Book, and the body of every good-looking monkey you ever wanted. How long do you want me to pay for our first encounter, Naama?"

"I don't need you to pay. I just want you to love me as you did before. Look at this body." She forcefully raised his chin. "I chose it for one reason only—because it looks like the innocent girl you took on our first night."

"And I still love you, damn it! As you well know," Azazel screamed painfully. "What else can I do for you? Become a

Fallen Angel, be excised by the Creator? What else, Naama, what else do you require of me?"

"Nothing of the sort. All I want is to be with you, to cuddle in your arms, and feel you inside my body. Let's disappear, my love, just you and me, to somewhere in a distant corner of Creation. Let's plead with the Creator to let us have our love forever!"

She pressed her body against his and kissed him passionately.

Frankly, I felt sorry for Azazel. An asexual, self-righteous Angel decided one time to have a bit of fun and got caught up in this monkey—no pun intended—business forever. I couldn't predict what would happen next, but I desperately wanted to be in his place caressing my Nora.

Azazel finally broke the kiss. "Then what will to happen with this body? It is not yours to keep. Shouldn't you return it to its rightful owner?"

"Then get me another one!" Naama cried.

"How? By taking it from another woman?"

"Ask Rafael to make me a new one."

"You know neither Rafael nor I can get you a new body without the Creator's sanction. Why would he give you another life after everything you have done? And even if he does, I am eternal and you are mortal. How many more bodies will you need to live with me forever? No, I may have done stupid things in the past, but I am still an Angel and must follow the rules of the Creation. There is no shortcut to life and death, and you have already taken more than your fair share of lives. Believe me, I wish I could spend eternity with you, but that is not what the rules permit."

"Oh, screw your damn rules! Did you think about the rules when you grew a male member and came on to me?" Naama sounded bitter, but she shed no tears, just like Nora when I betrayed and sold her to Kuza Bandar.

Azazel didn't answer. Instead, he gently squeezed her neck. His eyes were misty. "You are right, my love. That was wrong, too, and it is time to put everything back in order."

Alarm shot through me. Did he mean to kill her? And Nora along with her?

Naama was choking. Tears finally flowed down her cheeks as her life was leaving Nora's body. She must have understood that this was the end, and deep down in her soul she probably didn't mind. Six thousand years of struggle and disappointment must have made her tired of life.

"At least tell me you still love me," she said in a weak voice.

"Stop!" I yelled at Azazel.

But he kept choking her until she stopped breathing. She looked as if she had fallen asleep, beautiful, peaceful, and innocent. "Sleep, my love," he whispered. He kissed her forehead and turned away from me so as not to show his weakness. "I will remember you always."

I was shell-shocked. "Hey, what the hell! You killed Nora!" I grabbed his hand. "Bring her back, you callous bastard!"

Azazel threw off my hand. "Don't worry about your woman. I simply squeezed Naama's soul out of her body. I put Nora's soul into the Netherworld for the time being. When this is all over, I will ask Rafael to put her back together in one piece. One lost love was more than enough for one day."

I wasn't sure I believed him, but I was hopeful and held my tongue.

Azazel's eyes were puffy when he stood up with his fists clenched. He yelled so loud the mountains shook. "Damn you, Ashmodai! Damn you forever! Don't ever claim to be my son again, because you are the Devil's spawn and not worthy of existence. Come face me. I will tear your horns from your head, you filthy half-breed!"

Ashmodai didn't respond.

Suddenly, I heard the loud fluttering of wings and the thundering sound of explosions. Uzza flew straight to us, looking like a fighter jet blasting a full payload of Hellfire missiles. Ashmodai was right to keep an Angel next to him.

Azazel shouted a battle cry and flew toward Uzza. The two Angels started to fight, and everyone stood still, afraid to interfere. The fighting was fierce and brutal. I sure as hell didn't want to be anywhere near them, nor did anyone else. Angels in full armor duking it out was an awesome sight, but best observed from a safe distance.

In a few moments that fell like an eternity, Azazel got the upper hand. Uzza fell from the sky in a fiery ball with a loud *bang* and dissipated into the air. Azazel came down, breathing hard and bleeding profusely.

The Demons let out a hateful cry and started climbing up

the cliff. Ashmodai stood behind, apparently not daring to face his enraged father. I looked down the cliff. Demons were everywhere, as far as I could see. Even an Angel, especially wounded, could never take on them all and live.

"I'm not telling you what to do, Azazel, but if I were you, I would have called on Gabriel and his cavalry."

"Are you kidding me?" Azazel was still trying to catch his breath. "You think six thousand years of transgressions will just evaporate into thin air like Uzza did? They will crucify me for everything I have done. No, this is something I have to deal with myself."

I sighed. "If there's anything I can do..."

He turned to me. "You did well, kid, but this is not your fight." For the first time, he hadn't called me a monkey.

"Thanks. But—"

He gently touched my shoulder and I felt shivers going down my spine. "Your Reincarnation Rights have been restored. My report to Samael had only praises for your stellar performance. Go in peace, Son of Man."

Then he grabbed me and threw me off the cliff.

CHAPTER 5

The Heavenly Offices
Department of Defense

I looked around as I regained consciousness. The reception area in front of Azazel's office looked exactly as it always did, with his secretary busily typing as she responded to a call. "No, the Boss is not here, but he is expected shortly. Yes, I will leave him a message to call you when he gets back."

Once the pain from reincarnation subsided, it was time to assess the situation.

On one hand, I was safe in the Heavenly Offices with my Reincarnation Rights restored, and protected by a good report to Samael. In other words, I had nothing to worry about.

On the other hand, there was a Demon rebellion happening on Earth, and Azazel's chances of stopping it were slim to none. There was the Creator, of course, who could take care of anything in a split second, but I had no way of knowing what he had planned for us. After all, he'd allowed Ashmodai's plot to work so far. Maybe he had decided it was time to punish humanity for all its sins. Or maybe he wanted us humans to exercise our free will to get out of this bind.

If the former, nothing would save us. But if the latter, I was one of those humans with free will who could, and *should*, do something.

I ran out of Azazel's office and went straight to the Heavenly Department of Defense.

A couple of Angels in uniform stopped me at the entrance. "What are you doing here, monkey? This area is off limits for souls."

"I need to see Gabriel. I am with the Pilot Program," I said matter-of-factly and pushed their hands away.

The Angels' eyes went wide. "You must be joking. Maybe we should call the Creator, as well?"

"Look, you can laugh all you want, but there is a full-scale Demon rebellion down on Earth, and if you don't bring me to Gabriel immediately, you will have to explain to him why you didn't notify him in time when you had the chance. Want to be dishonorably discharged and take on the status of Fallen Angels manning some godforsaken Records Room?"

The Angels hesitated. They didn't want to risk being reprimanded by the Boss, and my reference to the Pilot Program must have added to my bona fides. They reluctantly called Gabriel's aide-de-camp, who was just as shocked by my demands as they were, but thankfully, like them, he decided to bring me to Gabriel to cover his ass.

The officer led me into Gabriel's office. In my mind's eye, Gabriel looked like a four-star general in a crisp uniform and the bearing of a soldier towering above his desk. Before the aide had a chance to extend his apologies and explain my highly irregular visit, I pushed him aside and barged in. Gabriel was taken by surprise.

Figuring I had no more than a minute before I would be thrown out, I swiftly unloaded the whole story. My speech was incoherent, but Gabriel understood and immediately ordered a meeting in the command center.

No one paid me any attention, so I silently followed Gabriel and his aide-de-camp, who didn't have the guts to ask his boss whether I should be allowed into the command center.

The room looked just like any other command center depicted in the movies—a dark room with huge monitors covering entire walls and rows of computer operators in front of their keyboards talking into headsets in hushed tones. As Gabriel walked in, the Angel Guard at the doors snapped to attention. The sudden appearance of the Heavenly Armed Forces' commander-in-chief was not a usual occurrence, and all heads turned to him, then quickly turned back to their computers before he noticed them losing focus on whatever they were doing.

Gabriel gave an order, and one of the wall monitors instantly displayed the village where I had been a prisoner just a few moments ago. Ashmodai shouting orders appeared in a close-up on another screen, and yet another showed the assembling Demon army. They were no longer wearing greasy overalls, but instead, combat gear with tactical helmets and goggles that concealed their horns and red eyes. Yet another video feed showed Azazel standing his ground, repelling the initial attack by the Demons. He was pretty beaten up and looked like he was at the end of his rope.

Gabriel grunted in disgust at the unseemly scene and barked, "Implement DEFCON 3 and summon the Archangels!" He continued shouting orders for various Angelic combat groups to move in, organizing a counterattack.

A few moments later, Michael, Samael, Rafael, and Uriel strode in. The Angels on duty jumped to attention again, welcoming the heads of the Heavenly Departments. A hushed murmur went through the room.

Wow! I could never in my existence have expected to see the entire Heavenly Cabinet in one place, and I would bet that none of the Angels present at the command center had ever seen anything like this in the past six thousand years, either.

The Archangels watched the video feed, shell-shocked.

Samael recovered first. "What in blazes is going on?"

"Apparently, the Demons and their boss have decided to rebel," said Gabriel matter-of-factly. "I understand Ashmodai has obtained the Book of Remedies and is now trying to end the Demon excision protocol, thereby gaining total control over humans. His assault force is being assembled as we speak."

"How in the name of the Creation did that happen?" asked

Michael incredulously and turned to Samael. "You are in charge of the Maintenance Department and it is your job to keep those red-eyed bastards in check. How could you allow this to happen?"

Samael was annoyed by Michael's overt backstabbing. "Don't put this on me! Azazel screwed things up. And how is it that you, as Comptroller General and being so fond of auditing my Department, never noticed anything?"

"Stop it, please!" said Gabriel, twisting his lips and raising his hands. "This is not helping. Save your blame for the Creator."

"Speaking of Whom…" chimed in Uriel. "Should we go to Him for help?"

"No!" The visceral reaction of the other Angels was unanimous.

Samael was the most energetic in his objection. "If the Creator wanted to get involved, He would already have done so. Since he hasn't, he wants us to deal with the situation. If we go to him now we can kiss our Cabinet positions goodbye. Gabriel, how much time do you need to get your troops on-site?"

"They should be there any moment now. Once they are, it should be quick. The Demons will be exterminated before they even have a chance to realize what hit them."

"Wow, wow, wow!" Samael raised his hand. "What do you mean, exterminated? Do you want to wipe out the entire Maintenance Department? Who would do the work then, your troops with yardsticks up their asses? Or maybe you want to train a human brigade to run Maintenance?"

"Samael is right," agreed Rafael. "We have to quash the rebellion, but we cannot destroy the Demons. Forget about Maintenance. The Creator would never allow the extermination of their entire species."

"Ugh." Gabriel groaned and said sarcastically, "So, what would you suggest, my fellow Archangels? Send Ashmodai a welcome delegation and offer a parley?"

"Can we just disable and disarm them, then wipe out their rebellious inclinations and send Ashmodai for reeducation? My team at the HHS can take care of the modifications." Rafael appeared very proud of his suggestion.

"Easier said than done," said Gabriel. "My troops would need to disable them before they can be delivered to HHS. Do you think Demons will just stand there and wait for you to modify their consciousness?"

Rafael scoffed. "Well, that is why we have an army, for crying out loud. Or did you think that was just for the parades and the Creator's Honorary Guard? Let the army get down and dirty for once!"

"Easy for you to say. It would not be your Angels dying out there," deflected Gabriel. He added after a pause, "This bickering doesn't help. You are right, though, we cannot exterminate the Demons." He muttered something to his aide, who saluted and ran to a phone.

"Hey, one other thing," said Uriel. Judging by the annoyed faces of the other Department Heads, he didn't command a lot of respect from them. "What do we do with Azazel?"

"What do we do?' responded Gabriel. "He was aware of this mess from the beginning, so let him pay for it." Gabriel turned to Samael with a dismissive wave. "That said, he is your jerk, so do whatever you will."

Samael paused and took a deep breath. I could see how much he hated Azazel and how tempted he was to just get rid of him. However, the righteous Angel in him took over pretty quickly. "He may be a jerk, but he is one of us and he is trying to stop the Demons. We cannot leave him there. Can you arrange for his extraction?"

Gabriel rolled his eyes, exasperated. "Anything else I can do for you, Samael?"

Samael ignored the sarcasm and turned back to the video feed. "We don't have much time. Is there a special ops team that can take care of this quickly?"

"There is, and they can." Gabriel gave another series of orders. One of the monitors showed a close-up of a group of special force Angel operators diving into the field like falcons swooping down on their prey. As they hit the ground, a seismic wave rippled through the field, sending Demons flying into the air. With expert precision, the Angels formed a semi-circle around Azazel, shielding him from the Demons, then cleared the area around them, unleashing a barrage of projectiles to keep the Demon attackers at bay. As the ops team continued to fire, two of the Angels grabbed Azazel and soared into the sky, momentarily disappearing from view. Their comrades on the ground finished off the attacking Demons then followed.

"I said no killing!" said Samael with a wince.

"I am not a miracle worker," Gabriel said.

It was funny to hear such a claim from an Archangel, and I couldn't suppress a chuckle.

Gabriel continued, "If you want to have your cake and eat it, too, be my guest and do it yourself. Besides, we didn't exterminate the entire Demon race. There were only a few casualties. Necessary collateral damage."

Samael waved a hand in resignation. "Whatever."

The extraction team instantly delivered Azazel to the command center. He was just a shadow of his former self, exhausted, beaten-up, his armor shredded to pieces, revealing ugly wounds beneath. His eyes, empty of their usual conceited confidence, now reflected only total exhaustion.

Samael clenched his fists. "How could you do that? You of all Angels, the Undersecretary of the Justice Department, how could you fall so low?"

Azazel grimaced, "Please, Samael, spare me the sermon. I've had enough rebukes for the day, and the last creature I want to hear from is you—sanctimonious prick and backstabber that you are. Just enjoy another victory over me, because the only way you will ever win is when I screw up."

Samael went pale and hissed, "I will ignore your tantrum and insults, but you will pay dearly for everything you have done." He turned to the guards. "Just take this filthy piece of work out of my face!"

The guards cuffed Azazel and took him away. As he passed me, I could have sworn he smiled and winked at me. I was unsure, but I gave him an inconspicuous thumbs-up, nonetheless. For the first time in my life after death, I felt a genuine respect for an Angel.

CHAPTER 6

The Battlefield

Once they had taken Azazel away, I shifted my focus back to the monitor showing the battle. The assault force had just arrived. They split into two groups and executed a classic by-the-book pincer movement, flanking the massive but poorly-trained Demon army. Expertly using the landscape, they kept popping up as if out of nowhere, catching the enemy off guard. Their movements were precise and calculated, showcasing their exceptional training and the awesome prowess of Angelic troops on the battlefield.

"Remember, the rules of engagement: the objective is to apprehend and disable. Minimal casualties," Gabriel reminded his troops.

A chorus of "Yes, Sir, mission objective confirmed," came from the loudspeakers.

The Angels had loaded their weapons with tranquilizers to

subdue the enemy. Once a Demon was hit by a tranquilizer, his body shrank and he was encapsulated in a gelatinous substance, unable to move. Disabled Demons were then dispatched to holding cells in the Netherworld.

The huge Demon army was now a scattered mess, their ranks in disarray and their movements disoriented. They attempted to reorganize and mount a defense, but even their commanders appeared discombobulated and lost.

Meanwhile, the Angels kept proper formation, executing the plan flawlessly. Terse reports from field commanders added to the businesslike atmosphere on the battlefield.

I was fascinated watching the intense battle unfold before me onscreen. As someone who had never served in the military— at least I didn't think I had—I was mesmerized by the Angels' precise movements and swift actions. It seemed like everything was going according to plan, perhaps even too smoothly.

Alas, the best-laid plans of mice and men often went awry. Indeed, chaos started to creep in and reports became frantic and scattered. What had once seemed an easy battlefield victory for the Angels now appeared uncertain and precarious.

The tables slowly turned. Although the Angel soldiers were unmatched in skill and strength, the sheer number of Demons was overwhelming them. Using their numerical advantage, they were finally able to organize a defensive line in the rear while the Angels were busy pummeling their front ranks. A quickly-assembled but determined company of Demons broke through their ranks and slowly pushed back against the Angelic army.

The pincer movement perfectly executed at the beginning of the battle had stretched Angelic troops too thin, separating their flanks and now putting their left flank in danger of being surrounded. As if that weren't enough, their orders to only disable and disarm rather than kill the Demons made their task almost impossible since a large group of Angel soldiers was occupied with processing the disabled Demons. The numbers on the monitor tracking Angelic casualties skyrocketed at an alarming rate.

Meanwhile, Rafael's team working in an overflowing mobile hospital did their best to save as many wounded Angels as they could, but it was an uphill battle against the never-ending tide of injured.

Gabriel's face showed disappointment and concern. I was sure he was blaming Samael for not letting his Angels decimate the bastards and get it all over with.

"Can you send reinforcements?" asked Samael.

Gabriel shook his head. "And leave the rest of the Creation undefended? No way. I think, gentlemen, it is time for us to intervene personally."

Samael raised his brows. "Absolutely not! A strike by Archangels may only be sanctioned by the Creator."

Gabriel opened his mouth to say something—offensive, from the look on his face—but must have thought better of it. I guessed he needed Samael's support. "Are you telling me there are no exceptions?" he demanded.

Samael hesitated. "Well, of course there are during exigent

circumstances when immediate action is warranted. But even then," he quickly added, "it must be authorized by the full Cabinet, and I will not sign off on less than a unanimous decision."

I could barely contain my laughter. This World and the Other World were different as night and day…except when it came to lawyers and bureaucrats. I fully expected an outburst of unstoppable rage from Gabriel, and was genuinely surprised by his calm response to Samael.

"Wouldn't you say, my dear friend and colleague, that the circumstances we find ourselves in are nothing short of exigent?" He turned to the rest of the Archangels expectantly.

"If we strike," Michael said slowly and deliberately, "the Demons will be wiped out. Didn't we all agree that we could not decimate the Maintenance Department?"

Gabriel countered, "We can do a targeted strike with extensive damage in the epicenter but with gradually reduced casualties outside the strike zone. Once we strike, I am pretty sure any Demons who have never seen an Archangel strike will surrender."

"And, if not?"

"Then we will wipe out the rest and go to the Creator with our tails between our legs pleading for forgiveness and asking for a new race of Maintenance workers." Frustration finally burst out from Gabriel. "I am sure Samael will be able to deliver an eloquent summation justifying our actions." Looking at the confused faces of his colleagues, he added contemptuously,

"Something tells me you have all grown fat in your posh executive offices and have forgotten how to fight a good fight. I don't think all this debating will bring us closer to a resolution. I move to vote. All in favor of us intervening?"

I looked in suspense at the Cabinet members.

Rafael and Uriel raised their hands. Reluctantly, Michael and Samael joined them.

Satisfied, Gabriel smiled. "Unanimous. Motion carried. Come on, let's suit up and show those miscreants the true meaning of shock and awe!"

The five Archangels put on battle gear and flew down to the battlefield…except, to my shock, there was no putting on the gear or going anywhere. The command center simply morphed into the battlefield with the Archangels standing there in full armor.

Since I was in the command center, I was also pulled along, and found myself on the edge of the fighting, not far from the village where I'd been held prisoner.

Once the Archangels joined the battle, it was a game over. Imagine armies engaged in conventional warfare when an alien spaceship armed with wonder weapons showed up and wiped out everyone in a couple of shots. Now, multiply that alien spaceship by five and you get the picture…or rather, a very remote approximation of the breathtaking sight I was privileged to witness. The limits of my imagination could not possibly have envisioned the assault by the Archangels.

They descended upon the battlefield in unbridled fury, the

very embodiment of wrath itself, their wings spreading wide and casting a looming shadow over all who dared oppose them. For a moment, it looked like the whole Creation receded, like an ocean before a tsunami wave, and a suffocating silence enveloped everything around us, broken only by the ominous *whoosh* of the wind.

They then unleashed a power of truly Biblical proportions upon their enemies. The very air crackled with divine energy. The ground trembled beneath my feet, and I could feel the raw force of their presence pulsing through my veins. As the wind of their fury subsided, the ground around the Archangels reverted to its primordial state of liquid magma, and the Demons outside the strike zone were reduced to nothing more than whimpering creatures cowering in fear. The rest of the Demon army lost all will to fight. They threw down their weapons, kneeling in submission before the overwhelming power that was second only to the power of the Creator Himself.

I wondered what Ashmodai was thinking.

Turned out, Ashmodai was not that stupid. As the command center morphed back from being the battlefield and Archangels changed back into their suits, a call came over the loudspeakers.

"Sir, the Head of Maintenance is on the phone demanding a conference."

Gabriel scoffed. "Demanding? That's interesting."

Ever a lawyer, Samael wanted to know all the facts first. "Let's hear him out since he has decided to talk. Put him onscreen and trace the call. I want this troublemaker apprehended as soon as possible."

Ashmodai's face appeared on one of the large monitors. He was grinning and didn't look in the slightest like a fellow who had just lost his cause, let alone his existence.

"Esteemed Members of the Cabinet, what an honor to see you all in one place. Thanks for sparing me the extra phone calls."

"What do you want, Ashmodai?" Gabriel asked in annoyance. "You lost, so the only sensible thing for you to do would be to surrender. I am sure Samael will give you a fair shake in the Courtroom."

"Not so fast, General. While your bluntness suits your rank, you may first want to hear what I have to say. Your exploits on the battlefield were impressive, to say the least, but not unexpected. So far, you have been so predictable that I was bored at times. The order to tranquilize and not to kill, with devastating consequences for your troops, and your valiant and glorious entrance to end the battle—I predicted all of that. You, on the other hand, seemed to have underestimated me."

Gabriel stood up straight. "I am tired of your posturing, Ashmodai. Say what you have to say, but know that none of it will make a difference. Your only choice is to surrender, and the sooner you do it the more merciful we may feel."

"All, right, straight to the point. I love you military types. So, here is the situation. While you were monkeying around on the battlefield, my Maintenance teams rigged all the maintenance tunnels with explosives. Unless you agree to my terms, I will blow up the entire service network of the Creation." He held up a device that looked like a remote detonator. "How's that for direct talk, General?" Ashmodai's tone changed from bantering to menacing.

To say the Archangels were stunned would be a gross understatement. Their faces reflected complete dismay. While no one doubted that the Creator could restore all the maintenance tunnels, blowing up the entire service network would require a major overhaul of the entire Creation…and effectively end their careers as Archangels.

Samael recovered first. "You wouldn't do that. If you do, the Creator will send you to Oblivion."

"Worry about yourself, Samael. Maybe I will pay for the explosion with my existence, but so will you. Do you want to risk your pampered Angelic hide?" Noticing that Gabriel was saying something quietly to his subordinate, Ashmodai quickly added, "General, please stop this phone trace nonsense. There is no way you can trace me through the service network, so dispense with the childish games."

Gabriel's face went red. "We heard your threat. What are your demands?"

"You help me manufacture enough anti-excision vaccine using the recipe in the Book of Remedies and allow all Demons to be inoculated with it. Once the threat of excision is removed, I will take control of all humans, with no interference from you."

"Aren't you forgetting something? What about the Creator?"

"Fair point. But let me worry about the Creator. I will plead my case before Him if and when he chooses to call me to the Courtroom. In the meantime, I demand your cooperation. I am a big fan of collective responsibility, so I would love your company by my side when I stand before the Creator trying to justify our collective actions."

I knew he didn't need the Archangels to manufacture the vaccine, his department was fully capable of doing it. What he really wanted was to make the Archangels his accomplices.

"Give us a few minutes," said Samael.

"By all means, gentlemen. Take your time. But not too long. I am getting antsy." Ashmodai's face disappeared from the monitor.

Gabriel pressed his hands tiredly to his head. "Any ideas?"

Uriel grabbed his moment for glory. "Let me flush the tunnels with gamma rays from a few supernova explosions. The blast should disable all connectivity with Ashmodai's remote detonator and render all explosives useless."

He didn't get to enjoy the glory for too long. Samael was pissed. "Come on, Uriel. If you blast the service network with your gamma rays, can you guarantee that no habitable planets will be destroyed in the process?"

"My Angels will do their best to produce a directed blast, but with an explosion of this magnitude there is no guarantee."

Samael threw up his hands and asked, "Gabriel, can your guys disarm the explosives?"

"No way am I sending my troops to clear the tunnels one by one. I could lose the entire army and half of the tunnels in the process."

"Does that mean we have no choice but to accept the demands of the extortionist?" Michael sounded incredulous.

It was clear to me that the Archangels had run out of solutions and were prepared to accept Ashmodai's terms. They had nothing to lose, of course, because it was humans who would be under the yoke of the Demons, not them. Why bother with creative and politically dangerous decisions when their own hides were not at risk? How typical of calculating and conniving Angelic bureaucrats completely devoid of any sense of compassion to choose the most rational and prudent approach, no matter the cost to everyone else.

I should have learned my lesson from them. Had I been a prudent man I would have kept my mouth shut. Unfortunately, prudence was not among my soul's virtues.

I cleared my throat loudly. "Excuse me, sirs. May I make a suggestion?"

All heads turned toward me, appalled at my impudence.

"Who is this…soul?" asked Samael in obvious disbelief that a monkey had somehow become privy to the most sacred proceedings of the Heavenly Cabinet. I could feel how much he had wanted to say monkey instead of soul, but using derogatory terms was apparently unbecoming of an Archangel.

"Oh, yes, I completely forgot." Gabriel's voice was full of annoyance. "This is one of Azazel's Pilot Program souls. He warned me of the rebellion. Can someone please take him out of the command center?"

Before the Angel Guard could remove me, I quickly shouted, "If I managed to bring the news of the rebellion to you against all odds, shouldn't you at least give me a moment to explain myself?"

Everyone in the room was shocked by my audacity, but after Ashmodai's brazen threats, it was a Chutzpah Day at the Heavenly Offices.

Gabriel raised his hand, stopping his guards. "Very well. One minute."

"Thank you, sir. If I may… I know for a fact there are Demons who are unhappy with the rebellion. If you would give me a proper weapon and allow me to make a maintenance call to one of those unhappy Demons, who happens to be a buddy of mine, I may be able to track down Ashmodai and eliminate him before he has a chance to blow up the service network. He would never allow an Angel to get near him, but he would not consider a lowly human monkey a threat. Once Ashmodai is eliminated, the rest of the Demons won't have the guts or the will to continue the rebellion."

Uriel, still upset that his supernova idea was rejected, vehemently objected. "Put our trust in a soul? No chance! What if he messes up?"

"You have a better suggestion?" Gabriel retorted. "I cannot send my Angels to search the entire network, and this soul appears to have a way into the Demon army. At least let him try. Better than going to the Creator with our tails between our legs."

"I agree," said Michael and Rafael simultaneously.

Samael nodded approvingly.

As with any governing body, the Heavenly Offices operated by consensus, and the majority just voted to give me a chance.

"Done." Gabriel always liked to take charge. He turned to me. "What do you need?"

"My body, one of your weapons, a maintenance ticket to the Demon Abaddon, and a full pardon for him in exchange for his cooperation."

"I can't fix his body fast enough," chimed in Rafael. "But I can outfit him with a substitute. I should have some spare bodies at the ICU."

I shook my head. "Unfortunately, sir, I need to use my own so Abaddon will recognize me right away. But it doesn't need to be completely fixed. Just make it more or less functional. I only need it long enough to get to Ashmodai."

"Okay, I will take you to the ICU and try to make it fast. I don't think we have a lot of time."

"I will buy you time," said Samael smiling. "My Angels will need to draft a cooperation and immunity agreement, and Ashmodai will need to review it. He has been part of the Justice Department long enough to know that the cogs of justice move slowly. But let me make one thing clear," he added forcefully. "Ashmodai should be disabled but not killed. I am not going to be responsible for an extra-judicial killing of the Head of Maintenance."

Gabriel raised his eyes heavenward. "I am so glad I am not in charge of lawyers, or I would have excised myself into Oblivion long ago." He turned to me. "My special ops Angels will take you to the battlefield and give you the necessary weapons. But remember, soul, if you try to play games or fail, the Movie Room will be the most pleasant outcome you can expect."

I nodded politely. "Thank you, sir. I won't fail you."

CHAPTER 7

Ashmodai Headquarters
in the Vicinity of the Battlefield

Rafael's Angels took me to the ICU and I was pleasantly surprised to learn that body repair could be done very fast and without endless waiting time. Once the retrofitting was done, I found myself on the night-quiet battlefield surrounded by Angels in combat uniform who looked like, well, like special forces types.

The team leader approached me. "So, you are the brave soul who decided to take on the Chief Demon, eh? I'm not sure if you are too dumb or too smart for your own good, but here you go." He handed me a pistol-looking device with a magazine stuffed with what looked like blue marbles.

"Um. What is it?"

"A tranquilizer gun. Once you are in the vicinity of a Demon, shoot one of those globes straight at him, but before you shoot you have to press this button to activate the globe." He pointed to a small button affixed next to the trigger. "You can also bury the tranquilizer in the ground like a landmine, remove the tiny button from the trigger, and when a Demon passes by, press it. The blast will also send a signal to us to come in and apprehend whomever you tranquilized."

"Don't you have something simpler, without an extra trigger?"

He made a face. "Oh, don't get me started." Clearly, the order not to kill had not been well received by the Angelic troops. "If we could use our normal weapons to destroy the material shell of a Demon, we would have destroyed their army in no time. However, the geniuses upstairs decided that was a no-go. Now the only way to disable a Demon is to use this tranquilizer that binds their spiritual part and swallows them like a giant jellyfish. What those geniuses didn't realize, of course, is that their spiritual part is made of the same stuff as ours, so any blast will also disable any Angels in the vicinity. Hence, instead of fighting, we have to stay outside the blast radius. And if one of us gets hit, it is just a question of who will reach him first—the Angels to get him to the hospital, or the Demons to send him to Oblivion. Blipping morons!"

As much as I enjoyed listening to his venting, I needed to proceed with my mission. "Thank you, commander. You should go now. I am about to call my Demon friend."

The team leader shook my hand. As he was leaving, he quickly added, "One more thing. You should stay well away from the blast. Since the blast affects the spiritual part of any being, it will most likely destroy or damage your soul to the point of no return. Not sure exactly how it works, but the tranquilizer gradually liquifies the human soul instead of binding it. Unlike bodies, souls cannot be repaired. Good luck, man. Go, get'em."

The Angel team silently disappeared into the night.

It took me a while to register his last statement.

Okay, then. So, when all is said and done, I am going to Oblivion, after all. If not through the Movie Room, then through my heroic actions to save humanity. Great.

But wait, who and what was I saving, anyway? Cushy jobs for a bunch of Angelic bureaucrats with chips on their shoulders and a deep-seated disdain for the whole of humanity? Awesome. Why did I go and volunteer for this mission where my future was more or less mapped out for me? Shouldn't I have left it to the Creator to deal with this entire mess?

On second thought, how could anyone know how the Creator would deal with the situation? Maybe Ashmodai was right, and the Creator had grown tired of this Earth-on-Earth degeneration with all its murder, sexual deviance, and lack of morality. Maybe He thought allowing Hell on Earth would result in a more orderly and less violent society…albeit controlled by not-so-nice Demons.

No, I wasn't prepared to accept that outcome. If that was what the Creator had in store for us, I would prefer Oblivion. Heavenly existence didn't sit well with me, and I humbly hoped to negotiate a second life term. But a second life term in a world controlled by Demons with their twisted sense of right and wrong? Nothingness felt better.

My soul-searching was giving me a headache, and I willed myself to focus on the mission. *Take it one step at a time.*

I sighed and issued a maintenance call.

Abaddon was hard to reach and responded only after I'd made a few calls.

He looked scared. "What are you doing, exposing me like this? I was surrounded by Demons when your ticket showed up. Did you want to get me killed? And how did you survive, anyway? I saw Azazel throw you off a cliff."

I lifted a shoulder. "He reinstated my Reincarnation Rights before he threw me off."

"O-oh." He frowned. "At least they could have done a better job with your body." He pointed to the multiple wounds and congealed blood all over me.

"No time. Had to take it as is. Look, here is the deal. Samael has promised you a full pardon if you get me close to Ashmodai so I can hit him with this." I showed Abaddon the tranquilizer gun along with a fancily-written full pardon bearing the Department of Justice's seal.

"How did you get to Samael?" he asked.

"Don't worry about that, just take my word for it. Do you know where Ashmodai is?"

Abaddon scratched his head. "I do, but getting to him is next to impossible. He is surrounded by cronies to whom he has promised various cushy administration posts, and they are behind him one hundred percent. We will be searched, and your tranq gun will be discovered. After that, *whoop*." His paw waved in the general direction of Oblivion.

Yes, that was a definite issue.

We both thought silently for a couple of moments. My previous thoughts came back to me with a vengeance. Now I had a great excuse to go back to the Heavenly Offices and proceed with the offered risk-free route to Heaven. Shouldn't I use it?

I thought about Nora, the human race, Azazel, the Angelic special ops team, the Heavenly Cabinet—even though I had zero sympathy for them—and all the innocent creatures in the World. The Creation was beautiful, and I liked it as it was—without Demons running things.

Which must be the answer, right?

What was one soul in the grand scheme of things…even if it was my soul? Besides, I kind of felt at least partially responsible for the current mess.

No, it was time for me to do something courageous, even if my soul with its ingrained fear of nothingness hated my decision and tried to hold me back.

I removed the magazine from the tranquilizer gun, removed a handful of tranquilizer globes, took a deep breath, and swallowed them one by one. Thankfully they were small, so swallowing them was easy. I then attached the tiny remote control button to one of my back teeth. I turned to Abaddon, who was dubiously watching me eating the globes.

"I'm not even going to ask."

"Why don't you take me as a prisoner to Ashmodai?" I suggested. "Tell him the truth—that I contacted you and tried to convince you to betray him. Bring me to him, and then walk away. The conceited bastard would no doubt love to have a chat with me."

Abaddon was still not sure, so I had to prod him. "Don't worry, these globes are just tranquilizers. He will survive."

"But you won't. You know that, right?"

"Yeah, yeah. I know. But at this point, I don't have much left to look forward to. I am a dead man anyway." I laughed bitterly.

"Well, suit yourself. For the full pardon from Samael, I will take you to Ashmodai."

"That's all I am asking."

Abaddon tied my hands behind my back and took me into one of the maintenance tunnels. We came out somewhere, I was not sure where, and we found ourselves surrounded by Demons. Dressed in combat uniform and armed with whatever their weapons were called, they looked tense. Clearly, they knew the battle was lost and that Ashmodai was playing his last trump card. Yet, their faces displayed a grim determination to fight to the bitter end.

"Where are you taking this monkey, Abaddon?" the one who looked like the commanding Demon asked suspiciously. His voice sounded familiar. I took a closer look, and, lo and behold, Baphomet's glowing red eyes shone from beneath the helmet.

"To Ashmodai," Abaddon said. "This is the monkey who called on Azazel. I am sure Ashmodai would enjoy talking to him." He gave them the full story about the maintenance call.

Baphomet approached and looked at me curiously. A lot of time had passed since our last card game and our trip to the Courtroom, but he recognized me. "Hey, buddy. Doesn't look like you are up for a game." He sounded unexpectedly friendly.

"If you want to play for my freedom, I'm in."

"Nah, can't afford those stakes. I suppose we'll have to find another partner for the next Texas hold'em."

"I suppose you should." I looked at him as if measuring him up. "Look at you, a commander of Ashmodai's personal guard. Who'd have thought? You never struck me as the fighting type."

Baphomet shrugged. "Maybe, you are not such a good judge of character. Besides, desperate times require desperate measures."

"Desperate times, indeed. Do you really think you have any chance of getting what you want? This rebellion is sheer lunacy."

My remark must have hit a nerve. Suddenly, the good-natured Baphomet was gone and I was looking at a ruthless commander of the Demon guard. He turned to his subordinates. "Search him, and search him well. This monkey is a trickster. It would be stupid of him to call on Abaddon just to be apprehended and brought here." He turned back to me. "You better tell me what you have in mind."

"Me? Nothing. Just came here to kick your furry asses. Oh, and to kill Ashmodai and the rest of you."

The Demons laughed. Why would no one ever believe the truth?

Demons searched both of us and found nothing, which made Baphomet even more suspicious. "Something doesn't add up. Let's take them both to the interrogation room and beat the truth out of them."

Abaddon's eyes opened wide. "What did I do? This is how you thank me for bringing in this monkey?"

I had to act fast. If they took both of us to the interrogation room Abaddon would break in no time and sing like a canary. In which case my beautiful plan would go to waste.

"Hey, Baphomet, look at me. Do you think this body can take an additional beating? If you try to interrogate me, chances are you will only have my dead body to show to your Boss. Something tells me that Ashmodai, who is looking forward to talking to me, won't be happy."

Baphomet hesitated, still wary of bringing me to Ashmodai.

I decided to help him. "Tell you what. Why don't you take this piece of shit Abaddon instead, and interrogate him as much as your heart desires?"

Abaddon's mouth dropped open in reaction to my brazen betrayal, preparing to tell everything to save his hide.

I quickly continued, not to give him a chance to speak. "And I will sit here and wait until you are done with him. In the meantime, the Angels will implement their plan and we will all happily go to Oblivion."

"What plan?" Baphomet demanded.

I almost had him now. "Well, you know. The plan only Ashmodai should know about, not a lowly Demon like you. But, hey, I'm not telling you what to do. You are a hotshot commander, and I'm sure you know better than I do how to deal with the situation."

He was still suspicious, not sure whether to believe me or not, but ultimately must have decided I couldn't possibly be a threat to his Boss. It was safer to let Ashmodai deal with me. Just in case, though, he ordered his soldiers to search us again to make sure we had nothing on us, then took us inside.

Ashmodai was sitting behind a makeshift desk, talking to Demons and issuing orders. A map of the service tunnel network hung on the wall next to his desk, with flashing red lights that must have indicated the locations of the explosives. Judging by the density of the red lights, the Demons had done a thorough job and the blast would wipe out not only the service tunnel network but half of Creation.

As Baphomet approached and whispered something into his ear, Ashmodai looked at me with a broad smile. "My, my. Who do we have here? The courageous monkey who stole the heart of my late mother and almost cost me the entire rebellion. I didn't expect to see you so soon." He turned to my captor. "Thank you, Abaddon, you can go. Your services will be rewarded in due time."

Abaddon quickly bowed and left, all too happy to escape Ashmodai's office...which was about to become a place of complete carnage.

The guards kept me away from Ashmodai's desk. Not knowing the blast radius of the tranquilizer globes, I was hesitant to push the detonator button. What if it only got the guards surrounding me? I needed to get closer to my target. As close as I possibly could.

"Happy to see you, as well, Ashmodai. How's the rebellion going? I heard you've lost your entire army."

He laughed. "Then you must also have heard I've rigged the entire service tunnel network with explosives. My army will be back with me in no time."

"I don't think so. As far as I could tell, the Archangels have no desire to acquiesce to your demands. In fact, I think they've decided to send their special forces team to capture you."

His eyes glowed red. "You are bluffing. They will never find me, nor would they risk damaging the service network."

I kept my face completely expressionless, which I was very good at thanks to my extensive experience playing poker with my Demon buddies. "You don't have to believe me. See for yourself. I think Uriel came up with a way to prevent the explosions using some kind of cosmic rays. But I am no expert in Angelic tricks. As for finding your location, have you forgotten how many of your soldiers are now imprisoned in the Netherworld? How hard could it be to extract a confession from one of them? I am pretty sure they'll capture you soon." I paused with a wave of my hand. "Or, who knows, the special ops guys might just botch the capture and send you straight to Oblivion. By mistake, of course."

Ashmodai growled. Whether he believed me or not, I had definitely unsettled him.

Time to go for the kill. "So let me ask you again, my furry friend. Was this whole rebellion thing worth it? Losing your mom, losing your cushy job, risking Oblivion—all for what? Being worshipped by a few human crazies? No, Ashmodai. You may want to pretend to be an Angel, but deep down you are just another grease ape suffering from the same inferiority complex as all the other Demons."

I could feel the rage building in Ashmodai. Finally, he snarled and approached me, his paws clenched and lips twisted. "Even if what you say is true, Samael will always strike a deal with me because he needs my Demons. You, on the other hand, will be shipped straight to Oblivion, monkey. Right now!"

He lurched close and grabbed me violently, anticipating the pleasure of tearing me apart. As his face came within inches of mine, I smiled and bit down on my teeth. The blast tore open my belly and almost certainly damaged my soul, but somehow I was still alive. I wished I weren't because the pain was unbearable.

The Demons around me were cowering on the floor, encapsulated in the potent tranquilizer. Ashmodai was being slowly enveloped by the gooey substance, shrinking before my very eyes and disappearing into the jellyfish-like tranquilizer bulb.

His bulging eyes projected confusion and fear. "What

the hell just happened?" he wheezed as the gelatinous shell swallowed him whole.

"Redemption, you hairy motherfucker!" I winked at him as my body was taking in its final breath, and I slipped into a coma.

CHAPTER 8

The Creator. Everywhere

Once my body died completely, my soul returned to the Command Center at the Department of Defense. One of the large monitors was streaming the Angelic special forces team apprehending Ashmodai and his guards, and disabling the remote detonation device. The rebellion was finally over and the Demons were being processed by Rafael's behavior modification unit.

The Archangels were elated, shaking each other's hands and laughing. Their jobs were secure, and they didn't have to suffer through an embarrassing report to the Creator.

No one paid any attention to me. My job was done and I had served my purpose. No medals, no handshaking, nothing. Angels did not understand the concept of gratitude. For them, everyone did what he was required to do to serve the Creation. I was nothing more than collateral damage, an insignificant element of the Creation, the absence of which would not be noticed in the grand scheme of things. No one tried to stop me when I walked out of the Command Center and away from the Department of Defense. I could feel my soul—which had unwittingly witnessed one of the most awesome…and embarrassing…events in the history of the Creation—was slowly starting to disintegrate, piece by piece.

Well, at least there would be no Movie Room. Straight to Oblivion for me.

Outside, the area surrounding the Department buildings resembled a large park, a strange combination of Hyde Park and the National Mall. I realized I had never paid any attention to what lay between the buildings as I rushed from one Department to another. The park was eerily deserted but really nice. I found a bench under one of the large trees and sank onto it, closing my eyes.

It dawned on me that in these, my final hours, I had no place to go and no one to talk to. Azazel's office was empty, and my poker buddies from the Maintenance Department were all being re-educated. I was a wandering soul, indeed. It felt like the only place I belonged now was Oblivion, but my soul stubbornly refused to give up the ghost.

Maybe Oblivion wouldn't be so bad. At least it was just one big nothingness without pain or remorse. Still, deep down I refused to accept nothingness, hoping that maybe, just maybe, the Creator would decide to save my soul. After all, the Creator was all-merciful, and in the end, I did well, all things considered. Possibly even redeemed myself in His eyes. Even if I didn't get another shot at life, at least He might move me to Heaven—whatever that meant—for an eternal R&R. Not what I'd had in mind, but in my soul's opinion a much preferable outcome than Oblivion.

My thoughts switched to Nora. Gosh, how much I wanted to have her! I had to believe Azazel would keep his word, no matter the circumstances, and ask Rafael to restore her soul to her body. Which would doubtless wipe out all her memories of past events. The altruistic part of me was happy she would be brought back to life. As for the selfish side of me, it was time to accept that I was dead, and think of our exciting adventure together as an unexpected parting gift from the Creator. I would cherish those tender memories as I was on my way to Oblivion.

Speaking of which…there was no rush, was there? No one was trying to speed up my soul's demise, so I might as well sit and enjoy the outdoor gardens a bit more.

The park was alive with the crisp, invigorating scent of fresh spring air. It mingled with fleeting hints of delicate flowers I couldn't quite place. I let my thoughts go, focusing on the lovely scents, the gentle sound of rustling leaves, and the caress of a soft breeze against my disintegrating soul. Every sound, smell, and touch felt like a sweet release, allowing me to fully embrace the supernatural beauty surrounding me.

Suddenly, a hand touched my shoulder. I flinched and opened my eyes. The aide-de-camp who had escorted me to Gabriel's office earlier stood above me. Had they finally remembered the unaccounted-for soul and decided to have someone nudge me toward Oblivion?

And yet, he didn't look like a messenger of doom. His eyes were wide open, full of awe and fascination.

"The Creator wants to speak to you," he said in a hushed voice, as if afraid to use the Creator's ineffable name in vain. "I will take you to Him."

My heart skipped a beat. I remembered the feeling of warmth and happiness I had experienced in the Courtroom. Was I really being given the honor of meeting the Creator himself? I could scarcely believe it.

As we rushed through the park, the aide gave me quick instructions. "Do not approach the Throne of Glory, stay outside the sapphire boundary. Prostrate yourself, and do not rise unless the Creator tells you to. Do not speak unless spoken to, and under no circumstances raise your eyes and try to look at Him, or your soul will burn in a split second." The aide's voice was full of envy. Meeting the Creator was an honor that even very few Angels ever received, other than Archangels and the Honorary Guard.

"I get it, I get it. Let's just go." My soul was on the verge of vanishing into Oblivion so every moment counted.

We exited the park and came to a large square that was paved with cobblestones and surrounded by a thick fog. The Department buildings and the park disappeared from view.

"I will leave you here," said the aide. "You alone were summoned, and no one is allowed in the presence of the Creator unless summoned. Don't forget, when you hear the sound of trumpets and see the Honorary Guard, prostrate yourself on the ground and do not lift your head or raise your eyes." He hastily left the square and vanished into the fog.

A strong wind *whoosh*ed through the empty square, and one by one the cobblestones turned to sapphire. I instinctively moved back, but the cobblestones under me remained as they were and the sapphire line stopped before me. I heard the loud sound of trumpets announcing the arrival of the Creator. The fog partially dissipated, and I saw a dense cloud shrouding a ball of fire with a brilliance surrounding it. A strong surge of energy coming from the cloud pierced the air around me, reverberating through every particle and spreading the crisp scent of lightning-produced ozone. It was so powerful I fell to the ground without any further reminders.

From my prostrate position, I heard the marching of the Honorary Guard and the ringing of their trumpets, then suddenly everything went quiet. I couldn't see what was going on, but I was filled with the same feeling of warmth and exhilaration, the same as I'd experienced in the Courtroom.

The Creator had arrived.

I fully expected a thundering voice to bellow in my eardrums. Instead, a quiet voice said, "You did well, Son of Man. Self-sacrifice, loyalty, love. Things neither Angels nor Demons are capable of. I believe your soul is worthy of being kept out of Oblivion. It shall be restored to you." He paused, letting me absorb my unexpected salvation. "You must have many questions for me. Don't be afraid. Ask."

I gathered my courage. "Why did you allow all of this to happen?"

"These are things beyond your understanding. Let's just say the Creation required an uplift. Also, you needed to be tested."

I was shocked. This whole mess was just to test me? No way.

"Don't look so surprised. Humans are the pinnacle of Creation, and you are sitting on that pinnacle whether you know it or not. Everything is done for you and your benefit. Angels and Demons are just servants—powerful, but servants nonetheless, devoid of free will and resourcefulness."

"But, seriously. The size, the gravity of it! Just to test one human soul?"

"Size doesn't matter. The entire Creation is puny in my eyes, and if it had to be shaken up for the improvement of just one soul, it was well worth it. You needed to be shown the proper way to use your free will, and you passed the test."

I was gobsmacked. "Didn't Azazel have free will when he did what he did?"

"Not in the full sense of it, no. No Angel can do wrong— that was how I designed them. I had to give Azazel a modicum of rebelliousness to allow him to falter. Now that he is back to his Angelic self, these events will haunt him for eternity. No punishment is worse than one's own sense of guilt and embarrassment. You also want to know about the Demons? They will stay where they are. The Creation needs maintenance and balance. And yes, I will deal with them, and they will remember their lesson for a long time. But Ashmodai is a good administrator, and he will eventually continue in his role."

Sensing my utter confusion, the Creator said, "Understand that nothing happens without me knowing about it. I loosened the reins here for a reason. Now I will tighten them up again. But I'll inevitably loosen them again when I deem it necessary." He paused. "Don't try to understand the workings of the Creation. They are beyond human understanding. The laws you need to follow were given to you in the various Sacred Texts. Certain other things are only understood by those who join me in the Heavens. The rest cannot be explained or shown, as it exists outside your World."

"But I'm wondering…"

Was I really that bold?

"But are you sure those are the questions that concern you the most?" He stated more than asked.

Encouraged, I decided to push my luck. "If You are saying I passed the test, wouldn't You want me to exercise my newfound skills in the World of Living? For some unfathomable reason, I seem to be important to You, to the Creation, since You did all this just to test me. Wouldn't it be worth giving me another shot at life to see if I can live up to your expectations, or if I just screw it up again?"

A warm wave ran through my soul. I wasn't sure what it was, but I thought it may have been the Creator smiling. "Don't flatter yourself, Son of Man. You are no more important than the greatest human king or the lowliest human servant. You are all equally important. As for your request…" He paused for a long moment. "The future is not for you to know. Maybe I will give you another shot at life, but then again, maybe not. But regardless of what happens in the future, first you must pay for your actions. You killed many innocent people and corrupted others. You may have thought you did those things for the greater good, but nothing justifies inflicting harm on others. Reward and punishment are the cornerstones of the Creation, and the only way to redeem yourself is to review and examine your life, understand your transgressions, and cleanse yourself of them. Only then will you be entitled to receive your reward."

My heart sank. "This is it, then. I will be sent back to the Movie Room, then either to the Heavens or to Oblivion."

"I didn't say that. Yes, you will be sent to the Movie Room, but I don't think Oblivion is in the cards. Otherwise, I would not have restored your soul. No matter how harshly your soul will judge you, you have enough to squeak by.

This was supposed to be a reward? "Is Heaven my only alternative, then?"

He sounded amused. "I don't know. You always have a choice. You can choose to join me in the Heavens—and believe me, it is not as boring as you imagine—or you can stay in the Pilot Program and continue your work there. Not exactly a new life, but you will be able to experience the World of Living again. Know, however, that should you choose to continue in the Pilot Program you are bound to commit more transgressions, and punishment will still await you for those new ones. Whether you want to play it safe and go through the Movie Room only once and then straight to the Heavens, or you'd rather take your chances in the Pilot Program and risk the additional pain of the Movie Room and maybe even Oblivion…it is up to you. The way the Creation is set up I can control everything, but I choose not to influence human free will."

I thought for a moment. The Heavens were no doubt great, but… The last few months and the beautiful face of Nora flashed before my eyes. Staying in the Program might give me a chance to see her again. I still hadn't figured out what attracted me to her so much in the first place, or why the Moffat mission had triggered such an emotional response. My past life was still an enigma that I very much wanted to solve.

Besides, I enjoyed the fast-paced missions full of twists and turns and unpredictable outcomes. Maybe I would have to face a few more unpleasant moments in the Movie Room, or maybe I would screw things up completely, but I figured it would be well worth it.

No, a quiet life in the Heavens was not for me. At least not for now.

I was about to open my mouth to tell him, then I remembered I was in the presence of the all-knowing Creator. "You already knew what I would choose, didn't you? What was that about not influencing free will?"

Another, much stronger wave of pleasant warmth rolled through my soul. The Creator must have laughed pretty hard at my cheekiness. "I think you've had enough of My presence.

One second more and you will lose whatever free will you still retain. Farewell, Son of Man. You have an exciting future ahead of you. Just remember, no matter where you are, I will be there, right by your side. Always."

That warning should have been alarming to me, but it wasn't. It felt…comforting.

Everything around me suddenly went quiet. The cloud of fog disappeared and the cobblestones turned back to their natural stony state. The Heavenly Offices buildings and the park around them became visible again.

I sat down, and my soul felt vibrant and cheerful. After being recharged by the Creator, I wanted to live, to feel, to experience, and face new challenges. In the end, did it matter whether my body was the one given to me at birth or one that had been made for me at the HHS? It was the soul that truly made one alive, and mine was once again full of life.

I got up and slowly walked toward the Department of Justice, hoping Azazel was back in his office by now, waiting for me with a new assignment.

About The Author

Born in 1964 in Baku, Azerbaijan—then part of the Soviet Union—Emil Buchman grew up in a world without video games, smartphones, or social media. With nothing but a state-sponsored TV channel for entertainment, he turned instead to books, devouring more than 1,500 volumes from his family's library. Classics, science fiction, and history became his lifelong companions.

After immigrating to the United States in 1991, Emil pursued law, graduating from law school and working as a transactional attorney at a large New York corporate firm. Yet even in the high-pressure world of corporate law, his passion for storytelling never left him. A life-long fan of Isaac Asimov and Robert Heinlein, Ken Follett, and Steven Saylor, as well as Star Wars and Star Trek series, Emil often dreamed of the sequels and prequels that never were.

So he decided to write his own. His debut, The Incredible Adventures of Chana in Judea, was a middle-grade—you guessed it, historical—novel written as a birthday gift for his granddaughter. His second book, Redemption Post Mortem, shifts into the supernatural—an electrifying thriller that fuses history, religion, and nonstop action.

Emil lives in Brooklyn with his wife Julie and their Wheaten Terrier, Chloe, and is ready to begin—work permitting—the next installment of the *Post Mortem* series.

To discover more about Emil and his writing,
please visit his website:

emilbuchman.com